WRONG

GIRL

GONE

WRONG

GIRL

GONE

Audrey Wilson

Wrong Girl Gone
Copyright © 2021 by Audrey Wilson

Content Editor: Brian Clow
Copy Editor: Emelyn G Ehrlich **and** Katie Schmeisser
Editor-in-Chief: Kristi King-Morgan
Formatting: Kristi King-Morgan
Cover Artist: Kristi King-Morgan
Assistant Editor: Amanda Clarke

Printed in the United States of America

ISBN- 978-1-947381-44-5

www.dreamingbigpublications.com

To all the women who have had to fight for the life they deserve... and to those who are still fighting.

Chapter One

My name is Joy Larson. I am a twenty-two-year-old female with dirty blonde hair, brown eyes, and a petite frame. My body will be discovered on the bank of the Kawanee River near Boone, Alabama, three-hundred and fifty miles east of Jasper, Mississippi. I'll be found face down in the mud, covered in cuts and bruises with fingerprints around my neck. My extremities will be swollen from the rising tide. Time of death will be unknown.

That's how the police will identify my body. That's what they'll tell you.

What they don't know and won't tell you is that my maiden name is Joy Elliot, and I lost more than my last name when I married Carl. Before being left for dead on the bank of the Kawanee River, I was a full-time mother, part-time waitress, and quarter-time wife. I list these jobs in order of importance. As I buckled my five-year-old son Jerry in the back seat of that 1974 Ford pinto station wagon and took a final look at our home, those last two jobs meant nothing to me.

My eyes felt hot and watery, either from crying or from the painfully low sun in the sky. I told myself it was the sun and poured the last few drops of gas from the canister into the car. Despite being fifteen years old, the station wagon still ran like rain. Thank God because I had no intention of hitchhiking my way out of my marriage. A single mother and her kid? We'd either be a target or avoided like the plague.

Wrong Girl Gone

I screwed on the cap and turned to John, one of my few remaining allies. If I'd known the first time that I waited on John at the diner that he was going to end up being the person I leaned on most during my struggles with Carl, I would have hugged him right then and there. Although most days I couldn't figure out who needed him more—me or Jerry. "Thanks for the gas." I looked from John to Jerry, who was obsessing over a slowly dying fly at the base of the window.

"It's gonna be okay," Jerry said to the fly. "You're just tired."

I turned back to John. "He really likes you, you know."

"Well, I really like him, too. Isn't that right, bud?" he said to Jerry through the open window.

"The fly died," Jerry said.

"Don't worry, little guy." John leaned down to meet Jerry's eyes. "There will be other flies."

"None like him."

"Can I get a high five for the road?"

Jerry grinned and slapped John's open hand.

John looked at me with those soulful eyes of his. "If you want, I could take Jerry for a while. Just until you get settled and find a place to stay."

I shook my head. "Thanks, but I don't want him to think he's losing both his parents. I just…" I told myself I wasn't going to break again and yet there I was, shattering like glass. "I don't know if I can do this."

"I understand. Hey—" He lowered his voice and lifted my chin. Now the tears were coming, and I couldn't do anything to stop them. "This doesn't have to be permanent. Just get away from him for a while. Clear your head."

I scanned our street for one of Carl's coworker's cars, silently praying he wouldn't be dropped off early. Usually, it was this guy named Earl who drove a cherry Volvo. I flinched every time I caught a glimpse of red. "What if he comes after me?"

"He's not going to know where you're going." Then after a pause, he said, "Where *are* you going?"

"East, probably. We'll take Interstate 20 towards Birmingham. I'm sure Kelly won't mind letting us stay for a few nights." I flinched when I noticed that Fiona, our neighbor and local gossip, was leaning in on our conversation with a keen ear as she watered her overwatered azaleas. I forced a smile. "Hi, Fiona."

She smiled back and waved. "Going somewhere?"

"Just visiting a friend."

The woman's bullshit detector was beeping furiously. "You have a nice trip now," she said and went back to watering her steroid-filled flowers. I swear that lady kept the Miracle Grow company in business.

I wiped my face and hoped she hadn't noticed how much I'd been crying, then lowered my voice to John. "Do you think she knows anything? What did she hear me say?"

"You're fine. She doesn't know anything."

"She's had to have heard the fighting before. She probably knows I'm running."

"Joy, you're gonna have to calm down. You're a wreck. It's stressin' me out." With each day, John's Chicago accent seemed to be more and more tainted with a Mississippi one. I think he preferred it that way. John was an actor back in Chicago, and he seemed to feel that his latest role of my confidant here in Mississippi was his best character yet.

"Yeah, I look like shit."

John brushed a stray hair off my face. "Very pretty shit."

"You know Carl would kill us both if he saw us together here, right?"

"Still not too fond of me, is he?"

"To put it mildly." I took a breath and pulled my hair back into a ponytail. "I've tried to convince him that I'm not your type, but he won't hear a word."

"Apparently he must think you're pretty desirable to men. Whether or not they're straight."

Wrong Girl Gone

I glanced at Fiona's house then back at John. "She still looking over here?"

"No, she's going inside. You're going to be okay." John pulled me close. "Carl doesn't deserve you." With a squeeze, he pulled away and opened the door for me, a chivalrous act I'd almost forgotten I missed. I got in and rolled down the window. "Call me from the road, if you can."

I promised him that I would. Then I checked my purse one more time for the envelope of money. The corners were starting to tear, so I'd wrapped a rubber band around it to keep the cash from falling out. At least half of it belonged to me, so I convinced myself I wasn't stealing. I was only taking my share.

I watched John's body slowly shrink as I backed out of the driveway. As soon as I was a few blocks down the road, I pulled out a cigarette and lit up, my hand shaking so much I could barely hold the damn thing. It shook as I passed the dilapidated sign on the edge of town that said, *You Are Now Leaving Jasper* as if it were a warning meant only for me. My hand continued to shake for the next fifteen miles after that.

"Where are we going?" Jerry said from the backseat.

"We're just going on a little trip, baby."

"To where?"

"I don't know yet. It's an adventure."

"Can we be pirates?"

My hand stopped shaking a little. "Aye," I said. "Of course we can be pirates."

"Arrrr!" He covered his eye with his hand. I really didn't want to be myself right then, so being pirates sounded pretty good.

It was all I could do not to slam on the breaks and turn the car around. But deep down, I didn't want to just turn the car around. I wanted to go back to when things still felt simple. To a time before I'd loaded up my life in the back of my shitty brown station wagon and left my pathetic hometown in a cloud of dust. Before I found myself black and blue and face down in the mud. Before my husband had taken everything from me. I could recall the day it all started like it was just yesterday. Maybe because it was. I was back in Jasper, picking up Jerry from the bus stop, like I did almost every day I wasn't at work, smoking a cigarette. I wasn't off today, but the diner was unbearably dead, so Dana sent me home early. Aside from missing the two hours' pay, I couldn't complain. It was an extra two hours I got to spend with Jerry.

I saw the school bus down the street and put out my cigarette. I didn't trust Jerry to not to let something slip to Carl about my smoking. Carl thought I'd quit. Said it was too expensive a habit for both of us to have, so I set aside a few quarters from my tips each night until I had enough saved up to buy the damn things myself. It's funny how Carl thought a buck sixty-five for a pack of Marlboros was too costly but gambling away half our life savings wasn't.

Jerry hopped off the bus and almost instantly started telling me a story about a boy who brought his pet toad to class for show-and-tell. The teachers always said Jerry was quiet in class, and even thought it might be a sign of autism when he started preschool. Because Jerry was chatty around me, I soon figured out that he was only quiet in school on the days after Carl had a particularly bad outburst.

"Everyone thought that because it was a toad it would give them warts, but toads don't give people warts," he explained as we walked toward the house. "So, no one wanted to hold him, but I did! I held him and he didn't even try to hop away. So, I've decided that for Christmas I want a toad, okay?"

In a moment, I went from listening to my son, with a light heart and a smile on my face, to having a fire of rage in me I'd only felt a few times before. I could no longer bring myself to hear a word Jerry was saying. My mind was focused straight ahead, straight on Carl getting out of a car that wasn't ours. It was parked just around the corner from our house, where it was almost out of view. He didn't pay the driver or shake her hand. Instead, he leaned his head through the window and kissed her like he was going to work for the first time after a weeklong honeymoon. You'd think he wanted to get caught. Like he was bragging about it.

Carl watched the woman drive away as if he were checking her out right through the rusted gold paint. When he turned to walk to the house, he spotted me and only hesitated a moment before composing himself and heading in my direction. I quickly walked Jerry to the house, waving politely at Fiona, who was looking between myself and Carl as though waiting for a show. The moment we were inside I sent Jerry upstairs.

"But you said you'd make me pancakes after school!"

"I will. For supper."

"Pancakes for supper?"

"Yeah, pancakes for supper. Now you go on upstairs while I get started."

"Are you gonna put chocolate chips in them? Not on top, but in the pancakes?"

"Yes, I'll remember the chocolate chips." I needed to get him upstairs, fast. My heart was racing and as much as I wanted to, I didn't think I'd be able to control my anger when Carl walked through the door. "You can watch TV in Mama and Daddy's room." That did it. His eyes got wide and he ran upstairs.

Once he was in the bedroom with the door shut, I went into the kitchen and tried to get my emotions under control. It wasn't the first time he'd cheated, but that didn't make it hurt any less. The first time I'd caught him with another woman, guilt got the better of him and he let me have the upper hand. The second time, I didn't have it so good. That time he beat the shit out of me for calling him a lying son of a bitch. Which he was.

If I didn't say anything now, he'd probably talk sweet to me all night, kissing me and helping me around the house here and there, motivated only by his own selfish guilt. If I did confront him, I was likely to end up covered in livid bruises.

Audrey Wilson

I heard the screen door open and grabbed the mixing bowl off the counter. Carl opened the front door and shut it behind him as I attempted to make chocolate chip pancakes with the weight of my rage bearing down on me.

Carl stepped into the kitchen. "Hey, baby," he said. I was prepared to hold my tongue. I was going to let him sweet talk me all he wanted, keep my lips shut as he kissed them. But when he tossed his keys down on the kitchen table and kissed me on the cheek, the very thought of him touching me any more than that turned my stomach to rot.

"Who is she?" I started to crumble before I'd even reached the boiling point of my anger.

He held his pose, his lips still inches from my cheek. I didn't even have to see his face to feel him grin. "You can't be serious."

"Just tell me."

"There's nothing to tell."

"I saw you down the street." I wasn't going to let myself cry, so I let my hands shake instead. I didn't care if the words that were about to come out of my mouth would leave me black and blue the next day. If anything, maybe the bruises would give him the guilt he deserved to feel. Either way, I couldn't hold back. "I just hope she was good."

That was all it took. Those three words were all it took to send my world spiraling. He hit me across the face, hard enough to knock my whole body down. I tried to stand, but before I could even get to a kneeling position, he had his fingers around my arms again, digging his nails into me and piercing my skin.

"You think you have the right to accuse me of anything?" His spit hit my face. "I'll do whatever I goddamn please and there's nothing on this earth you can do to stop me. Just like you do. I'm not blind. I see the way you look at John fucking Wrightman. You really want to tell me nothing's happening there?" Even with his piercing blue eyes burning into mine, I didn't look away. Let him think I was sleeping with John.

Wrong Girl Gone

Whatever made him feel even a fraction of the pain and anger I was feeling. "Well? You got something to say for yourself?"

"You're hurting my arms," I said.

"Oh, am I? Well, I'm sorry, baby. How does this feel?"

His nails drew blood.

"Carl, please. You promised—" Before I could say, "Promised not to do this again," he was spitting in my face again.

"And you promised me something, too." He leaned down next to me, holding onto my arms again, his anger bringing him to the verge of tears. "You promised to love me, to honor me, to obey me, all of it. And you're not doing any of that now, are you?" I didn't answer him. In some sick way, I think he actually believed I was at fault. "Are you, darling?" His voice was a mixture of sweet falsetto and seduction. "Answer me, baby doll." When I still didn't speak, he grabbed my hair, lifting my face so he could scream at it. "I know how you spend your days, flirting with any guy who so much as looks at you. You wear those tight little shorts like you're just begging for it. Do you have any idea how much it hurts me to see you looking like that for someone else?" I wished I could harness Carl's beautiful way of turning the blame for anything he'd done wrong around a hundred and eighty degrees and use it on him. He let go and stood up, taking a step away to survey what he'd done. "I don't even know who you are anymore, Joy," he said. "You made me do this. I hope you know that. You brought this on yourself." With a force of rage that I knew was meant for me, he kicked the wall and headed for the door. The late-day sun burned my eyes as the screen door swung roughly shut behind him. At last, I was safe. Alone was safe.

I tasted blood in my mouth. My head was throbbing, and my face felt like it was on fire. Tears began building up in my right eye since my left one was already swollen shut. I felt sick. I wanted to vomit, but having not eaten that day, I knew nothing would come up. It'd been over eight months since he did me in that badly.

14

Audrey Wilson

My legs gave out from under me as soon as I got on my feet and I collapsed again. I couldn't do this anymore. My body just couldn't take it. My heart just couldn't take it. I couldn't do it anymore, and yet I knew I would. Because without the money, without the means, and without the courage, what choice did I have? I was stuck with the bastard. And the saddest part was, I'd learned to be okay with that.

"Mama?" Jerry said, slowly coming down the stairs.

"No! Jerry, don't come down." My voice was shaking so much I almost choked on my own blood.

"Mama! Are you okay?" He was crying.

I couldn't stand it. I refused to let him see me like this.

"Jerry, I'm fine. Please, go upstairs and watch TV," I said, trying to strengthen my voice. "Don't worry, baby. Mama's okay."

Then I crawled over to the sink to spit the blood out of my mouth.

Chapter Two

Trees surrounded me on either side of the two-lane highway. I'd almost forgotten I wasn't alone when Jerry, half asleep, asked me what time it was, then fell back asleep before I could answer his question. The car clock was broken, so I honestly couldn't say. I'd asked Carl to fix it a hundred times, but there was always something better to do.

Whatever time it was, it was dark, and it had been dark for a while. Although it didn't feel like we'd been driving for very long, I knew we might need to stop at a hotel before I started to doze. The hum of the radio was all that was keeping me awake. That and the throbbing pain behind my eye from yesterday's beating. The swelling had gone down around my eye, so it was starting to look semi-normal. That's all that mattered in this world anyway, right? As long as you looked decent, no one could judge you. Even Jerry only asked about the bruises he could see.

But I wouldn't have to feel that pain again. I'd never have to hear Jerry look at my swollen eye and say, "Mama, why is your face turning black?" or see me changing and point to the bruise on my back, asking, "Did Daddy do that?"

No matter what happened, I wouldn't go back to Carl. I promised myself that as I took the highway farther and farther away from Jasper, farther from him. I silently made that promise to Jerry too. I just hated that I was so bad at keeping promises.

Audrey Wilson

Ours was one of the few cars in sight, but when I checked the rearview mirror, I saw a pair of headlights a good distance behind me. I felt both comforted and unnerved that we were no longer the only ones on the road. I dismissed my uneasiness and took my exit towards Alabama.

My uneasiness instantly returned when the car behind me followed us off the same exit. Even though the headlights were closer, I still couldn't make out the type of car it was. I had the sudden thought that it might be Earl's cherry Volvo and that he and Carl had been following me. Maybe I was just paranoid, but being married to Carl, I had a right to be. Besides, paranoid people live longer. If I hadn't been so paranoid all these years, instead of being twenty-two, I'd probably be dead.

I decided to pull an old trick that Mama, who was also paranoid, had taught me: If you think you're being followed, take three left turns, and see if they keep following you. I took a left on the first road I saw. At first, I thought I'd lost them. Then I saw the headlights round the corner. For the first time, I could see that it wasn't a car. It was a large, white van. When I pulled up to the next intersection, I made another left. For probably half a mile, I felt relief. But that relief was soon washed away by those bright, white lights. I stepped on the gas, going twenty over the speed limit. The van didn't speed up, but it was still following me. Finally, I did the final test and made my last left turn. My eyes flashed between the road ahead of me and the rearview mirror, waiting for headlights to appear. When they didn't, I let out a long breath.

"Mama?" Jerry said from the backseat.

I hoped he couldn't hear my heart beating in my chest. "Yeah, baby?"

"Are we there yet?" he yawned.

"Not yet, baby. Go back to sleep." For once, he did what I said. Most likely not by choice.

17

Wrong Girl Gone

I tried to keep my hands steady as I lit up a cigarette and smoked it out the window. For the rest of the drive, my eyes spent more time on the rearview mirror than on the road.

Chapter Three

While Carl was out getting plastered the night I found out about his latest infidelity, I laid in bed letting the pain of that afternoon's fight fully sink in. I liked to think Carl was drinking to try to drown out his guilt, although he was probably just looking for sympathy. He knew how pathetic he was when he was drunk.

You'd think the cheating and the beating would have been my last straw, but it wasn't. Maybe that made me strong, maybe it made me a coward. I was too exhausted to figure it out. The only thing I knew was how alone I felt whenever he did something like this. Not just the beating, but the lying. I wanted to hear someone tell me that he was a piece of shit for cheating on me. I wanted someone to try to convince me that I should leave him, just so I could fight them with the few good qualities Carl had. I wanted someone to validate me.

I tiptoed past Jerry's room so I wouldn't wake him and shuffled downstairs into the kitchen, where I stared blankly at the phone. There were three people I could call to confide in, and I felt like I rotated between them. There was John, who would get pissed as hell and insist I leave Carl. There was Mama, who I might tell about the cheating but definitely not about the beating. Denial was her favorite place of residence. Then there was Kelly, who would most likely empathize with me and gauge what I wanted to hear, which was probably the same thing I would have done. I guess it's a twin thing.

I picked up the phone and dialed Kelly's number.

"If you can't call Mama, you need to call John. Someone needs to be on your side there, Joy," Kelly said over the phone after I told her what happened. I shouldn't have even been bothering her. She'd just started her fall semester at Birmingham-Southern and didn't need my marital woes interfering with her elementary education classes. She needed to learn how to mold young minds, not fix ones that were too damaged to be molded. I guess that's your punishment when you're the "good" twin. You get the burden of dealing with the screwed-up one all your life.

"I can't. It's complicated," I said, even though it really wasn't.

"Just because Carl was one way when you fell in love with him, doesn't mean he'll always be that way."

"Yeah," I laughed. "That's becoming pretty obvious."

"Do you want me to come there?"

"God, no. You need to focus on school."

"You're more important. Besides, I haven't seen you in a while."

"I know. Almost two months." Kelly had visited us in late July. She only stayed for two nights when she was supposed to stay four, but I guess there was some issue with her roommate, so she had to leave early. Part of me didn't believe that, though. She just seemed off. All I could hope was that it was nothing I'd done. That was the thing about Kelly. You may have said something once that bothered her for years and she wouldn't tell you until so much time had passed that you had no memory of the incident whatsoever. I winced from a stab of pain that radiated down my back. "Distract me. How's school? You doing okay?"

"I have my good days and my bad," she sighed. "I just— I miss you. I miss Jerry. I think I'm just feeling lonely. When do you think you'd be free to get together?"

"Let me take a look at my work schedule and check with Carl." Kelly was silent on the other end of the phone. "Hello?"

"Sorry, I'm here. Oh, I have a new number, just so you know. Want to write it down?" I got a paper and jotted down the number as she read it off.

"Did you move?" I asked.

"Not yet. I can tell you more when I see you. Just let me know when you're free. You sure you'll be all right?"

"Yeah. I'll be fine. I'm just tired and emotional."

"John's there for you if you need him too, you know."

"I know. I just don't want to burden him with all this." That's exactly what I needed to do. Burden John with my problems, listen to his advice, then shoot it down, just like I was doing to Kelly.

"If you don't do it, I will. Do it for Jerry," she said. The truth of her words stung. Of course, she was right. I needed to look out for Jerry above everything else, but I just couldn't bear the idea of being someone else's burden tonight. I told her I'd call John, even though we both knew I probably wouldn't.

***

Around 2 a.m., just as I was finally starting to fall asleep, I heard Carl burst in through the front door, calling, "Baby," over and over again. Desperate for him not to wake Jerry, I limped out of the bedroom and hobbled downstairs. He saw me coming and stopped on the second step, holding onto the railing, and swaying like he was on a boat lost in a storm. "Joy…" He was crying loudly now. "God, forgive me. Oh, baby, please forgive me."

I tried to shush him, but I didn't think he heard me, so I just guided him to the couch instead, as far away from Jerry's room as I could get him. He put more weight on me than my body should have been able to handle, but somehow, I managed to get this stumbling, crying, two-hundred-pound man to the couch, where he collapsed into a sobbing heap.

"I'm so sorry. Baby… I'm so sorry…" he cried. I shushed him some more and helped him out of his boots so if he did get up again, his steps would at least be quieter. "You deserve better. I'm a fucking asshole." He started sobbing again. "An asshole at a shit job… You should leave me. Just fucking leave me…"

I hated seeing him this way. Not because I felt sorry for him, but because I felt like I was being tricked. How could the person who beat me black and blue be the same, sobbing mess in front of me right now? My brain couldn't make sense of it. I reached out my hand and began stroking his messy brown hair, the way I did when we first started dating. Maybe it would trigger some lost feelings of love. And maybe if he loved me enough, he wouldn't hurt me.

Carl had finally stopped crying, his breathing heavy and slow. "I don't know what's wrong with me," he said. "I think it's this house. Every fucking corner reminds me of my father. I hate it. And now I'm turning out just like him." He choked on his words and cleared his throat. I really hoped he'd say something else, so I didn't have to lie and tell him that he wasn't just like his father. That if he kept drinking and hurting us, he wouldn't end up dead from choking on his own vomit. Thankfully, he spoke again. "We should move."

"I don't think we could afford to live anywhere else."

"I don't care," he slurred. "I don't deserve either one of you. Jerry's growing up right in front of me and I'm missing all of it."

I did my best to offer Carl the words he wanted to hear. "I think he misses you playing with him," I said. "You guys used to go to the park all the time. He loved that."

"There's just no time," he said. "Working these late nights at the shop is killing me. This is why we need the money…"

He trailed off, on the verge of passing out. I assumed he was talking about the cutbacks at work. Longer hours, less pay. Although we'd been tight on money before, this was worse. I could see the stress it put on him. I wished there was something I could say to him. Some magic words that would sober him up and bring back the Carl that he used to be, if there ever was such a person. But there just wasn't anything. There were no words. There was just that damn reality.

"Are you still gonna see her?" I ask cautiously.

"Who?"

I resisted the urge to push him off the couch. "That woman."

"What? No, of course not. Baby, it was so stupid. I'll never see her again, I swear."

I stroked his hair with my numb fingers. "Do you love me anymore?" It probably wasn't the right question to ask, but I was still compelled to ask it.

"Why would you even ask me something like that? Do you know how much that hurts me?"

"I'm sorry. I don't want to hurt you," I said. He got silent again. "You're not gambling again, are you?"

"Of course not. What is this? First, it's all this 'Do you love me anymore?' shit, and then you start accusing me of something I gave up months ago."

"I was just asking." And I was just asking. It was something that had been bothering me for some time. Even after I got his answer, it still bothered me.

His chest heaved. "I'm sorry. God, I'm sorry. Jerry hates me, doesn't he? He has every right to hate me."

"He doesn't hate you."

"He does. I know he does."

Carl sat up, knocking me off balance.

He stumbled off the couch and used the furniture to walk himself to the staircase. "I need to ask him… I need to know if he loves me…"

I quickly pulled myself up and went after him. "No, no, no—don't do that, Carl. He's asleep."

"You can't tell me what to do. I need to know."

His feet missed the first few steps but somehow, he managed to make his way up the stairs and into Jerry's room.

Wrong Girl Gone

I followed him, even though I knew there was nothing I could do but stand outside the door as Carl searched the darkness for Jerry's bed. "Hey, buddy... You awake?"

I heard the mattress squeak as he sat down next to Jerry, who stirred and slowly woke. "What's going on?" he said.

"You love me, don't you? Jerry?"

"Of course, Daddy. But I'm tired."

"Say it. Say you love me."

I leaned against the wall, just watching the two of them. I had been tricked, and I hated myself for it. I hated myself for thinking for one second that Carl actually loved me and Jerry more than he loved himself. He couldn't love anything more than he loved himself. I learned that years ago, yet a part of me still pretended there was a chance it would change. I thought it would change when he first put his tarnished class ring on my finger, or when we got married and he gave me promises he'd thrown out as quickly as he'd made them. I thought it would change when Jerry was born because he wouldn't have had a choice but to put his son before himself. But he didn't. He only ever loved himself. He couldn't even go to sleep unless he knew others loved him as much as he did.

"I love you, Daddy," Jerry said. And we could all go to sleep.

Chapter Four

Jerry was still asleep in the back seat when I pulled off the dark road into the gas station for a fill-up and some food. He'd always been a light sleeper and woke just as I turned off the engine.

"Mama?" he whispered.

"Hey, sleepyhead." I turned around to face him. He had his pillow pressed up against the door and was lying with his head flat on the seat. I'd felt the car getting cold a few miles back and draped my old jean jacket over him to help him keep warm. It was starting to slide off, so I reached back and tucked him in better.

"Where are we?" he asked.

"We're at a gas station. I'm going to find a place for us to sleep soon, okay?"

He rubbed his eye. "I'm hungry."

"I'll get us some snacks."

"I want Ho Hos," he fussed. "And chocolate milk."

"I'll do my best."

"You have to get them, though!"

"Yes, I will." Now was not the time for a temper tantrum. "I'm going to lock the doors. You lay down and stay here, okay? Don't open the door for anyone, except me. Got it, baby?"

He nodded and turned over under the jacket. I got out of the car and locked the door, taking my purse and the money with me.

Wrong Girl Gone

The lights in the gas station were a greenish-yellow and made my hands look sickly. I grabbed a couple packages of Suzy-Q's and Ho Hos, a box of Pop-Tarts, a couple dry sandwiches, and two bottles of milk—one plain, one chocolate. I thought about getting a Dr. Pepper, but the caffeine would just keep me up all night. There was a stand of overpriced, cheap-looking watches by the door next to a display of sunglasses. I did my best to pick out the most attractive one, then took my purchases to the front counter. I paid for the food, gas, and watch. Then I asked the attendant where the nearest motel was. He said there was one about twenty-five miles up the road. It was called the Best Way Inn Motel. I laughed and asked him if that was really the motel's name and he said yes. Before I left, I checked the clock behind the counter and set my new watch five minutes fast to keep myself on time.

I walked out of the gas station with my bag of goodies and stopped dead when I saw a man standing just out of the light of the service area, staring at my car, as if studying every detail, down to the license plate number.

"Hey!" I shouted. The man looked at me, then slowly walked off down the street into the darkness. I ran over to the car, trying to catch a glimpse of his face but also terrified to see it. But he was nowhere in sight. All I could see were trees; my eyes weren't good enough to see very much in the dark. With my heart nearly pounding out of my chest, I got in the car and drove down the road as quickly as it would take me.

"What's going on?" Jerry said from the backseat.

"It's okay, baby. Go back to sleep."

"I wasn't asleep," he said, though his voice was weary. "Who was that?"

"Who?"

"The man."

I tried to keep my right foot steady. "You saw the man?"

"Why was he looking in our car?"

"What?"

"He tried to open it, but he wasn't you, so I didn't let him in."

By the time I found the voice to respond, Jerry had already fallen back asleep. I was torn between wanting him to wake up so he could talk to me and wanting him to sleep so he didn't have to. My eyes flashed to the rearview mirror every fifteen seconds to see if the man was following us. Or to see if that white van was following us. For all I knew, they were one and the same. Just because I didn't see the van at the gas station didn't mean it wasn't there. Now that we were on the road again, it was too dark to see very far back, which both eased my nerves and heightened them. Finally, I willed myself to stop shaking and turned on the radio. I needed the hum.

Chapter Five

The morning after the beating, when I awoke with my face throbbing, I started to wish I had called John. Because John would have suggested he beat the shit out of Carl for banging me up so bad, and I might have actually taken him up on it. Usually, Carl made sure to hit me below the neckline, so no one would see the bruises, but I guess he decided to break his own rules this time. I did my best to cover the bruises on my face with ten times the makeup I'd normally wear, although it didn't help much.

Carl didn't say anything when I set his coffee cup down in front of him that morning. I wasn't sure if he even remembered the drunken apology that he'd thrown at me the night before. Then, as I turned to go back to the counter, he gently grabbed my wrist, causing me to flinch.

"How you feeling today, baby?" He stroked the inside of it with his thumb, a motion that used to make me weak at the knees but now just made me nauseous.

I nodded my head. "I'm fine." He kissed my hand, gave it a squeeze, and turned to his coffee. With his guilt showing and Jerry upstairs, I figured it was as good a time as any to mention paying a visit to Kelly. He owed me that much. "I was thinking of visiting Kelly next weekend."

Carl didn't say anything at first. He just took a long sip of his coffee. When he set the cup down, he gave a sharp little laugh, and I instantly knew I picked the wrong moment.

"Why do you have to do that? We're having a perfectly nice morning, and you have to make trouble."

"I guess I don't see why me visiting Kelly makes trouble."

"Honestly? I don't think she's good for you. Last time she was here, you brooded for days after because she left so quickly, thinking it was your fault."

"I know, I overreacted. She just had some issue come up with her roommate."

"But don't you see what that did to you? You're so invested in what she thinks of you. Being around her always does a number on your self-esteem."

I hated to admit it, but part of me agreed with him. "Even so. She's my sister."

"Well, I might be working next weekend, so no one will be here to watch Jerry."

"I could take him with me," I offered. I knew he missed her as much as I did.

"I don't think that's a good idea. I don't want her knocking down his self-esteem like she's done to you." He stood up and walked over to me, resting his hand on my less bruised cheek. "Let's hold off on any big trips right now. Okay, baby? You've been through a lot lately."

He kissed my forehead, and in that moment, I hated myself. Because for one, brief second, I let myself feel protected by him. Because I needed to feel something.

***

When I limped into work at Hank's Diner for my shift that day, my coworker Veronica immediately asked what happened to my face, despite the layers of makeup. I mumbled something about walking into an open cabinet in my kitchen, then faked an embarrassed laugh. She seemed to buy it at the time. Then, when it was time for my break, Dana gave me an extra fifteen minutes for no reason, when she usually made me cut it fifteen minutes short. I figured Dana and Veronica were too self-absorbed to care about what happened to me other than for their own gossiping purposes and took the extra fifteen minutes without question.

I sat in the back corner of the half-empty diner, eating a cheeseburger with relish. Normally it would be one of my favorite meals, but my jaw hurt too much to enjoy it. I was passing the time by trying to remember where I got each of the random stains on my faded pink apron when John walked into the restaurant. He walked directly over to me.

I was about to tell him he shouldn't be here, that if one of Carl's friends saw us together, we'd both be dead. But John sat down across from me in the booth before I could put any words together.

"I got your message," he said.

"What message?"

"The one you left on my machine last night. That fucking piece of shit. How could he keep doing this to you?" I thought for a moment before it hit me: Kelly. We had the same voice, after all. Sometimes it really pissed me off when she didn't listen to me. Other times I was grateful when she didn't. "How you holding up?"

"It hurts to eat. You want the rest of my burger?" I pushed the plate across to John.

"That bad, huh?"

I nodded and sipped on my water. John sighed and picked up the burger. "You want to talk about it?"

I shook my head. John took a bite of the burger. He knew me well enough by now to know not to push me. "Did you talk to Kelly at least?" I nodded. John took a breath, shaking his head. "You've got an angel looking out for you there, Joy. A lot of them. Don't push them all away so fast. They don't get their wings from standing by idly, you know."

"No, they get them when someone rings a bell."

"It takes a lot more than that. The bell is just their graduation march after they've done all their angelic duties."

I mustered a tired laugh and was suddenly reminded of the early days when John and I first met. Maybe because things actually felt normal for a second. He was a regular at the diner and always sat in this very booth, so he always got me for his waitress. He'd come over during his lunch hour almost every day and we'd talk the whole time. He'd tell me stories of his days in theater back in Chicago and I'd share with him whatever funny thing Jerry had done that day. For how little we had in common, we really clicked.

John zeroed in on my eye and, for the first time, really got a good look at the shiner that was slowly seeping through my makeup. "Goddamn him," he said under his breath. Then he rubbed his eyes beneath his glasses. "Goddamn him." John had been trying to convince me to leave Carl since the first time I showed up at the diner with a shiner and he could tell I was lying about falling on a coffee table. "I'd help you, you know. If you ever wanted to get away from him. I'd do whatever it took to keep you safe. You know that, right?"

Yeah, I knew. And I was more grateful for him than he'd ever know. He was completely right. I should leave him. I had enough sense to know that. The things I didn't have were money and courage. Maybe I was wrong, but I couldn't think of any other single mothers who could get by working part-time hours as a waitress.

I looked over John's shoulder and saw a newer waitress named Melody conversing with Veronica, both of whom kept glancing over at John.

"What?" John turned to look at what I was looking at and immediately both women occupied themselves with busywork.

"Nothing," I said. John shrugged and took another bite. "How's the burger?"

"Delicious," he said. "I don't know how you ever thought to put relish on a cheeseburger, but you're a genius."

"I think it's the only way my mama got me to eat vegetables as a kid." I stole a fry back from the plate. "Thanks."

"They're your fries," he said.

"No. Thanks for coming here. I don't know what I'd do without you. I'd probably have given up a long time ago."

31

Wrong Girl Gone

"Just not today," John said and took another bite of the burger.

Before John left, I remembered I still had the Chicago Cubs sweatshirt he'd loaned me a few weeks ago when I'd gotten locked out of the house on a rare cold night. Or, more specifically, Carl had accidentally locked me out of the house while he was passed out drunk. I'd been keeping it in my locker at work, afraid Carl would stumble upon it and take it as proof that I was sleeping with John.

On the way to my locker, I passed Veronica, who was getting ready to clock out.

"Your friend still here?"

"John? Yeah, I'm just returning his sweatshirt." I pulled it out of the locker and tried to smooth it so it wasn't too wrinkled.

"Hopefully he washed it before he gave it to you."

"What?"

Veronica rolled her eyes. "One of the regulars decided not to eat here when they walked in and saw him sitting there with you."

"Why not?"

"Let's not play dumb, alright Joy? It's an old act."

That would have been fine, only I wasn't playing dumb. "I'm sorry. I don't—"

"It's just better if people like him stay out of the restaurant when we can help it. If he comes in on his own, we have to serve him, but when someone sees one of them talking with a waitress, they're gonna wanna stay away from our food."

Instant rage burned inside me. "Why is that?"

"Jesus, Joy, he's queer as a doorknob. No one wants to think about that while they're having lunch."

"What are you afraid of, Veronica? Huh? That he'll touch our food and contaminate it and make everyone in this godforsaken town gay?"

She laughed. "Of course not." Then she turned all serious again and lowered her voice. "That he'll spread... you know."

"No. I don't know."

32

She glanced around. "AIDS."

Despite all the violence that's been done to me, I am not a violent person by nature. But at that moment, I wanted to hit her. I wanted to hit her so hard she knew what it felt like to be me under Carl's fist or to be John when he was fourteen behind his high school back in Chicago.

I held John's sweatshirt with one hand and slammed my locker shut with the other. "John doesn't have AIDS and even if he did it is not carried that way." My voice and every part of my body was shaking. "It isn't a 'gay' disease or whatever the hell you think it is and you need serious help if you're judging people who have it anyway."

I pushed past her and out to the dining area where John was waiting for me. He saw the tears in my eyes and redness in my face before I could hide them. "Joy, what's wrong?" he asked.

I shook my head and handed him his sweatshirt.

"What happened?"

"People are assholes."

He took a breath. "I don't have to visit you at work anymore if it makes things difficult."

"No. I want you to. Don't let them stop you."

John stepped off to the side with me and lowered his voice. "Look, I knew what I was getting into when I moved here for my stupid sales job. People are cruel and... well, they can be ignorant too. But how people treat me doesn't define me and it doesn't define you."

I nodded and fought the tears. It sounded like something my daddy would have said. From what I remembered of him, at least.

"Thanks for lunch." I gave him a quick kiss on the cheek and ran to the back before the customers could see me break down.

I curled up in a dark corner near the storage room and held my knees to my chest like a child in time-out. I felt like I did when I was ten after I'd tried to defend a nest of baby bunnies on the playground at school. This girl named Tiffany kept trying to poke them with a stick even after I told her not to. We started getting into it pretty bad, but she crossed the line when she called my dad a retard. I shoved her down into the wood chips then went over to the swings and cried. People could call me any names they wanted to or hit me as hard as they'd like, but the minute they came after someone I loved, they'd have hell to pay.

After about fifteen minutes, my boss—or as the ten-year-old me saw it, the principal—Dana came over to take me to her office.

I sat down across from her in the small, cigarette smoke-filled room with more cleaning supplies in it than paperwork and waited for her to tell me what a bad girl I'd been. While I waited, I looked at the wrinkles in Dana's skin. I'd never known exactly how old she was. She looked like she was about sixty-five, but that was probably just thanks to alcohol and cigarettes. She was likely closer to forty.

Dana took a puff of her cigarette and set it in her crowded ashtray.

"I'm not firing you, Joy. So you can wipe that scared look off your face," she croaked. I didn't know if that was good news since I wasn't losing my job or bad news since I hadn't even considered being fired a possibility. "And I really don't give a rats' ass what goes on in your personal life so long as you keep it there." I wasn't quite sure if she was referring to the bruises that were starting to show through my makeup or the situation between Veronica and me, but I wasn't about to ask. "Look at you," she said. "Your skin's discolored, your eyes are bloodshot. You're a mess. How much do you drink daily, anyway?"

I didn't really know what to say, so I dimly blurted out, "I don't drink, ma'am."

"Then how'd you get that shiner? You don't end up looking like that running into a cabinet."

I should have just humored her and said falling down drunk was what gave me all those cuts and bruises. That would have been the simpler answer. "I'm just… kind of clumsy."

She looked at me for a long minute, trying to decide if she should believe me or not. "I see," she said, almost as though she'd been hoping for a different answer. "Maybe you should take the rest of the day off. Take it easy and we'll see you back here in the morning."

I nodded and tried not to make eye contact with Veronica as I walked out of the diner. But if I'd known that was going to be the last that she'd see of me, I would have.

Chapter Six

I could tell from the moment we pulled into the parking lot that the Best Way Inn Motel didn't deserve the title of "best" in any sense of the word. I asked the man in the office what town we were in. He said we were in Clinchmore, Alabama. I didn't even remember passing the sign that welcomed us to Alabama.

I paid him the twenty-five dollars for the night from the envelope of money, then went back to the car to retrieve our luggage. Jerry began unloading the backseat while I opened the trunk. As I lifted out my suitcase, I caught a glimpse of white and turned to see that white van turn into the parking lot. I froze, my hand gripping the handle of my suitcase in case I needed to use it as a weapon.

"Jerry, get in the car and shut the door."

"Why?"

"Just do it."

Jerry did as he was told. The van parked by the front desk. I waited for someone to get out. I waited for *that man* to get out, but he didn't. After a moment, the van slowly backed out, turned around, and got back on the road. I watched it brazenly as it drove past, seeing if I could catch a glimpse of the driver. Even though I couldn't see him in the dark, I was convinced it was the same man from the gas station. It had to be. Whoever he was, he gave me an awful feeling. I let myself breathe again, really hoping I was just being paranoid.

Audrey Wilson

When I opened the door to our hotel room, I could see dust floating through the air. The thick air made it hard to breathe and when I did manage to get a breath in, the smell rotted the insides of my nostrils. I locked both locks on the door and tried to shake the image of the man and the white van out of my head. Part of me wished I was the only one who had seen him at the gas station and not Jerry. That way I could convince myself he wasn't real.

I sat down on the bed. The powder blue sheets were cold and damp and matched the heavy curtains. My guess was that they bought the whole set when McRae's Department Store was having a going-out-of-business sale fifteen years ago. I tried not to think about all the people that must have slept in that bed and what they might have done there.

After hitting the air conditioner with my fist a couple of times, it finally came on, blowing icy air that smelled like burnt rubber. Jerry was wide awake by then. He'd already gotten a hold of the bag of contraband and was attempting to open a packet of Ho Hos.

"Open it." He handed me the Ho Hos.

"That's dessert. Eat your sandwich first." I handed him a tuna sandwich, the only kind in the gas station I knew he'd eat.

He tossed the sandwich on the bed and shook the Ho Hos at me. "No! Ho Hos first."

"Sandwich first."

"Come on!" He shook the Ho Hos harder, his little face turning red.

"Fine." I took the Ho Hos away from him and handed him the sandwich again. "No Ho Hos at all then."

He pouted and I prepared for the meltdown that was sure to come, but instead, he glanced at the sandwich and picked it up. I enjoyed my minor win as I watched him take a bite.

"Where are we?" he asked after we ate for a few minutes in silence.

"Clinchmore, Alabama."

Jerry giggled. "That's a silly name."

37

"Maybe a silly person named it."

Jerry smiled but I could tell something was on his mind.

"What are we doing tomorrow?" he asked. Before I could answer, his eyes got wide. "Can we see *Back to the Future 2*?" We owned the first one on video and Jerry had watched it so many times the tape had started to go bad. I think he was more excited for the sequel than he was for Christmas.

"It doesn't come out till November, baby."

Jerry took a long breath and processed this unfortunate news. "Then where are we going?"

"We're going to see Kiki." For a two-year-old, Kiki was a lot easier to say than Aunt Kelly. The nickname just seemed to stick.

Jerry started jumping up and down. I knew how he felt. I was looking forward to spending some time with her too, despite the unfortunate circumstances.

Once he'd emptied the chocolate milk bottle, he didn't hesitate to ask me where the remote for the TV was. I looked at the dinosaur of a thing. It was a big, old, brown one from the fifties, rabbit ears and all. When I told Jerry there wasn't a remote and the only way to change the channel was by turning the knob under the screen, he looked at me like I was crazy. After adjusting the antennas for ten minutes, I finally managed to get some old movie with Fred Astaire to come through. He and Ginger were soft-shoeing across the screen. Him in a dark-colored suit, and her in a long, luxurious evening gown that sparkled and radiated even in black and white. Watching the two of them made everything feel normal again, even if only for a moment.

It was almost two in the morning when the movie finished and Jerry began complaining of a tummy ache. I knew all those sweets were a bad idea. I gave him some water and antacid, then I laid him on the bed and gently rubbed his tummy.

"Mama?" he mumbled. "When's Daddy coming home?"

"Daddy's not coming here tonight."

For a moment, I thought he was asleep. "Mama?" he said.

"Mmm?"

"Will you keep us safe?"

"Of course I will."

"Promise?"

"Promise."

I rolled him onto his tummy so he could be more comfortable. Then I brushed his hair out of his face and rubbed his back in soft, circular motions. Just as I was tucking him under the covers, he reached his little arm out from beside him and locked it around mine.

Just like Mama had done for me so many times, I sang to him in my softest voice. "You are my sunshine, my only sunshine. You make me happy when skies are gray…"

As I sang, I thought about Carl. I tried not to, but it was a habit, I guess. Had he gotten home yet? If so, did he miss us? I had a hard time picturing Carl missing anything. Past Carl, maybe. But that Carl was different. If he were still Past Carl, maybe I wouldn't be sitting in a dumpy hotel room with our son and an envelope of stolen money.

Emotional damages, I decided to think of it as.

Chapter Seven

I had about two hours before Jerry got out of kindergarten after Dana sent me home early, so I decided to get a head start on my errands. The entire time there was an awful feeling in my stomach, constant ache in my cheekbone, and massive migraine steadily growing between my eyes.

Carl had been getting home later every night because of all the cutbacks he was taking at work and the amount of money he brought home grew smaller by the week. I was pressed to stretch our money every cent I could, even if it meant driving to the next county to buy Carl's beer and cigarettes because the sin tax was two percent less there. Sometimes I felt like the money he brought home just didn't add up next to the number of hours he worked, but whenever I'd brought it up to him, he just said, "Jesus, Joy, what do you think 'cutbacks' mean?"

We hadn't been this tight since Carl went on his last gambling binge, just after New Year's. I prayed that wasn't what was happening now.

"I'm gonna win it all back," he'd said.

"We'll never have to pinch pennies again," he'd said.

"Baby doll, I'm at Red's bar in Jackson and I had to sell the Buick to pay my debt, can you come pick me up?" he'd said.

After I'd picked him up, I yelled at him for all he put us through, thinking he'd be too drunk and ashamed to hurt me, especially while I was driving. I was wrong. We just had to pull over on the highway so he could hit me. When we finally got home, the alcohol started leaving his system in the form of tears, and he promised he'd never gamble again and if he did, I could leave him.

And to my knowledge up until that point, he had actually followed through with that one.

Part of me got mad thinking about the money we would have had if that whole incident never happened. At the same time, I knew Carl was trying. If I was going to stay with him I might as well be happy with the little things he did accomplish.

After I picked Jerry up from school, the first place we went was Mama's trailer in Sunnyside Mobile Home Park, the same one Kelly and I grew up in. She wanted to give Jerry his birthday present. Jerry was five years and three months old. She took "better late than never" a little too literally.

She made him a grilled cheese sandwich and gave him some toys from Dollar General. Mama didn't make much working part-time as a teller at the bank, but it was enough to get by on. And to Jerry, her grilled cheese and cheap toys were the best belated birthday presents ever. I was grateful he was still young enough that he couldn't see the shame in her eyes when she gave him the presents wrapped in newspaper. But I wished I hadn't seen the fear in her eyes when she stared just a little too closely at my bruises. I'd done my best to apply more makeup after crying it off at work, but in the overheated, tin can trailer, I was already starting to sweat it off.

While Jerry was packing up his new toys so we could leave, Mama took me out of his earshot and spoke in a whisper. "Sweetie, what happened to your eye?"

For a second, I was so tempted to just tell her about everything Carl did to me. She deserved to know. I owed her that much. At the same time, I just didn't know if she really wanted to know. She liked to live in denial, and I decided I might as well join her.

Wrong Girl Gone

"I walked into a cabinet." I was glad she couldn't see any of the other bruises on my body or imagine the throbbing I felt in my chest.

"Oh, for heaven's sake, Joy!" she said, practically relieved. I knew deep down she only bought it because she wanted to. "You need to be more careful. You always rush through tasks and end up hurtin' yourself. Like that time last spring when you walked into a door." More like Carl's fist slammed into my shoulder, but sure. We'll go with the door.

As we left, Mama mouthed, "Be careful," to me in an extravagantly expressive manner. I smiled and nodded, but, just once, I wished she wouldn't buy it. I wished that she would call me out on my shitty lie and convince me to leave Carl. Deep down, I was certain she knew what he did to me, the same way I saw all the empty wine bottles hiding around her trailer but pretended not to.

By the time we finished our visit to Grandmother's House, it was already four forty-five. I had so badly wanted to get home before the five o'clock meltdown started, and I knew I still had to make a run to the currency exchange to pay the gas bill before the day's end. It was the last of my money, but Carl got paid tomorrow, so I figured I was safe.

We drove to the currency exchange. I left a very fussy Jerry in the car with the doors locked, went in to pay the bill, and returned to the car. Finally feeling relief, I began to drive us home. As soon as I allowed the relief to just barely sink in, the gaslight on the dashboard went on. I panicked. I had fifty-four cents in my purse, forty-two cents short of a gallon of gas at the nearest station. To add to my stress, Jerry was now crying in the backseat, complaining that he was hot and thirsty.

After waiting at the stoplight for what felt like ten minutes, I felt that surge of relief again as the light turned green and I was allowed to press on the gas. The car stalled.

So long, relief.

I struggled with the ignition until I finally got it going another few feet.

Audrey Wilson

Then it stalled again.

I took a breath, made sure Jerry was buckled in tight, then I pushed that car over a mile home, blinkers going all the way.

There was no way in hell I could call Carl and ask him to pick up gas on the way home from work. He'd do it, and then he'd damn well teach me a lesson after. I could call John, but I didn't want to worry him more than I already had at Hank's. If I'd had any money at all, I would have taken Jerry, walked to the gas station, and picked up a gallon myself, but the house was bare.

My first plan was to transfer gas from the lawnmower to a canister, then into the car. When I had managed to get myself pinned under the lawnmower for the third time, I realized that I was simply too scrawny to lift a lawnmower upside down by myself and gave up.

As soon as that plan failed, I was forced to move to Plan B before any of the neighbors heard the crash and came to see what I was doing.

Plan B: Go sofa cushion diving and scrape together just enough for a gallon.

Jerry and I made a game of it, which helped lighten our moods temporarily. I needed something, anything, to keep my mind off the hell I'd face if Carl came home early. He let me have the car three days a week, and I knew I'd lose that privilege if one of his coworkers dropped him off at home to a dead car and a soon-to-be-dead wife.

Jerry started by searching through the drawers in the kitchen while I stuck my hands in the sides of the sofa. We'd been looking for half an hour and the most either of us had found was twenty-seven cents, an old, half-licked cherry sucker, and part of a candy cane from at least two Christmases ago.

Just when I was close to giving up, I slid my hand under the seat of Carl's easy chair and thought I'd struck gold when I felt paper. I pulled out what I'd hoped was going to be a crisp, twenty-dollar bill. I wasn't that lucky. It was just a folded piece of paper. I noticed writing on the inside and opened it:

Carl. We had a good game last night. You know how to pick them. I enclosed your share of the winnings, plus what I borrowed the other day. The total should be $975. See you Saturday for poker. -Dan

Saturday? Saturday a week ago, or Saturday last year? I hardly stopped to think. A minute later I was upstairs in our bedroom, tearing the whole place apart. He was keeping the money somewhere. He had to be. If he were keeping it from me, he wouldn't hide it in the bank, at least not our bank, where Mama worked. He wouldn't be that stupid. That was the thing that threw you about Carl. He acted like a redneck and enjoyed playing dumb, but he was often much smarter than he appeared.

I grabbed drawers out of the dresser and dumped them upside down on the floor, searching through his socks and underwear. The rage that had built up inside me was finally rearing its ugly head and I couldn't help but think to myself that destroying his belongings might act as some form of therapy. They probably make people pay to do that sort of thing in a clinic.

After opening and dumping out every box and container in the closet, I came to the realization that I had finally lost it. The note was probably old, leftover from his gambling days. I took a deep breath and began trying to put things back how I'd found them. When I picked up one of Carl's Playboy magazines that I "didn't know about" to add to the stack, a heavy, worn-out envelope fell out.

Jerry's voice sneaked up behind me, causing me to jump as I reached for the envelope.

"Mama? Did you find any money?"

I held the envelope in my sweaty hands. "Not yet."

"Then who won?"

I released the air from my lungs before I fainted. "We're going to find out." I ripped open the envelope and immediately saw crinkled green paper sticking out. I counted the money quickly, just to get an idea of how many lies he'd been hiding in our closet.

There were over fifty, hundred-dollar bills in that envelope. My hands were shaking so furiously I began to laugh. I could think of a thousand names to call that man I was married to, none of which Jerry should hear, but I couldn't think of anything else. All I could see was green in my hands when my eyes were open and red behind my eyelids when I blinked.

You don't earn that kind of money with a job like Carl had, dealing with "cutbacks" and paying countless bills every month. In fact, you don't earn that kind of money at all. You win it.

That lying son of a bitch.

"Never again," he'd said.

"I'm done with it," he'd said.

"If I ever do it again, you can leave me," he'd said.

Well, he did it again and he wasn't done with it. So, I could leave him.

My sweaty hands and sudden rage were damaging the paper in front of my eyes. How could I have, for one pathetic second, thought he was done gambling? Of course he had been gambling. Playing poker with his friends, driving to the casino behind my back when I thought he was working… whatever it took. Gambling meant money. Money meant everything. He must have been saving it up for something.

But what?

My first thought was that he was going to leave me. Wait until I was at my weakest, then sell this house, take Jerry, and leave me with not a penny to my name. I'd be right back where I started—in a trailer in Nowheresville with nothing and no future. But he didn't care what he did to me. He didn't care at all. And why should he? Money was what could buy him happiness. If you have happiness, you don't need anything else.

Wrong Girl Gone

John came over about fifteen minutes after I broke down and called him. He even brought a gallon of gas with him, too.

"You should take it," he said when I showed him the money. Of all the possible responses, I hadn't expected him to give that one. "Pack up Jerry, take the money, and get out."

I didn't know if I could, but I knew I wanted to. So, so badly. I wanted to get away from this man I was married to. This lying, cheating, abusive scum. I finally had the money, now all I needed was the courage. But the sad truth was, I was still afraid of him.

"I don't know if I can."

John took my hand and looked me in the eye. He wasn't afraid to look people in the eye like I was. "Joy, I can't stand to see you like this," he said. "Please, get out before he hurts you again. Don't give him that chance. Next time it could be Jerry."

"No…" I said in disbelief. "No, he wouldn't hurt Jerry."

"Why not?"

"He's just a child."

"For now. But what happens when he gets older and talks back to his father? You think Carl is going to stand for that?"

I didn't answer. I just tried to wrap my mind around the idea that Carl could harm my son, a possibility that I'd somehow refused to believe.

John leaned in closer to me. He had that look in his eyes like when he's describing the plot of an intense movie or raving about the beauty of a Van Gogh painting, only this time there was a burning flicker of desperation behind his pupils. "You can bet the day will come when Jerry does something that sends Carl over the edge and nothing is going to stop him from laying into your son with those hands of his. Not even you."

"You don't know that. He loves Jerry."

"Yeah. He loves you too."

That was the moment. The glass-shattering moment that I'd been waiting for those past six years. Carl did love me. He loved us both. And if he could hurt someone he loved the way he hurt me, what was stopping him from one day doing the same thing to Jerry? Whenever Carl was about to lose it, I always sent Jerry to his room. I made sure he was safe before I even considered my own safety. I could recover from the scars, from the bruises. Jerry was too young to experience that heartache and for as long as I was alive, he wouldn't have to. Jerry would never have to feel the same pain from his father that I did. I swore on my life that I'd never let Carl lay a finger on him. I was dispensable. Jerry wasn't.

John helped Jerry pack while I watched out the front window, keeping an eye out for Earl's cherry red Volvo, or one of Carl's other coworkers' cars. Maybe even his new friend's car, whatever the fuck her name was. With my luck, this would be the day he came home early.

The phone rang, and I was certain everyone in the house was suddenly holding their breath. John stepped out from Jerry's bedroom and took a few steps down the stairs while I answered the phone in the kitchen after the third ring.

"Hey, babe." When I heard Carl's voice on the other line, my heart pounded uncontrollably. It felt so big I didn't think I could swallow. "Just wanted to let you know that me and a couple of the guys from work are going out for beers and some food, so I won't be home for supper," he said.

"Oh, okay." I let myself breathe again. "Do you… have enough money for that?"

"Huh? Yeah, I have a few bucks. Some guy tipped me a twenty today for fixing his Mercedes. What a life that must be, right?" He laughed with that bark of his.

My blood began to boil, but still, I kept my cool. "Yeah. What a life."

"I gotta run. I'll see you later. Love you, babe." He hung up on his end and I did on mine. My insides were numb. I didn't see how that man could love anything.

Chapter Eight

Jerry and I ended up sleeping later than I'd planned and stopped for breakfast at a diner in a town called Pletcher. Even though I felt guilty sitting with my child in the smoking section, my nerves were too on edge to not have a cigarette with my coffee. Jerry melted down just as we were leaving the restaurant because I wouldn't let him have a packet of peanut M&M's at the register counter. If he hadn't just finished off an entire stack of chocolate chip pancakes, I may have considered it. Everyone stared at me as I carried a kicking and screaming Jerry out of the restaurant like I was the worst parent this side of the Mississippi.

As we left the restaurant, my heart jumped when I noticed a white van pulling out of the parking space in front of me. It was a little less intimidating in the daylight, but still. That damn white van. I could have sworn it was the same one, but there were a lot of white vans on the road, especially right off the highway. It couldn't be the same one. Or if it was, it was just someone coincidentally headed in the same direction as I was, right? Right. I was just imagining things. I was paranoid from living with Carl for six years and delirious from lack of sleep and too many Ho Hos.

We got back on the road again and, with a few oldies playing on the radio, Jerry calmed down. I, however, was still a little uneasy. I wanted to give Mama a call but was worried she might let slip to Carl where I was headed. Still, I knew she was probably worried about me and I hated to make her worry. After much deliberation, I finally decided. I'd call her from the next payphone I came across just to let her know we were okay, but I wouldn't tell her where I was. Good plan.

As soon as she answered, I regretted my decision.

"Joy? Joy do you have any idea what chaos and hell you are putting me through? You think this is funny, I'll bet. You decide to just take off on a little road trip with my grandchild—"

"Mama, listen—"

"No. You listen to me. You've got absolutely no right to just go off as you please with no word to Carl or anyone else where you're going!"

"Mama, you're going to have to listen—"

"I'm not listening to a word you have to say until you tell me exactly where you are."

"Mama, would you please listen to me for one second?"

I could hear her next word catch in her throat before she paused and let out a defeated sigh. "I'm sorry. Go ahead." That was a lot easier to do than I thought it would be, although I knew she was only listening because she was scared.

"I don't think you realize what I've been living with for the past six years. Carl isn't the nicest person, in case you haven't noticed." It took me by surprise that those words turned out to be a lot more difficult to say than I expected. They almost hurt coming up, in fact. "I needed to get Jerry away from him for a while. He's been keeping money from me, Mama. A lot of money. I think he's gambling again."

When I'd finished speaking, she uttered, "Dear Lord, Joy. Even so, you can't just take off without telling anyone. I've been worried sick…" followed by the sound of her taking a gulp of something. After years of cleaning up empty wine bottles from her bedroom, I knew better than to think it was just water. Memory bottles, as she liked to call them. "Memories are just heavy air that can fit anywhere," she'd say. When she had a memory she didn't like, she'd drink the poison from the bottle to make room for her own heavy air.

Wrong Girl Gone

"I thought you weren't drinking anymore."

"I'm not." She cleared her throat. "And don't tell me what to do." Her voice softened slightly. "Do you need anything?" Just less pain, a good life for my kid, and maybe to see my daddy again. The same things she wanted. But Daddy left me with nothing but an old harmonica and sad smile eleven years ago, and I hadn't spoken to him since, so I was pretty sure that last one wasn't going to happen.

"No thanks, Mama. We're okay." I had a cigarette in my mouth when I spoke and hoped she didn't notice. Probably the same way she'd hoped I wouldn't notice the sip from her memory bottle.

"Well, I'm here if you need me," she said. "Take care of yourself."

"Thanks, Mama."

"And Joy?"

"Yeah?"

"Don't smoke around Jerry."

I guess even poison from her memory bottles couldn't numb all her senses.

Chapter Nine

When we stopped for gas, I called Kelly at the new number she'd given me. I didn't tell her about the money yet, just that I needed to get away from Carl for a while. I said we were headed towards Birmingham-Southern and asked if we could move our visit up a bit since we were only an hour and a half away.

"You know you're always welcome to stay with me. But I'm sort of between places right now," she said.

"What do you mean?"

"Long story. Can I meet you somewhere along the way? There's the Silver Bell Motel in Ashville. It's a bit remote, but it's not too bad."

To be honest, I was curious how she knew about this place, but I didn't ask. The last thing I wanted Kelly to feel was judged for how she chose to spend her free time. "Sure," I said. "That works."

As we drove, I still felt anxious and seeing that van again didn't help. I'd seen enough crime and kidnapping shows to know that white vans were never a good omen.

Jerry worked diligently in his coloring book most of the way to Ashville, so I didn't have much to occupy my thoughts. When "Blue Suede Shoes" started playing over the car speakers, my wandering mind landed on my daddy. It was his favorite song, and the first one he learned to play on the harmonica. Like a broken projector, the morning he left flickered into my mind. I remembered less and less of it as I got older. Now all I could recall was the early morning sun illuminating my room in a blue tint, Kelly asleep in the bed next to me, and our daddy sitting by my feet, all dressed as if he were going to work, even though it was a Saturday.

"Joy?" he said gently. He reached under his hat and took out a small rectangular box. "I, um, I want you to have this." I opened the box. Inside was his old harmonica. "I want you to have it. Keep it safe and think of me when you play it. Okay?" I looked down at the tea-stained box with the torn, flaky label, not quite sure what to make of his gift so early on a Saturday morning. "I—I'm sick, Joy. I need to go away for a little while, to try to... you know, try to get better."

"What do you mean you're sick?" A knot had formed in my stomach as I waited for his answer.

"I just... have to go away for a while. But I'm going to write every day. And I'm going to call, too. And Mama's going to take care of you, all right? You and your sister are going to be okay," he said, reassuring himself more than me. "Okay?" With that, his mouth twitched into a small smile that matched his eyes and he stood up. "Okay," he repeated, answering his own question.

He didn't hug me or anything. Then again, he never did. It wasn't that he was a cold person, he just didn't like to be touched.

He wrote for a while after he left, but I never wrote back. I was young and resentful and didn't understand the concept of people leaving for reasons unknown and being gone forever. When I was old enough to understand, Mama told us that two weeks before he'd left, he'd been admitted to the hospital for attempted suicide. Neither Kelly nor I knew anything about it. We'd just thought he'd been away on a business trip that week. After that, he knew he needed to go away so he could try to get better. I just wished he could have gotten better with us.

With my memories clouding my mind, I started to swerve into oncoming traffic and was honked back into reality by a very angry truck driver.

"Jesus Christ!" I turned the wheel like a maniac and with my hands shaking and numb, pulled over to regain my mental consciousness.

"Did we almost die?" Jerry asked, sounding more excited than scared.

"No, we didn't. We're okay."

"We almost hit a car!"

"Jerry, just be quiet for a minute." I let myself get a breath of air and began to frantically check the mirrors before pulling out. "The last thing we want to do today is get into an accident."

"Why is that the last thing we want to do?" he said.

To be honest, I didn't have an answer to his question. I let out a laugh. "You're right," I said. "It's not the last thing we want to do. How about we just knock it off our list altogether?"

I focused my eyes back on the road and pretended I didn't see a white van in the other lane three cars behind me.

***

Setting my watch ahead five minutes didn't really do me much good with getting us to the Silver Bell Motel any earlier. As I pulled into the lot and surveyed the other cars, I breathed a sigh of relief; no sight of the white van.

I also didn't see a little blue hatchback, so I assumed Kelly wasn't there yet. Then, by the front entrance, I saw her sitting there with her bags, biting her nails. She saw us pull in and waved. Instantly, I felt safe. Up close, I could see Kelly had on sweatpants and a light-wash jean jacket. Her hair was dyed a light, chestnut brown and tied back in a ponytail. Aside from the darker hair and lighter jacket, I was watching myself for a moment. All that was missing was a cigarette.

"Kiki!" Jerry hopped out of the car as soon as I'd parked and ran up to her.

"Hey, Jer Bear!" she said, picking him up. "Oh! You've gotten so big. How did you grow so much in two months?"

Wrong Girl Gone

She carried him back outside with her then set him down so he could get his toys out of the car. She gave me a hug and took the suitcase out of my hand. "You doing okay?"

I let out a bitter laugh. "Ask me later. How did you get here, anyway? I didn't see your car."

"Took the bus."

"Where's your car?"

"I sold it last month. Just couldn't afford it anymore."

The casualness of her voice almost shocked me. I was about to ask her a dozen questions all at once, but I knew I should get a room for us first. I went inside to the front desk, the envelope of money burning in my back pocket.

When I got back, Jerry was very animatedly giving her a detailed account of our close encounter with the car.

"And then they honked their horn, like, six times! And Mama almost hit the car in front of us! But then she didn't, and we lived. It was crazy."

"Oh, really?" She turned to me. "Hittin' the bottle hard today, Joy?"

"You must be confusing me with my husband."

After a pause, she said in all seriousness, "You aren't drinking, are you?"

"No. Of course not. You know I don't drink. I don't want to end up like her either. Besides, how would I have time to drink when I'm busy taking care of a drunk at home all the time?"

As far as I knew, Kelly didn't drink much either. I think the two of us had watched painfully and helplessly one too many times as Mama knocked herself out with the stuff. My sister and I were identical twins, down to our birthmarks. Normally, Mama could tell us apart instantly, so we were rarely able to get away with playing *Parent Trap*, but when she was drinking, telling us apart was a damn near impossible task. I think sometimes she thought only one of us was in front of her and she was just seeing double.

We got to our room and finished unloading the car. Jerry instantly moved from the adult conversation to hunting through the empty dresser drawers for things people left behind. I sat my suitcase down by the double bed closest to the door. "I need a cigarette."

When I grabbed the pack out of my purse, I noticed just how many suitcases Kelly had brought with her. "How much did you pack for an overnight trip?" I asked Kelly.

"Enough," she said.

I eyed her for a moment before saying, "Jerry, stay inside and watch some TV. Looks like this one has a remote." I picked up the remote and tossed it on the bed.

"Are we eating soon?" he asked.

"Yeah, we'll get something to eat. Just hang tight for a little bit. We'll be right outside."

Kelly shut the door behind us. I took a cigarette from the pack and offered her one. She shook her head. When I struggled with my lighter, she took out hers and lit my cigarette for me.

"Thanks," I said.

"You might want to watch what you say about Carl's drinking in front of Jerry," Kelly parented. "He'll get a bad image of his father when you go back to him."

Her lack of confidence in my life choices stung. I took a long drag on my cigarette. "I'm not going back to him."

"Good."

"I'm not."

"I said, 'Good.'"

"You think I will."

"I don't want you to, but I wouldn't blame you if you did. Are you going to tell me what happened that made you decide to actually run away from him this time?"

"I don't want to talk about it."

"You made me sit on a hot bus for over an hour only to tell me you don't want to talk about it?"

I didn't say anything. I didn't even know where to begin. I just took a puff of my cigarette then clenched my jaw until I heard it pop.

Wrong Girl Gone

"Come on, Joy, your phone calls were so vague I didn't even understand half of what you said. Please. I know he's been hurting you, but he's done that since day one. Something must have pushed you over the edge."

I pulled out the rubber band-bound envelope from my purse and set it on the white paint-chipped banister. She looked inside. "Jesus Christ." She gaped for a moment as she thumbed through the money.

"He hid it from me. Jerry and I have been scraping by on coins from the sofa cushions. Literally. And he's been saving up all he can. Most of it probably from gambling."

Kelly's jaw tightened. "After everything you've done for him? After how hard you work?"

"Maybe I haven't done enough." I wasn't expecting my voice to crack, but it did. "Maybe I deserve this."

"Hey, don't you dare." She interlocked her arm in mine and kissed my forehead. Then the tears started to come. I couldn't stop them. "You don't deserve this. You deserve so much better. He's an asshole."

"But he's Jerry's father."

"He's still an asshole."

"I don't know what I'm going to do," I said finally. I wiped my face with the back of my hand and took another puff from the cigarette to calm myself down. "I don't know where I'm going to go. I mean, I just up and left my job. I didn't call them or anything. This money's not going to last forever, I'll have to settle somewhere eventually. I just know I can't go back there because if I do, God knows what he'll do to me." I tapped the ashes off my cigarette. "What do you think I should do?" Part of me was really hoping she'd tell me I'd made a mistake. Part of me wanted her to tell me that I should go back to him, go back to my simple little life. That would be so much easier than whatever path I was trying to find now.

"I think you did the right thing."

"Really?"

Kelly sighed and looked past me, off down the road and trail of trees. "Really. He's not a good person, Joy. I think you did the right thing, leaving him."

"What if I'm not strong enough to stay away? What if I cave and go back to him?"

"Are you kidding? I don't think I would have even had the nerve to run away."

"You wouldn't have been in this position in the first place."

"You don't know that."

"Yes, I do. You wouldn't have ended up with a guy who hauls off and smacks you if you track mud on the floor you just cleaned. You wouldn't have gotten yourself pregnant and had to drop out of school. You wouldn't have made any of the same mistakes I made, and you know it."

She didn't say anything at first. "You stayed with Mama."

"What's that got to do with anything?"

"It's got to do with courage, Joy. She needed one of us there and you chose to stay. You're better at handling life than me."

"No, I'm not."

"Would you stop negating yourself for one second and listen to me?" I listened to her. "You've got a lot of guts, Joy. I'm not just saying that either. You didn't have to keep Jerry. You chose to."

"I chose to because I was afraid of getting an abortion."

"No. That's why you say you kept him. I know the reason you kept him. Because you loved him from the moment you knew about him. You have more courage than I ever will, and I know you'll never admit it. It would have been a hell of a lot easier to have an abortion or even give him up for adoption than it was to keep him and raise him like you're doing. And from what I can tell you're doing a fine job."

I wanted to say, "Thank you," because that's what you say when someone says something as nice as that but thanking my sister would mean I was agreeing with what she said. I couldn't do that. Instead, I changed the subject.

Wrong Girl Gone

"I thought about Daddy a lot on the way here," I said.

"You know his birthday's coming up."

"Yeah. The twenty-third." I began falling into the dark hole of my mind. "I hope he's okay."

"He is." She began rubbing my back just like I had done for Jerry the night before.

"How do you know?" My heart jumped a little. "Are you in touch with him?"

"What? No. I just assume he's fine. He still writes those checks to mom every month, doesn't he?"

"Yeah. I just hate that that's the only way we know he's okay. From a check every month with no return address." Despite the relaxing motion of her hand on my back, I felt that familiar wave of anxiety spread through my veins. "I just wish I could call him up sometimes. Even if we didn't have much to say."

Kelly opened her mouth like she was going to say something, but all that came out was a sigh. The silence between us was filled by the sounds of belated June bugs and distant traffic. I felt a whole seasons' worth of memories finding their way back to me. "Remember when we used to sneak out of the trailer late at night?" I said finally.

"Yeah." She smiled. "Yeah, I do. Hank's Diner sure kept us out of trouble, didn't it?"

"We'd save all our allowances up just to have enough cash to each buy a burger," I said.

"All those burgers never did help either of us fill out like we thought they would either," she said.

I laughed. "Yeah, but you're so beautiful I'm sure most guys never notice a lack of anything else."

"Joy, what mirror have you been looking into?"

"Oh, come on, Kel, you're gorgeous. The boys couldn't keep their hands off you. And here I'm the one who got knocked up." I took a drag on the cigarette. "You're lucky you got out of Jasper while you could."

"I didn't go back to school this semester."

My stomach dropped. I turned to her. "What?"

Audrey Wilson

"There's no point. I barely passed my classes in the spring. It's just too much." She took my cigarette from my hand, took a puff, and placed it back between my limp fingers. "I'm not cut out for it."

No. No. No. No. She couldn't just quit school. This was the girl who had more discipline than anyone I knew and here she stood telling me she couldn't do it anymore. I stayed behind in Jasper with Mama so that, in some way, Kelly could go on, so she could live the life that I didn't get to live. Knowing that made my life okay, somehow. It made me feel like I was doing something worthwhile for once, even if it was vicariously. She was the smart one, the ambitious one. Her success was going to make up for my lack thereof.

Then, for a brief, terrible moment, I felt better about my life. Instantly afterward, I hated myself for it.

"What about teaching?"

"I'm not smart enough. I've been thinking of getting back into photography again. Something you don't need a degree for."

"What have you been doing all this time?" I asked.

"Working for an insurance company. And I lost that job last week." This was all wrong. My world was supposed to be the one that always fell apart, not Kelly's. "I told my roommate I wasn't coming back which was great news for her. I just want to save up enough money to maybe move to Dallas or Chicago and see if I can get a photography job, maybe even sell some of my pieces."

"That's why you packed so much." I was slowly putting it together. "Look if you need money, let me give you some of Carl's—"

"You know I can't accept that."

Of course I knew. But it was still worth offering. "Is that why you've been so distant from me this past month? Were you afraid of what I'd think?"

She nodded a little. "Among other things."

"What other things?"

"There's something else I've been needing to tell you."

Wrong Girl Gone

"You're going to drop a bigger bomb on me than dropping out of school?"

I expected her to laugh, but she just kept looking out ahead, frozen. I could see tears building up in her eyes. "Oh my God, Kel, what is it?"

She shook her head, her hand shaking as she tucked a stray piece of hair behind her ear. "Back in July—"

Before she could get another word out, the motel door opened, followed by a loud, "Mama, I'm hungry!"

"Just a minute, baby. Go back inside."

Kelly shook her head and quickly wiped her tears. "No, he needs to eat. It can wait."

"Are you sure? He'll be fine—"

"Mama! My tummy's growling! You said we were gonna eat soon."

"We can talk more later," she said. "We should get something to eat."

"I saw a diner down the road on my way here." I took a final puff of my cigarette and put it out on the railing. "I'll go grab us a few specials and be right back. Then promise me we'll talk more after we eat, once he's asleep. Okay?"

Kelly nodded and gave me a sad smile. I went into the hotel room to grab my purse with Jerry on my heels. "Are you going to get food? What are we having? I want a cheeseburger. Can I have a cheeseburger?"

"Yeah, I'll get you a cheeseburger. Kiki's going to watch you, but I'll be right back." My purse was lying open on the bed with the contents spread all over the comforter. I'd let Jerry empty out my purse *one time* to give him something to do and now regretted it as I grabbed the contents and shoved them back into my bag. Then I took the folded envelope of money out of my pocket and stuffed it into the side pocket of my suitcase.

"I'm leaving the money in my bag," I said in a low voice to Kelly. "Just make sure you keep the door locked, okay?"

She saluted me and knelt on the floor by Jerry, who was pushing his DeLorean across the carpet at lightning speed.

"Try to avoid almost hitting a car on your way there," Kelly said on my way out the door. I appreciated her advice.

***

Simon's Diner was a crappy little place with only the letters S-M-O-S and N-E-R lit up on the sign out front. Like the outside, the inside of the restaurant was pretty much dead too. I tried not to make eye contact with the beady-eyed, bearded man at the bar looking me over and quickly ordered two meatloaf specials and a plain cheeseburger.

"Fifteen forty-five," the waitress said. I took my wallet out of my purse, only to discover it was not actually my wallet. It was a turquoise one with little studs on it. I flipped it open and saw Kelly's driver's license inside. This was precisely why I shouldn't let Jerry play "Let's Empty Mama's Purse!"

There was some cash in it, so I used that to pay for the food and reminded myself to pay Kelly back later. In the fifteen minutes I waited for our order, I pretended not to see three different cockroaches. Finally, they brought out the order and I left with the greasy brown bag of food.

It had started drizzling when I went into the restaurant and by the time I got outside, it was pouring. I made a run to the car and got in, suddenly feeling utterly alone. There didn't seem to be anyone around for miles other than the three cars in the puddle-ridden parking lot, none of which was a white van. It was the kind of rain that hit the front window so hard I felt like I was underwater. I took a breath to calm myself. As much fun as it was to psych myself up in the middle of a horror movie, it wasn't nearly as rewarding in real life.

I reached the Silver Bell and pulled into a parking spot near the side of the building, so I could quickly get under the awning and hopefully not get more soaked than I already was. I got out and started toward the motel, protecting the food under my jacket. The moment I took two steps in the rain, I saw the white van parked in front of our room. A shadow fell out of the open motel door and instantly I lost all coherent

Wrong Girl Gone

thought. I froze, dropping the sack of food, my worst fears slowly being realized in front of me. I ran around to the side of the motel and stood with my back to the wet brick wall so I couldn't be seen. This wasn't right. No one should have been outside our room. But I could see a man's shadow when I peered around the corner. Then I could see the rest of his dark outline through the storm. The man was wearing an olive-green jacket and had a pair of oversized glasses sliding down his nose. Then I saw something else. Something I'll never forget.

He was carrying a large, heavy, black bag out of our room.

The man in the green jacket opened the back door of his van, tossed the bag inside, and closed it up, like a zookeeper closing a cage. Then he turned around and shut the motel door behind him like he was never there. I didn't know what to do or think or feel. I ran to the van like my life depended on it. Because if anyone I loved was in that bag, I would never be able to live with myself if I didn't do everything in my power to save them.

Just as the man started the van's engine, I opened the door and climbed inside.

Chapter Ten

The back of the van was empty except for the bag. There was no window that connected the back-storage area to the front seat, so I couldn't be seen. I stared at the black bag, waiting for the thing inside it to stir. The car began to move, and my knees hit the floor of the van, the bag inches from me. The rebel in me considered myself an atheist, but right then I prayed like I'd read the bible every day of my life. I prayed that within that bag were cleaning supplies. Bricks. Garbage. Anything but what I feared it was.

Everything that mattered to me lived in that moment when I pulled the zipper back and saw my own reflection staring lifelessly back at me. I didn't touch her. I didn't cry. I didn't do anything because she wasn't dead. That wasn't possible. Any minute now, she was going to blink. She was going to start breathing again.

"Kelly," I whispered into her ear. When she didn't answer, I whispered it again. And again. And again. I kept looking at her, trying so hard to get her to look back. But she never did.

I wanted to scream so badly my throat hurt. I wanted to punch the metal walls of that death trap until my fists bled. All that ran through my mind was a film reel of every moment, every image I had ever had of my sister. I saw her crying with a hairbrush tangled in her hair. I saw her laughing with me as we threw handfuls of flour at each other in the kitchen when Mama was out of the room. I saw her face light

Wrong Girl Gone

up on Christmas morning when she got her first camera. I saw her screaming at me when I spilled grape juice on her favorite vintage dress. I saw her holding me in her arms in the hospital right after Jerry was born, telling me what a brave girl I was. My thoughts froze on Jerry. I didn't know if he was in the hotel room or out in the rain or if he was even alive. He'd learned to hide from his father over the years. I just prayed he'd hid when this man came into our room. I looked at my sister's lifeless eyes. In that moment, my only salvation was that Kelly was the only body in the bag.

I composed myself as best I could, and gently closed her eyes. The thought that that was the last time I'd ever see them was more than I could bear. With an uncontrollable tremor in my hand, I zipped up the bag, making sure not to catch her hair. The van hit a bump, jolting me into the realization that I had no idea how in the hell I was going to make it out of this van alive.

For the first time since I'd been in there, I noticed the beating of the rain on the roof. Then I heard thunder and felt it, too. Mama used to tell us that thunder was just the sound of God bowling. I looked down at the heavy, black body bag at my feet. I guess God was too busy bowling to do his job, so he let the devil take over for a while.

We had been driving for what felt like half an hour. I looked around the van. There was only a faint amount of light coming in from a sunroof, so I couldn't see much. There were a few boxes pushed up against the wall, covered in a black sheet. I crawled over and pulled off the sheet. Underneath were some clothes, mostly dark ones, a few fishing rods, and some bait. There was also a crowbar and a roll of duct tape. Exactly what someone would need to commit a murder. I started to pull the sheet back when I caught a glimpse of silver. With a closer look, my heart nearly stopped. It was a police badge.

I balanced myself as I stood on the swaying floor of the van, holding the badge up to the light. The badge read: *Harrison County Police 714*

Audrey Wilson

Harrison County didn't include Jasper. But it was the next county over from ours. Did this belong to the man? Was he a cop? Or had he *killed* a cop?

The van began to slow down. I pocketed the badge, grabbed the crowbar, and shoved it in the back of my jeans. Then I opened the door and watched the concrete blur come into focus. Finally, we stopped. I set my beliefs aside, said a silent prayer for Kelly, climbed as quietly as I could out of the van, and crawled underneath it, softly shutting the door behind me. When I forced my breathing to stop, I realized I'd been clutching the crowbar so tightly my fingers throbbed.

The rain was much quieter outside the van than in it, but it was still falling hard. The van's headlights were turned off, limiting my vision, but from the smell of pine, I knew we were near the woods. I watched his feet splash in puddles as he walked around to the back door. It was all I could do to hold my breath when I wanted nothing more than to take in as much air as I could, savoring the reminder that I was alive.

The man opened the doors. A second later, the bag fell to the ground with a thud. I cringed, trying not to vomit. He shut the door, picked up the bag, and headed for the trees. I could have gotten back in the van and tried to hot-wire it like Carl had shown me once. I could have stayed where I was, laying on the ground, hoping he wouldn't notice me when he came back. I could have gotten up and run the other way till I found help. I could have. I should have. But I didn't. With anger burning inside of me, I crawled out from under that van and followed him through the rain.

***

I stayed a good distance behind, so all I could see of him was a dark outline of his and my sister's bodies when the lightning hit. I dragged the crowbar behind me through the mud, and a couple of times almost lost my footing on unstable ground. We were walking downhill. If I hadn't caught myself, I probably would have fallen face-first down into my own personal mudslide. We must have walked for over a mile. I felt dizzy and tired like I was on the verge of waking up from a nightmare. All that kept me going was thinking about the things I wanted to do to this man and the pain that I wanted him to feel. My sister deserved better than a grave of mud to mask the fingerprints around her neck.

I was trying to get a better grip on the crowbar, when suddenly I saw him stumble up ahead of me and drop her body for the second time, churning my stomach. It was all I could do not to come up from behind and crack that crowbar through his skull. I didn't care how it was done; I just knew I wanted to cause him as much pain as he'd caused her. I wanted him to suffer until she was back here with me, and Jerry was safe in my arms.

The path started to get a whole lot brighter and the trees were fewer and farther between. Through the hissing sheets of rain, I saw his outline in a clearing ahead of me. I stumbled the rest of the way down the hill and kept a safe distance from him, hiding behind the damp trunk of a tree. The whole area was bare, and I realized we were right where he wanted to be. We were on the edge of a cliff and below it was a huge river. There was only one river that big around for miles: The Kawanee River.

For the first time, I saw the man as clear as day under the lightning-scattered sky. He was broad-shouldered, around six feet tall. What little hair he had was very thin and soaking wet. He was probably no older than forty-five, but his skin was so pot-marked, and his chin so covered in stubble that he looked like an aging sixty-five-year-old. The drops of rain rolled down his forehead, off a nose that was too big and crooked for his face. He dropped her body on the mud-covered ground and when he bent over, I could see his profile even more clearly. The stubble-covered chin jutted out and up slightly, his mouth tightly shut. Then there were those glasses. Those big, square, clear-rimmed glasses with thick lenses that magnified his eyes. I caught the glimpse of a mustache under his nose, as thin and wiry as the hair on his head. He unzipped the bag and dumped her out in a broken heap, then folded up the bag and stuffed it into his backpack. He didn't even carry her body, he just dragged it, like she was a piece of meat being fed to the sharks. As soon as I could move, I was going to do it. I was going to run at him and hit him with that crowbar until his whole body bled.

But I couldn't move.

I watched, frozen, as he pulled her body around in a half-circle, right up to the edge of the cliff. I couldn't bring my body to move even an inch forward. Like a statue in the rain, I stood, the crowbar glued to my hand. I looked down at her lifeless body, instantly aware of what this man was capable of. Up until that point, I had followed him blindly, somehow feeling invincible, believing he was incapable of doing to me what he'd done to Kelly. Believing I could get revenge with a piece of metal and whatever strength I could muster. I was wrong. I was stupid. In my blatant stupidity, I let my jaw hang open as I watched him throw her off the cliff and lean over the edge to make sure she landed just right.

Even through the rain, even through the ringing in my ears, I heard her body hit with a soft thud. Blood fully drained from my face. My hands went limp. I could feel the crowbar slip through my fingers, my reflexes too delayed to grab it. It landed with a clank on a rock, enough of a noise to snap me back to reality. And enough of a noise to catch the man's ear. He looked over his shoulder and locked eyes with mine. Almost instantly, he bolted towards me. I reached down and managed to grab the crowbar off the ground. There was no point in running. He would grab me before I could escape. I gathered all the strength I had in me and whacked him across the face with the crowbar. I hoped it would be enough to at least get away, but before I could turn, he reached out a hand and grabbed the stick of metal, trying to pull it away from me.

Wrong Girl Gone

But I wouldn't let him. I yanked the bar back, causing him to fall on top of me, his bloody face just inches from mine. I refused to let go of the crowbar and started kicking him as hard as I could. With a rush of adrenaline, I shoved the bar against his jaw. With one thrust, I heard his teeth clamp together, his pain just enough of a distraction to get out from under his body.

As soon as I managed to get to my feet, he grabbed my leg and pulled me to the ground. Instantly, pain radiated up through my spine as I felt a sharp, paralyzing stab of a rock against my tailbone. I couldn't move. I couldn't breathe. I rolled over onto my side, holding my lower back, and gaping in agony. My whole body suddenly seemed to go completely numb. All I felt was the rain hitting my face like I was drowning with my head above water. I could see the outline of his body standing over me in the darkness, holding the crowbar in his hand. All the numbness faded, and the pain shot back. For a second, my mind flashed to Carl, about to strike me with the back of his hand. At that moment, I would have taken a thousand blows from his fist over what I knew was coming next.

He whacked the bar down across my right leg. It was more pain than my body could handle, more than my darkest thoughts could have imagined. Before I could even scream, the metal hit the back of my head. Not hard enough to kill me, just hard enough to make me see red. My eyelids started to grow heavy, but I forced them not to. I needed to stay awake. If I didn't, I knew he'd kill me.

But my will to stay awake wasn't enough. My thoughts grew distant like I was somewhere deep inside my body and everything that was happening to my outer shell echoed from far away. I felt something tighten around my wrists like someone was loosely binding me with soft ropes. Suddenly, the pain slowed. Everything slowed. I had rolled off the edge and was falling through the rain, racing each drop to the surface of the river. The only thing I could think was that this was what dying felt like.

Chapter Eleven

When I was little, I used to play a game. It was one I really liked because I could play it by myself and no one else knew the rules. I played it when I had to get up in the middle of the night to go to the bathroom. I'd get this irrational fear that a man with a gun was standing in the dark, some three feet away from me. I'd pretend to see him when I went out into the hall, standing there with his back against the darkest wall in the house, blending in with all the other deadly shadows. The only time I was safe was when I was in the bathroom with the lights on and the door closed at half-time. I'd do my business then mentally prepare myself for what was waiting for me in the hall. The lights would go off in the bathroom and the chase back to my room began. He'd be on my heels the whole five yards there. Only when I was back under the covers at home base could the referee yell, "safe" and the man with the gun couldn't chase me anymore.

Now, it isn't a man with a gun in the hall. It's a man with a crowbar in the woods. And it's no longer a game. It's a fight to live.

I begin my half-time.

With my face on the ground, I take my first conscious breath and choke on mud. At first, I can't tell whether my eyes are open or not. I'm afraid to look anywhere, so I try my best to keep them shut. When I attempt to pull my right arm up next to me to roll my body over, I realize it won't move. I breathe again and this time choke on water, swallowing a

Wrong Girl Gone

big gulp of mud along with it. My body isn't letting me lift my head and there isn't a single muscle that doesn't throb beneath my skin. The only part of me I can move is my left hand, which doesn't do me much good without the use of my shoulder. I then try to move my legs, which sends my mind into a state of panic when I realize I can't feel them. I manage to turn my head to the left a little and get my mouth off the ground. Warmth hits my skin and I peel back my eyelids. It's bright. Very bright, hurting my eyes even more, like someone had been pressing them shut with two iron thumbs all night.

I look around as best as I can without the use of my neck. Half of my body is underwater, and the other half is slowly following suit. I claw at the ground with my usable hand until my fingertips begin to bleed on rocks, but I don't stop. When I've finally pulled my legs and lower back out of the current, the numbness in my lungs starts to dissolve and I can breathe a little better than before.

Every time I move a muscle, I'm certain I'm that much closer to knowing what hell feels like. I manage to pull myself out of the riverbank and onto a flat rock a few feet ahead of me, my legs dragging uselessly behind my body.

I lift my head and see my new body for the first time. My right arm doesn't look terrible, although the back of it is scraped raw, with red glistening through the dirt and bruises, and my left wrist is swollen to twice its normal size. I can't see my legs beneath my jeans, but I can tell from the agony that something's wrong, especially in the right one, which sears with pain at even the slightest movement.

Just when I think I can't possibly feel any more pain, I think of Kelly and Jerry and my heart sinks. She's dead. My sister, half of me—the better half—is dead. I'm no longer sharing this world with her. I'll never have another conversation with her again. I'll still talk to her, of course, but she won't answer. And for every response I don't hear, my heart will break a little more.

Audrey Wilson

But Jerry. My everything. Air catches in my lungs as fear sweeps over me. He's alone in this godforsaken world if he's even alive. No. He is alive. I can't think otherwise if I want to live too.

My mama said that when I was born, I came out fighting. Kelly was quick, she told me. She slid right out before the doctor could even say "push." It took her another nine hours of hard labor to give birth to me. Mom would have none of that C-section business. She was determined to have me the old-fashioned way, even though her lower spine had been killing her all through the labor. I was a pain in the ass right from the start. I fought to stay in my mother's womb, and I fought her on everything else since then.

So, here I am—A twenty-two-year-old female with dirty blonde hair, brown eyes, and a petite frame. My body will be discovered on the edge of the Kawanee River near Boone, Alabama, about three-hundred and fifty miles east of Jasper, Mississippi, face down in the mud, covered in cuts and bruises, with fingerprints around my neck, my extremities swollen from the rising tide.

My body might be discovered, but I won't be.

For the first time since opening my eyes, I am completely awake. I'm not going to die out here in the middle of the woods. Kelly wouldn't want me to. My mama wouldn't want me to. Jerry wouldn't want me to. For them, I don't want me to. My son is alive. His heart beats with mine, and mine is still beating. I know he's alive. To allow myself to die when Kelly's life had been taken from her would mean she died in vain. I can't give up when she didn't even have the option to. I refuse to stop fighting.

This isn't how I die. Not like this. Not yet. Jerry's sweet face flashes into my mind. I can hear his voice. I'm going to hear his voice again.

I pull myself off the rock, then drag my broken body into the wet leaves, into the woods as far as I can. The brush around me is heavy and unkempt. About twenty minutes after I start crawling, my palms are skinned raw. I can't tell what's dirt and what's blood. I find myself shivering from the cold breeze. My hands are throbbing as I crawl, and I know I need to stop the bleeding. I manage to take off my tee-shirt, rip the material in half with my teeth, and wrap a side around each hand. Even though the blood stains the gray quickly, it's still better than nothing.

Even with my minor movements, my arms are killing me, and I know I'll never make it to the road without walking. I look to my left and see a tree with a few dead branches sticking out of it and grab onto one. With all my strength, I heave myself up onto my feet, although my right one seems to want nothing to do with standing.

I grab hold of a thick branch to use as a crutch and hop forward, falling flat on my face. But I don't give up. I can't if I ever want to see my son again. I use the next tree ahead of me to pull myself up again, this time managing to get three more feet before falling a second time. By the third time, I'm exhausted. Finally, on the fourth try, I'm able to keep moving forward on my one working foot, stopping only to rest on occasion when I can't stand any longer.

After what feels like hours, things start to get fuzzy. To wake myself up, I think of Jerry. I think of him playing with the water hose in the backyard. Or playing with his brick-printed cardboard blocks in the living room, building forts and telling me to come and see his house. Sometimes I was too busy and said I would soon. Sometimes I never got around to it. I'd give anything to have those moments back right now.

The sun is low by the time I hear something I never thought I'd miss. There's a car horn from somewhere up ahead. It's faint, but I hear it. And it wakes me up better than any alarm ever has. I wince through a surge of pain and keep going. Every time I take a breath, the broken ribs in my side pierce my lungs with a stabbing pain, so I try to use my breaths sparingly, and only inhale when I know I can bear the hurt. My body, my mind, my will to live—everything is about to give out when I finally see a break in the trees up ahead.

Audrey Wilson

The sky is getting darker, but the path is slowly brightening. I move as fast as I can up the hill to the opening.

When I finally scrape my way out of the brush and onto harder ground, the sun is almost set. The road is just a few feet away from me and I can see down the street both ways. As though my body has gotten me as far as it possibly can, I collapse, and my face hits the dirt.

I don't know how long I'm lying there. All I see are flashes of bright lights beaming red through my eyelids. The lights dim and fade, then come back again, then fade again. When the headlights warm my skin, I'm on base, safe in the bathroom with the light on. When the lights go out, I see the man with the gun waiting in the shadows. Only it isn't the man with the gun. It's the man with the crowbar. And he's waiting for me. Then I get the horrible feeling I'm falling, and my heart races, and I finally come to just before I hit bottom.

This time when the bright lights come, they don't fade. The silhouette of a man is walking towards me. My breath turns sharp and rapid. I hear myself making choked, high-pitched noises that don't even sound like they're coming from my lips. Like I'm asleep and I'm trying to wake myself from a nightmare. This man wants to hurt me. I can't tell if he's the man with the crowbar, but I know he wants to hurt me. I've played this game too many times to know how easily it could become reality.

The man is even closer now. I reach out my arm and watch it fall to the blacktop. I try again to get away from him, but my nails just scratch at the road, leaving prints of blood on the ground. When I crane my neck to get a glimpse of his face, the bright lights swallow him whole and all I see is a dark, disoriented, skinny outline of his body. When he leans down in front of me, I choke out another scream. He tries to shush me, but I keep screaming. I try to hit him and push him away, but it does nothing. I might as well be a fly on his shoe. I try to pull myself away from him. I try to call for help. I try to move my arms. I try everything. Then I black out all over again.

Chapter Twelve

I'm not sure if I'm dreaming, or just waking up. If it is a dream, the dream neighborhood is something out of *Pleasantville*. Each house is painted a different, subtle color and each lawn is the exact shade of green that it should be. All the doors on the houses are painted white, except for the house at the very end of the street. This house is gray with a black door. Something about it feels tainted and unsettling, not just the color, but what lies inside it.

When I get closer, I see that there is no door, just an open space where a door would be. The stark contrast of the darkness of the house in this sunny, picturesque village frightens me, but it also brings out my curiosity. I walk up the front path and through the dark doorway. It's a relief to see that the inside of the house doesn't match the outside. It's simple, familiar, and safe. It's my home.

I put my hand on the banister, expecting to see dust on my finger when I remove it, but it's clean. Everything is exactly the way I left it, only no Carl, which is fine with me. I'm about to go into the kitchen to fix myself something to eat when I hear Jerry call me.

"Mama," he says from upstairs. "Mama, come see what I did!"

All my thoughts of food vanish, and I run up the stairs to see my child again. As soon as I reach the top he comes out of his room, closing the door quickly behind him.

"All right," he says. "Now you have to close your eyes and don't open them till I say." I nod my head and close my eyes. He leads me into his room. "Okay, you can open them now."

I open them. All Jerry's brick cardboard blocks are on the floor in the form of a fort, but the fort's slightly too small for what's inside. I see two feet sticking out of one end. The fort has no roof, so I am looking down on the body inside. My sister is laying on the floor, the blocks built evenly around her. She's looking straight at me. Jerry takes his plastic saw and begins attempting to saw off her feet.

"Jerry, don't do that, sweetie," I say to him. Even though it's my voice, calm and complacent, they're not my words. "It's disrespectful."

"It's fine," says Kelly, her eyes still blank and wide. "I don't need them anymore anyway." Then her jaw begins to move side to side, popping and cracking. I look over at Jerry. He's succeeded in sawing off her right foot. I was worried there would be blood, but there isn't any. Just dirt and sand pouring out of the ankle stump. "Kelly?" she says.

I shake my head. "You're Kelly," I say.

"Kelly, stop it," she says. "Take care of Jerry while I'm gone."

"I'm not Kelly. I'm Joy."

"I'm Joy."

"Kelly, stop this."

"Kelly, stop this." Her jaw continues to pop and crack. Side to side. Side to side.

"My name is Joy Elliot Larson," I say.

"My name is Joy Elliot Larson," says Kelly.

"My name is Joy Elliot Larson," says Jerry.

I am now the one in the cardboard box made of bricks, looking up at myself and watching Jerry saw off my feet. The dirt and sand turn black and watery.

"We're going to miss you, Kelly," Kelly says. She is holding a box of cockroaches. "We'll bury you tomorrow." She spills the insects on top of me. I can't move, so I let them crawl. They tickle. They bite. They crawl into my ears and my mouth and my nose and tickle my insides. I look at my arm and see them moving under my skin. They don't hurt. They feel like a massage. Then I start to get antsy. They're making me nervous and antsy. I pinch my skin to grab one, but it cries, so I let go. I can feel the box I'm in getting smaller. I kick my legs and knock over the blocks. I roll to the side to get out of the fort. I think I'm going to stop rolling as soon as I'm free, but I don't. I keep going. My whole body is spinning down a hill. Then it starts to get out of control. I hit a bump and fly into the air, holding my breath until I hit the ground, rolling again. Finally, I reach the end of the hill, my legs now dangling over the edge of a cliff. I grab onto a root and try to pull myself up. The root starts to come up from the ground.

Kelly and Jerry are standing over me again.

"Don't let go," Kelly says, "Not today." But I do anyway. And I fall. Before I hit, I open my eyes and wake up.

The first thing I see is the sun glaring through glass, and I wish I'd kept my eyes closed. Then I see branches coming from a tree outside the window and realize I'm upstairs. My eyes close and open again, one slightly slower than the other. The wallpaper in the room is blue. A very dusty blue. With little pink dots all over it. When my eyesight sharpens, I see that the dots are really flowers.

As always when I wake up, my first thought is Jerry. I always took comfort in knowing that I could walk right into his bedroom and see him playing with his toys or sleeping in his bed. But now I have no idea where he is. The last place I'd seen him was the hotel and God knows how long ago that was. I suddenly can't breathe. I need to leave. I need to get away from wherever the hell I am. I need to get to Jerry. Even though Kelly may be gone, I can still save my son.

The second I move my arm I feel the pinch of a needle in it. I look down to see an I.V. plugged into my skin, the bag of liquid dangling from a stand beside my headboard. But something isn't right. I'm not in a hospital. I'm in someone's home. For all I know, I'm in *his* home. I rip off the tape and

Audrey Wilson

pull the needle out of my arm. It hurts like hell and when I see that I'm bleeding, it hurts even more. My lungs feel like they're caving in on me, preventing any air from getting in. Everything is spinning and I just want it to stop.

My mind runs in circles over where Jerry could be. I tell myself he's alive, that he's safe, but maybe I'm just being optimistic. Maybe I'll never see my son again. In a flash, I'm back in the throes of crippling anxiety.

My legs feel like they're filled with lead. I search everything within reach for some clue as to where I am or how I can get out. I look at my clothes. I'm wearing a large, white undershirt and a pair of boxer shorts. In the corner of the room is a wood crate with a baseball bat, a basketball, a football, and a few other sporting goods sitting in it. Although there's no record player, there is a large collection of vinyl sitting under a desk with no chair. On the nightstand next to me are a few decorative candlesticks with no candles and an old alarm clock. It's a quarter after nine. I check the time again ten minutes later. It's still a quarter after nine, which explains why I haven't heard it ticking. There are four books in the nightstand drawer. I recognize one, which is Albert Camus' *The Stranger*. Two of the others look like fifty-cent drugstore mysteries and the fourth is olive green and very old. The date inside is December 1918. It has a bunch of poems in it but in my current state, I don't care to read any of them.

The floor creaks on the other side of the room, where the only door to the room is. I sink down under the quilt and wait helplessly as someone turns the knob and opens the door.

"Get away from me," I say with broken vocal cords before I even see their face. I knock over something on the dresser next to me when I grab a heavy candlestick. "I swear, just stay away."

The man enters the room. He's tall, with dark skin, black hair, and dark brown eyes. He isn't the man from the woods, but I still wouldn't have trusted a single being that walked through that door. For all I know, this man could be working with the one who killed Kelly. The killer could be in this house right now. He could be downstairs in the kitchen, sitting at the table, biting into an apple as he reads the paper. As soon as I'm unconscious again, the two are going to rape and brutalize me until my body finally gives out. Then they're going to take me back to that same spot in the woods and throw me into the river.

"No, it's okay. I'm—" He moves closer, and I swing the candlestick at his hand with all the strength my weak arms can muster before he finishes his sentence. It isn't much, but it's enough to break the skin. He pulls his hand away. "Please try to calm down. I promise, I'm not going to hurt you." He reaches out his uninjured hand towards the bed.

"No! Get away from me!" I reach for the next closest object to me, the I.V. stand, and push it at him. He isn't going to hurt me. I'm not going to let another goddamn man hurt me.

He pulls the I.V. stand over to me. "You need to keep that in your arm," he says. "You'll get dehydrated." He reaches for the tube.

I pull my arm away. "I'm fine."

"There are antibiotics in there. They're helping you recover." He moves toward the I.V. again. "I promise I'm not going to hurt you."

"Then stay away from me." I'm now shaking so severely my jaw is clenched in pain.

"You're shaking," he says, but I ignore him.

"Where's my son?"

"What?"

"My son!" My voice shakes along with the rest of my body. "Where is my son?"

The man stammers, his hands extended in front of him in surrender. "I—I don't know where your son is."

I'm about to grab the other candlestick when I realize that this man is the only connection I have to the outside world. He's my lifeline to Jerry. "Can I use your phone?"

"Yeah, of course." He leaves the room and returns a minute later with a phone that he plugs into the jack next to my bed. I do want to use his phone, but I also want to know if he'll let me use it. He passes the test.

I quickly reach for the phone, like it could be taken away from me at any second. The man moves back, giving me my space. "Let me know if you need anything else." He heads for the door.

"Wait." He turns to face me. "What's your name?"

"Clay," he says. "Grady."

"Which is it?"

"Clay Grady."

"Where am I?"

"Boone, Alabama. About forty miles from Northchester." He says it like I should know where Northchester is. "That's where I live. This is my mother's house."

"How long have I been here?"

"It's been two days since I found you on the highway."

"You found me..." I feel like a parrot. "On the highway?"

"Yeah. You, um..." he runs his hand over his head. "You weren't wearing your shirt. Looks like you may have wrapped the material around your hands."

"Yeah, I did." I try to recall what happened. All I can remember are flashes of lights, passing car horns, and a faceless figure walking towards me that must have been him. "I don't remember much. Sorry."

He seems surprised and almost smiles. "You're sorry you were unconscious?"

"No. I mean, yes. I guess so." I glance over at the I.V. stand and feel another wave of paranoia wash over me. "Are you some kind of evil veterinarian or something?"

He looks perplexed and mildly amused, but says with all seriousness, "No, of course not."

"Then why do you have an I.V. stand? And why didn't you just take me to the hospital?"

Wrong Girl Gone

"I didn't know if you'd make it that far," he stammers. "I figured it was better to just bring you here. My mother's a nurse, that's why she has the I.V. She's been helping me take care of you. Like I said, this is her house. Well, it was mine too, before I moved out. I knew my mother could patch you up as good as any doctor. Which she did. You have a grade one to two posterior cruciate ligament sprain in your right leg." I glance under the covers at my legs. The left is bruised and kind of sad-looking, and the right is wrapped up with a splint and a makeshift cast. I don't know what a posterior cruciate ligament sprain is, but I do know it feels more like a grade ten.

"If my leg is that messed up, how did I walk over a mile through the woods?"

Clay shrugs. "Adrenaline maybe? She said it seemed like the initial injury was agitated. Maybe from you walking on it." After a silence, he says, "I'll let you make your call. The phone number is on the back of the phone if you need it."

My first thought is to call the police. But then I remember the badge in the van. Kelly's killer may very well be a cop. If he is a cop, that means I can't trust any cops, something I already have difficulty doing. The cops were little help when the neighbors would report a domestic disturbance of one of Carl's drunken outbursts.

I want to call Mama and tell her I'm all right. I want to tell her Kelly is gone. I want to tell her everything that had happened to me in the past week. I want to, but I can't. There is no way I have the strength to talk to her. I punch in the numbers on the phone and wait for the ring.

The second ring comes, and he answers. "Hello?"

"John?"

"Yeah?"

I can picture his face in front of me and I would give anything for him to be here. "It's Joy."

"Jesus Christ. Joy? Oh my God, where are you? Are you all right?"

"Yeah, I'm okay. John, where's Jerry?" My voice cracks. I'm terrified of what his answer might be.

"He's safe." My eyes fill with tears. He's alive. My baby is alive. I take a deep breath and try not to let my heart beat out of my rib cage. "Carl picked him up. I guess he'd reported your son kidnapped and your car stolen." Of course, he did. "Where are you? Should I call the police?"

"No, no. Don't call the police. I'm okay, I'm safe. I can't tell you everything because there's just too much to tell. A man killed Kelly."

"Oh God, Joy…" John's voice is muffled like his hand is covering his mouth.

"He dumped her body in the Kawanee river. I followed him through the woods."

"Jesus Christ."

"I don't know why I did it. I wanted to hurt him, I guess, for what he did. But he caught me. He beat me up real bad, left me for dead." As soon as the words come out of my mouth, I realize they don't sound right. He could have made sure I was actually dead. He could have killed me. But he didn't. I still had a heartbeat when he left me there. I still had a pulse.

"Do you think he meant to kill Kelly?" John asks, his voice frantic. "I mean what if he was after you and accidentally killed her instead?" My heart beats quickly. He has a point. The man could have been after me and thought Kelly was me at the hotel. Aside from the hair, everything about us was the same. Even our DNA was identical. "Do you think Carl…?"

"No," I say quickly. "If anything, maybe Carl sent him to get the money and something went wrong. Carl wouldn't have me killed," I say to myself more than John. "But now, I don't know where this man is, and I don't know if he's going to try to come after me again. I need you to keep it quiet that you talked to me, all right?"

"Yeah, of course."

Wrong Girl Gone

"After he beat me up, I made it to the highway. A different man was driving by and found me on the side of the road. I'm in his home in Boone, Alabama."

"You're staying with some stranger?" John's voice borders on hysterical.

I lower my voice. "His name's Clay Grady. So far, he seems okay, but I just can't trust anyone right now. Here, let me give you his number..." I give John the phone number on the back of Clay's phone and he writes it down. "Also, the man who killed Kelly. I think he might be a cop."

"What?"

"I found a badge in his van."

"What did it say?"

I shut my eyes, trying to remember what the badge said, but I can't seem to grasp it. Even if it was only two days ago, it feels like a lifetime. "I can't remember. I'll call you tonight to check in and maybe it will come to me." Before we hang up, I ask another half dozen favors of my dear friend. "Do you think you could get a hold of my mama and just let her know I'm safe? Don't tell her anything else, just that I'm safe. She's probably worried sick. And can you keep an eye on Jerry? Make sure Carl's taking good care of him?"

"Of course."

"And John?"

"Yeah?"

"Thank you."

After we hang up, I feel dizzy again and lay back down. I wrack my brain trying to think of the number on the police badge I found in the van, but I can't. I feel like my brain is trying to keep it from me. Like it's trying to erase the whole incident from my memory.

***

Half an hour later, there's a knock on the door. I tell Clay he can come in.

"Everything okay?" he asks.

82

"Thanks for letting me use your phone." I glance at the bandage on his right hand where I hit him with the candle. "Sorry about your hand."

Clay shrugs. "It's okay. You're scared. I get it. I probably would have done the same thing."

We're silent for a moment, then I say as a precaution, "I called John." This man is slowly gaining my trust, but I want him to know that someone else knows I'm here. That I'm not alone.

"John?"

"Yeah. He's the man I'm supposedly having an affair with." Before Clay has a chance to get the wrong idea, I correct him. "I'm not. He's my friend, but my husband Carl thought there was more going on." I'm quiet for a moment. "He said my son is okay."

Clay lets out a sigh of relief, which surprises me because he only learned of Jerry's existence half an hour ago. "Good. I'm glad he's okay." He stands there for a moment, glancing around the room and avoiding my eyes. Finally, he says, "I'll bring you something to drink," and leaves the room.

I'm about to ask for a bottle of whiskey, but with his hospitality, this man would probably bring me one.

Chapter Thirteen

Clay comes back into the room couple of times throughout the rest of the day. We don't talk much. He doesn't seem like he's much for words and I'm still trying to figure out how much I trust him. If he is a killer, he isn't a very smart one. He gave me his phone number, which is real. John's called me back twice so far this afternoon to be sure of it. He asks me both times if I can remember what the police badge in the van said, but I still come up empty.

It's now late in the afternoon and Clay is downstairs and I really have to pee. I tried the bedpan once earlier after my pathetic attempt to walk failed, but I only made a mess for Clay to have to clean up, so I feel like he'd appreciate me not doing that again.

"Clay?" I call. "Clay!"

What feels like half a second later, his footsteps run up the stairs and land in my doorway. "I'm here," he says, out of breath. "What do you need?"

"I gotta pee."

"The bedpan should be—"

"Is there a bathroom on this floor? Maybe I—"

"I can carry you." He lifts me out of the bed like it's nothing and carries me into the bathroom. Even though this is probably the least romantic reason a man could have for carrying a woman, there's still something chivalrous about it. It eases my embarrassment.

Audrey Wilson

After I do my business, Clay carries me back to bed before heading back downstairs.

He returns ten minutes later with a tray of food. "Sorry it's just leftovers," he says. "My mother's the cook in the family. She's working a double tonight." I look down at the food; meatloaf, mashed potatoes, and carrots, each nicely placed on a white plate with little roses on it. The arrangement is just a little extra something to add to my guilt. I feel like I'm Clay's sick, bedridden wife who he's obligated to wait on. I wonder if Carl would have waited on me if I were bedridden. He probably would have, but I'm sure my meal would have ended up in my lap on more than one occasion.

***

When it's finally dark, I can't sleep since I've been in bed all day. I let my mind wander to Jerry and ultimately to Carl. Not present Carl. But past Carl. The Carl I fell in love with. The Carl who could in no way be even partially responsible for Kelly's death.

I can still fall into our little whirlwind romance like it started yesterday. Carl first joined our friend group when we were fifteen. Our "group" was just me, Kelly, and our friend Peggy. Carl was funny and charming and added a little needed testosterone, so we liked having him around. For the longest time, I was convinced Carl only wanted to hang out with us to get closer to Kelly. I think that only made me more smitten when I realized I was the one he was interested in.

One day after school, Kelly had a photography project she was working on and Peggy was in detention for faking a sick note, so I was walking myself home when I heard Carl's voice behind me.

"Joy!" he was running, actually *running* to catch up with me.

"Hey," I said.

Wrong Girl Gone

"You walkin' home alone?"

"Yeah."

"Want me to walk you?"

I thought he might want to talk to me about the spring dance coming up. I'd had a feeling he wanted to ask Kelly and maybe wanted my advice or something. "Sure, why not."

As we walked, he started making chitchat—about the weather, school, teachers—basic stuff. It was nice. He was chatty, friendly, and easy to talk to. I was so caught up in the attention that I'd almost forgotten that he probably preferred my sister.

"So, are you going to the spring fling?" he asked. I snapped back to reality.

"Oh, I don't know. Maybe."

"'Cause I was actually wondering…" Here it came. Kelly already had her eye on Chris Ramsey, but an offer could only boost her ego. "If you maybe wanted to go with me?"

"If I wanted to go with you?" It must have come out all wrong because Carl looked offended all of a sudden, like I'd put the emphasis on *you* instead of *I*.

"Yeah. Would you want to?"

"I thought you liked Kelly," I blurted out.

He laughed. "Kelly? I mean Kelly's great and all, but I like you."

That was all it took. *A boy liked me! A boy liked me!* If only I could go back in time and slap the pen out of teenage Joy's hand as she wrote "Mrs. Joy Larson" all over her notebook in purple ink.

So that was it. We started dating. We still hung out with Kelly and Peggy, but I think they got fed up with us from time to time, especially when we became more interested in making out than conversing. We started spending all our time together. When Carl's dad wasn't home, we'd hang out in his garage. Carl wasn't allowed in the garage without his father's permission and except for when he was at the bar, his dad was always in the garage. According to Carl, all he did was sit in his garage in an old lawn chair, drinking beer and reading cheap porno magazines he'd mail-ordered from a catalog. Carl never even knew his mom. She left when he was barely two. He grew up not knowing where she went or what she was doing with her life. Then, soon before we'd met, he found out she'd committed suicide in her apartment in Houston after killing her husband and his lover.

Carl and I bonded over our screwed-up home lives, which probably wasn't the best basis for a relationship, but we didn't know any better.

Despite Carl's family, he was the epitome of the word "gentleman" when we started out. He had rich, messy brown hair, a flirtatious grin, and what I thought were kind, pale blue eyes. Every time it rained, he said that God was crying because He missed His favorite angel so much. He said he was the luckiest man on the face of the earth because he got to have me in his arms. A guy who looked like him could say that to any other fifteen-year-old girl and I guarantee you they would have gone weak at the knees just like I did.

One night, Carl and I were nestled in this old stone bridge that tunneled a small section of the freight train tracks in Jasper. Our "spot" was a small nook in the middle of the tunnel, just big enough for the two of us. It obstructed us from passersby just enough where we could make out and no one would see. The train only passed through once each night, but the nook kept us out of harm's way. Still, we always made sure to get out before the train came, just in case.

We'd been kissing and necking for a good half hour when Carl pulled away and brushed a stray hair off my cheek. It was probably close to one in the morning, around the time the freight usually came through, which meant it was almost our cue to leave. But he was looking at me with those dreamy blue eyes that made time melt away around him. I couldn't bring myself to tell him we should go.

"What is it?" I said.

"Nothing."

"You're thinking something."

Wrong Girl Gone

He sighed and to this day I swear there were tears in his eyes. "You're beautiful, Joy."

Like any girl, I blushed.

"I mean it," he said. "You're beautiful. And I love you."

My heart practically burst out of my chest. I could feel my hands starting to sweat. I wanted to ask him so many things. Had he ever been in love before? When did he first know he loved me? When had he first wanted to say it? The neurotic in me had endless questions, but instead of ruining the moment, I said, "I love you too," and kissed him back. I found myself so enchanted by his words that even when I heard the distant train horn growing louder, it didn't seem to register. Only when the white light made me see red through my eyelids did we pull away from our embrace.

"Shit! Go, go, go!" Carl shouted, grabbing my hand, and pulling me through the tunnel. We emerged and rolled away down the slope of grass as the train roared past us. He pulled me close, protecting me from the train's thunderous roar. Our hearts raced as the train's last car passed. We looked at one another for a moment before breaking out in laughter, blissfully unaware of how close we'd just been to death.

"We're all fools when it comes to love," Mama always said. As the lovesick fool that I was, I believed every word Carl fed to me and gave him all I had to give. A year after we started dating, I was pregnant.

The first person I told was Kelly. We were standing in the bathroom while Mama was at work, and I was holding the positive pregnancy test in my sweaty, shaking hand.

"Shit," she said, her eyes fixated on the blue-tipped stick. I burst into tears.

She hugged me and tried to tell me these things happened all the time, that it wasn't my fault. She said there was a place I could go where I didn't have to tell Mama and I could have it taken care of safely. I nodded and knew I didn't really have any other options.

When I told Carl about the baby, I was prepared to follow up the news immediately with my plan. Kelly had written the number and address of a clinic in Jackson on a piece of paper that I'd put in my back pocket. But Carl's response wasn't at all what I had prepared for. Carl got down on one knee and took my hand. Then he gave me his tarnished class ring right off his finger and asked me to marry him. I felt that piece of paper burning through my back pocket, but I willed myself to ignore it. Instead, I behaved like the stupid teenager I was and pretended I was in a movie scene at the end of a romantic comedy. I imagined that I was beautiful and looked like Audrey Hepburn with Gregory Peck at my feet. Then I responded with a "yes" and a smile.

God, I was so stupid. Not for having Jerry. Never for having Jerry. The first time I held Jerry in my arms and looked into those wide, glazed, innocent blue eyes, I felt sick with myself for even having considered giving him up. I loved him from the moment I saw him and every moment after that. In fact, it seemed the less love I gave to Carl, the more I had leftover for Jerry. It was a good balance, I'd say. I'll admit, at first, I was overwhelmed at the idea of being a mother, but I was also excited by it. He was mine. Jerry was always mine, never his, and taking care of him was the one thing I knew I could do right.

Chapter Fourteen

The moment I finally drift off to sleep, I see a man with no face staring at me. I'm lying in the same bed in the same house, but the room is darker. It's bathed in soft candlelight, only I don't see the candle anywhere. The man is sitting in a chair in the corner. He's in the darkness, barely visible in the shadows of the light. He's not moving, just sitting there watching me. Even though he has no eyes, I know he is watching. I stare back at him. I want him to move, but he just sits and stares. Suddenly the room gets very hot. I want to find the candle and blow out the flame, but I can't find it. I look at the man again. He still doesn't move, and I am beginning to wonder if he is even a man at all. Maybe he's just a doll or it's a trick of light. I feel a prickling sensation in my toes and look down at my body. I see then that I have no toes. I have no feet. I have no legs. But I already knew that, so it doesn't come as a surprise.

Suddenly, I hear Jerry crying in the other room. I want so badly to get out of bed and comfort him, but I have no legs. I look over the edge of the bed to see how far it is from the ground, and I see water. The room is filled with at least three feet of water. Even if I can't walk, I can still swim.

I pull myself out of bed and land with a splash. The water cools me off and lets me escape the heat for a moment, but it doesn't feel wet like water should. It just feels like thick, cool air.

Audrey Wilson

I use my arms to swim through the water to the door. When I get there, I turn to look at the man. He's gone, but not really gone. I know he's there somewhere, even though I can't see him. I drift out of the room and into the hallway. It looks a lot like the hallway back at home, and Jerry's cries are coming from a bedroom a few doors away, where his room would be. Through the darkness I see a yellow glow illuminating the rim beneath the door of Jerry's room, and swim towards it.

His cries are getting louder, and the room farther away. I try to go faster, but I can't. The harder I swim, the colder the water becomes, the farther away the room becomes, and the louder the cries are. Finally, time speeds up and I'm right outside his door. The cries are so loud by now it's like he's screaming in my ear. My hand barely reaches the doorknob, it's so high. I open the door and swim inside. All the furniture is floating in the water, with Jerry's crib in the far corner of the room. I swim over to it. By the time I reach the side, the crib has shrunk, and I have grown. I am standing there, looking into the bed. Inside is this tiny little thing. Bald, shriveled, and hairless, it doesn't even look human. But I know it is. I know it's Jerry.

I reach in and pick him up as gently as I can. He barely seems to weigh an ounce and easily fits in the palm of my hand. I stroke his little golf ball-sized head, trying to soothe him into calmness. But he doesn't stop crying. The crying just keeps getting louder. Then I hear a voice calling from behind me.

"Kill he," the voice says. I turn around to look at the door, but the door is gone, and the faceless man is standing there in its place. "Kill he," he says again. His voice sounds like it's a hundred miles away, even though he's standing only feet from me. I look back down at the little Jerry in my hand. I don't want to kill him. I don't know why I would ever want to kill my child. "Kelly," the man says. This time the word makes sense to me, and I feel reality rattle me slightly. I look up from Jerry. There is no man. There is no door. There is only a mirror, and I'm in it.

"Kelly." The words come out of the mouth in my reflection, but not in my voice. "Kelly," my reflection says again. "Kelly, wake up."

That's when reality takes over completely and I open my eyes, squinting in the sunlight. There is a hand on my shoulder. "Kelly?" Clay is looking down at me. "Are you all right?"

I rub my eyes. "What?"

"You sounded like you were having a bad dream."

I don't know if I'm hearing him correctly or if I'm still dreaming. "No, what did you just call me?"

He sets a tray of breakfast on the nightstand beside me. "Kelly."

"Why did you call me that?"

"That's what it said on your ID."

"My ID?"

He opens the top drawer of the dresser and takes out a turquoise wallet. I don't own a turquoise wallet.

He hands it to me, and I flip it open. Inside is sixteen dollars, a Visa, a MasterCard, a receipt from Piggly Wiggly for a packet of gum and a Milky Way, Kelly's student ID, her driver's license, and three scraps of paper. On one is Mama's address, on the second is mine and Carl's, and on the third is "Daryl Elliot 235 E. Burch St. Raycene, Alabama 70812." Daddy's address. She had his address. And his address is just a few hours from Jasper.

For the first time since she died, I'm angry with my sister. Truly angry. And hurt. I didn't know people could still hurt you after they died. For some stupid reason, I thought you had to be alive for that.

The corner of the paper is damp from the sweat of my hand. Eleven years. I haven't seen him in eleven years or heard from him in ten, and in my hand, I hold his address. And she kept it from me. Had she only just gotten it? She couldn't have since we talked about him that night she died.

Had she been in touch with him? Had she been keeping him all for herself?

My eyes burn and well up. It hurts so much to be angry at her. Especially when I remember she'll never know it.

I safely tuck the paper back in the wallet before my sweat or tears have a chance to blot out the ink. I don't want Clay to ask me what's wrong. I don't want to think about everything that's wrong. I close up the wallet and make sure Clay doesn't see me wipe my face.

"It's not mine." I toss the wallet down on the bed. "It's Kelly's." I remember how I had accidentally taken it instead of my own when I'd gone to get us food back at the hotel. I wonder if Kelly had picked up mine, and if she had it on her when she was killed, what that would mean when they found her body. *If* they found her body. "She's my sister." No, not is. Was. It's *was* now. But I can't bring myself to tell Clay that just yet. "My name is Joy." I look for any way to quickly change the subject. "I'm not kicking you out of your room, am I?"

Clay finishes folding a blanket and lays it at the foot of the bed. "Technically, yes. This was my room, and it is where I usually stay when I visit, but it's no problem. I've been using the pull-out in the den."

"I'm sorry I'm disrupting your normal sleeping arrangements."

"It's fine, really."

"Am I keeping you from a job or anything?"

"I work at Segar's. It's a hardware shop back in Northchester." After a pause, he adds, "The owner, Walt, is a good guy. He's planning on retiring soon and I think he's been grooming me to take over."

"That'd be good. You going to do it?"

"We'll see."

"Did he give you time off this week?"

"No." Clay pulls the blanket up over my feet. "I was already on vacation."

"Am I keeping you from a vacation?"

Wrong Girl Gone

"What? Oh, no. Not a real vacation. Not really." He seems jittery, like he isn't used to holding a conversation for this long. "I was planning on staying around here anyway. Just working on some home projects, helping my mom and such. You know." I take that as my cue and don't ask any more questions. "Anyway, I'll leave you to your breakfast."

He turns to leave, but I don't want to be alone. "Clay?"

He stops and looks at me. "Yeah?"

"You wanna… play cards or something?"

We play rummy while I eat my breakfast. We play casino while I eat my lunch. I beat him a few times, but he comes out on top in the end. When we play poker, we bet miniature oatmeal cookies. He definitely isn't a talker, but I don't feel much like talking, so we balance each other out.

Chapter Fifteen

I wake up screaming with no idea why. When I open my eyes, the sun is low in the sky and Clay has his hand on my shoulder. I pull away from him, disoriented.

"It's okay," he says. "You're okay."

I wipe my hair off my forehead and realize my face and whole body are drenched in sweat. I look at my hand. It's shaking.

"I'll get you a towel." Clay leaves and returns a minute later with a damp washrag. He pats it on my face. My instinct is to pull away, but I tell myself to relax and let him take care of me.

"I guess I had another nightmare." I feel my heart rate slow as the cool cloth dabs my face. "What time is it?"

"Half-past eight." I told John I'd call him at eight, but I must have dozed off right after dinner. He's probably worried. "Your friend John called around eight," Clay says as if he's read my mind. "I let him know you were sleeping and would tell you he called. He seemed a little suspicious and asked me to have you call him as soon as you woke up."

If I didn't feel so lightheaded, I would have chuckled over John's inherent protectiveness. "Thanks."

Clay stares at me for a moment, his brow furrowed. "I don't mean to pry, but what happened to you?"

I'll have to tell him sooner or later, so I might as well throw it out there now before I have to start coming up with stories to cover up the truth. I tell him everything. I tell him about Kelly, the man, the body bag, Jerry... I stop myself before I tell him about the money. I don't want him to know I'm a thief.

And to be honest, the money hasn't even crossed my mind since the incident. I assume either Carl or Kelly's killer took it. Even if one of them did, I don't care. If Carl sent the man to get the money back and kill me in the process, then he's even crazier than I thought he was. I know Carl, and that isn't something he would do. He might hunt me down to get the money, he might beat me senseless, he might say awful things, violent things, but he wouldn't hire someone to have me killed. As sick as it is, he loves me too much. Although I wouldn't put it past him to hire the wrong guy to get the money from me. Carl knows some seedy people. Part of me wants to spend hours playing detective in my head, putting together the pieces of my sister's death and who I should hold responsible. But another part of me wants to live in deep denial because right now, none of it matters. I don't care what Carl or Kelly's killer intended to do. All I want is to get back to my son.

When I'm done talking, Clay lets out a long breath. "Jesus... It really is a miracle you're alive."

I feel a pang of guilt. After all the lies and running and hiding, I feel a strange need to be honest with Clay, even if it means him thinking I'm a thief. "My husband had been keeping money from me. A lot of money. Money that we needed to buy food and pay bills. I stumbled on it one day, tucked away in his Playboy. He's a gambling addict and he'd spend all our money at the casino while I was saving and scraping together everything that I earned waitressing. Some days I didn't even have enough to feed Jerry a proper meal or put gas in the car. When I found that money, I looked at it like this was my chance. Jerry and I could start a new life together. I could make a better home for him, away from Carl. But I shouldn't justify stealing."

"No," he says quickly. "You did the right thing. That shouldn't even be considered stealing. You're married. Half of that money is yours." Clay rubs his face. "Do you think we should call the police?"

I shake my head. "No. I think the man who killed Kelly might be a cop."

He lets out a sigh. "You know, when I first found you on the highway, I thought you might be a cop."

"Why would you think that?"

"I found that badge in your pocket."

My heart races. I sit up. "What?"

"The badge. In the pocket of your jeans."

"Can I see it?"

He goes over to the dresser where he'd taken my wallet from before and hands me a silver badge. I read it carefully: *Harrison County Police 714*

"This was what I found in the van." My voice is shaking. "I think it belongs to the man who killed her. I need to call John."

"Of course." Clay leaves the room so I can make my call.

"Joy?" John says after only one ring.

"Yeah, it's me."

"I was just about to call you again. I called at eight. Did he tell you I called?"

"Yeah, he told me. I was just sleeping. Sorry if I worried you."

"No, you're fine." He sounds tired. "You okay?"

"Yeah." I look at the badge in my hand. "John, can I ask you for another favor?"

***

"My mother should be home from work soon," Clay says around three o'clock the next afternoon.

"Can't you tell her I'm in no shape for company?" I stare out the window at a blue bird sitting on a branch near the top of the tree. I haven't heard anything from John since I gave him the badge number last night. He said he'd try to call the

97

Wrong Girl Gone

Harrison County police force this morning and see what he could find out. But the phone hasn't rung yet and I'm feeling restless. "Besides, we've been living together for less than a week. I think it's a little soon for me to meet your mother."

I feel Clay staring at me. "Are you always this sarcastic?"

"Only on good days." I look over at him. He gives a half-smile, half-laugh. I see teeth. I didn't know he had any up until now.

His mother, Winnie, comes home around three-thirty. She's a round little lady, probably in her late fifties. She isn't much shorter than average, although next to Clay she's the height of a child. Her gray hair looks practically white against her dark skin, and there are years of crinkles around her eyes when she smiles. I can tell instantly that she's one of those people you can't help but like as soon as you see them.

"Hi, sugar, how you doing?" she says when she sees me, like she's known me all my life. Before I can respond with more than a nod, she lifts the covers to look at my legs and gently prods the area above my damaged knee. "Looking good, darling! I do damn fine work if I do say so myself." She looks at the dangling I.V. tube next to my right arm. "Clay, why isn't the I.V. in her arm?"

"She refused it," he says.

I look over at Clay. "I did not refuse it."

"Honey, you've got to keep this in, or you'll get dehydrated." She reaches over me for the needle, replaces it, and sticks it gently in my arm. It hurts, but not nearly as much as when I ripped it out myself.

"She doesn't like needles," Clay says.

"And I'm the only one who doesn't?"

"And she gets sarcastic when she's sick," he adds.

My eyes narrow at Clay, who gives me a small twitch of a smile.

Winnie chuckles. "Well, you two are certainly getting along well."

My instinct is to point a finger and yell, "He started it!" but I restrain myself.

Audrey Wilson

Winnie fashions a brace around my knee that allows me to bend it only slightly. It still hurts to move it, but the pressure of the brace helps. "Alright, missy." Winnie puts her hands on her hips. "Time to get you out of bed!"

"I tried that. I don't walk so well."

"Of course you don't. You've still got your sea legs! Let's get you moving, and you'll be walking like a champ in no time. That knee isn't going to heal itself."

I sit up on my own, and with the help of both Winnie and Clay, pull my legs over the edge of the bed. After putting too much weight on my bad knee, I have to sit back down. A few minutes later, I try again. And I sit. And I try. And I sit. And I try again.

"Right foot… Good, good. All right, now left…" she says. I find it ironic. Two people I hardly know are teaching me how to take what feels like my first steps. For the second time in my life, I'm learning how to do one of the things you're never supposed to forget. Just when I think I've pushed through the pain, Jerry's first steps pop into my mind and I feel my heart ache.

When I feel strong enough, I ask them to let me try it on my own. I do it. I shuffle across the room like a little old lady. At one point my knee twists and I start to fall, but Clay catches me before I hit the ground.

After Joy's Big Walking Adventure, Winnie seems to realize I smell or something and decides to stick me in the bathtub. My knee looks gross and swollen beneath the water, but she adds some Epsom salts and after a few minutes it's already feeling better. Finally, she leaves me alone in the tub after asking if I need anything else a hundred and fourteen times. But I don't mind her mothering. I haven't had any in a while.

Once she's left the room, I close my eyes and rest, soaking up the heat and bubbles. When the bubbles start to disappear, I can see my body through the water. Although I've always been trim, now I'm starting to look downright scrawny. Carl would have hated it. He always preferred curvy girls. I think he would have made me gain weight if I could have.

Winnie must have a tub timer because just when I'm starting to prune, she knocks on the door to see if I need any help getting out, which I do. She helps me out and dries me off, just like I do with Jerry twice a week. Once in the winter.

Once I'm in a pair of her fresh pajamas, she walks me back into the bedroom. The bed is all nicely made, and the covers are turned back.

"Now, I've let Clay know not to bother you anymore tonight. You need to get some rest after the eventful day you've had," Winnie says as she tucks me in. I can only hope I'll eventually have days a little more eventful than this one, but for now, it's enough.

Chapter Sixteen

"Well, you were certainly in a mood yesterday," I say to Clay the next morning when he comes in with breakfast. I think it's a good conversation starter. He needs those a lot, I've noticed.

"What?"

"*She refuses the I.V.,*" I quote.

"You did refuse it."

"Yeah, but you don't have to tell your mother that."

"I thought maybe you'd listen to her."

"I listen to you."

He lets out another one of those grunts masquerading as a laugh, then changes the subject. "Those pajamas more comfortable than mine, I hope?"

"They are. Thanks." As soon as he sets down the tray of food in front of me, I grab a piece of bacon and take a bite. "Your mom's really sweet."

"She has her moments." He leaves the room and a minute later comes back out with a small mop and a bucket. Then he begins mopping the hardwood floor, even though it's relatively spotless since Winnie had mopped it herself less than ten hours ago. He stops mopping and looks at me. "Do you mind?"

"Not at all. Do whatever you need to do." I take a bite of scrambled eggs. "Thanks for breakfast," I say.

Wrong Girl Gone

"No need to thank me." Clay rings out the mop in the tarnished metal bucket and continues cleaning, leaving little streaks of water droplets on the wood floor.

"Where's your father?"

"He died three years ago."

"I'm sorry."

"It's all right." He hesitates a second before continuing. "We owned the peanut farm behind this house. One day he was out on the tractor. There was a cat running around in the field. He saw it heading towards the machine and tried to stop, but his foot ended up getting caught between the wheels and he fell out." He pauses again. "The tractor ran over him."

"Oh my God." It's one of those moments where I know, "I'm sorry," won't cover it.

"The cat was okay," he says. "I think Dad wanted my brother Russell and I to take on the farm, but neither of us wanted it. It had always been his passion, not ours. We sold the farm to our neighbor and put the money into the house for Mom. She makes decent money as a nurse, but not enough to keep up with this old place. I moved to Northchester with my girlfriend at the time, took the manager job at Segar's, but Russell didn't quite have his footing. After some floundering, he joined the army. Dad's death hit him hard. I think that's why he was so quick to get out of this place."

He finishes cleaning and props the mop up in the bucket, then he stands there for a moment, looking at something I can't see.

"You can sit down if you want. I don't mind."

"All right." He sits down on the end of the bed, his hands in his lap like an awkward schoolboy. "So," he says, like he's looking for the right conversation starter. "What do you do?"

"Besides be a shitty mother and avoid getting killed by men in white vans? Not much. I'm just a waitress."

"That's important."

"Not really."

Clay smiles a little. At least I think it's a smile. "What do you want to do?"

"I really have no idea."

"No dreams?"

"Plenty of dreams. Just no ideas. I guess I always wanted to help people with their problems or work with kids, maybe teach."

"Like a social worker?"

I've never heard it put into those words before. They sound good side-by-side. "Yeah, I guess that would cover both, wouldn't it?"

"Where are your parents?"

"My mom lives in Jasper, Mississippi. My father left us when Kelly and I were eleven. I haven't seen him since."

"Have you read *A Time to Kill?*"

I stare at him blankly. "What's that?"

"It's a novel by a guy named John Grisham."

"Never heard of him."

"I guess he hasn't written much else. But he wrote that one. It's pretty good."

"Okay." I'm having a hard time connecting this conversation to the one we were just having.

"Oh, it's set in Mississippi."

"Ah." There's the link.

"Why haven't you seen him?" Clay asks after another pause. "Your dad."

"We just lost touch, I guess." I can't bring myself to open the old wounds of my family. That he left because he felt he wasn't good enough for us, not knowing it was the most painful thing he could have done. "I only just found his address in Kelly's wallet."

"She had his address and didn't tell you?"

It hurts to hear it said that way. Probably because it's the truth. I nod my head. "We'd even talked about it the night she was killed. I'd said how I just wished I could talk to him and know he was okay. And she didn't say a word about it."

"Had she been in touch with him then?"

Wrong Girl Gone

"I'm sure she was. She had his address. She seemed pretty certain that he was okay. It's not her fault, really. I mean when I got pregnant with Jerry, the attention switched to me pretty quickly. He was probably all she had left that was hers."

"He was your father too."

"Is. *Is* my father." I've had to remind myself of the difference between *is* and *was* a lot lately.

"He *is* your father too," he corrects himself. "She should have told you."

I can't bring myself to thank him, so I just offer up a small smile. "I promised myself I was going to be a better parent than my own. That I'd never leave my son." I let out a hard laugh. "Now look at me. Mother of the year."

Clay looks over at me, a stern expression on his face. "You're a good mom."

I don't know what to say. I want to rebut his compliment somehow. I don't deserve it. No one, not even my own mother, has ever said I'm a good mom. Not once. It was always about how inexperienced I was and how I'd never be able to raise a child at such a young age. If I'd gotten pregnant ten years later than I did, they might have thought differently. If I'd gotten pregnant five years later, they might have thought differently. But for a teenager, it was all bad press.

Finally, I say the only thing I can think to say. "Thank you."

Clay breaks the brief silence. "Have you thought about writing to your dad?"

I hadn't thought of that. I don't know why. My palms begin to sweat. "Yeah," I say. "Could I have some paper and a pencil?"

Clay immediately gets up and goes into the other room. When he returns, he doesn't just bring back a piece of paper and a pencil; he brings back a whole stationery kit.

Once I'm all set up, he goes downstairs to make some tea, leaving me alone with my thoughts and a blank piece of paper.

104

Audrey Wilson

First, I write "Dear Daryl." But that sounds stupid, so I erase it and write "Dear Daddy." Then I erase that and just write "Dad," but that sounds cold. Finally, I give up on the intro and try to jump into the letter. After a few minutes of staring at the nearly blank piece of paper, I realize that I should just stick with rewriting the introduction repeatedly because there is no way I am ever going to get past it. How can I possibly write a letter to the father I haven't seen in eleven years?

I plan it out in my head:

Dear Dad,

It's been so long. I hope you're doing well. I am bedridden in the house of a man named Clay. Up until last night, I have been wearing nothing but his boxer shorts and shirt. Don't get the wrong impression. He is a very respectable man with good intentions (I think). In other news, Kelly is dead, (too bad it wasn't me, right?) I can barely walk, and Jerry has recently been abandoned at a local motel. It's all my fault, of course, but what else is new? And don't worry, Jerry's fine, other than a little emotional scarring. He is in Carl's care. (Notice I didn't say "safe" care.) Isn't that great? I'm so proud of Carl for coming to the rescue like the hero he is and saving my child from any immediate harm after enduring years of physical and emotional abuse from him.

Wrong Girl Gone

Hopefully, Jerry will remember the "Oh no Daddy's Drunk" hiding places I showed him next time Carl comes home hammered. Anyway, sorry for the slight overload of information. I look forward to paying you a visit soon.

Sincerely,

Joy

P.S. Now might be a good time for you to consider changing my name.

Something tells me that little rant might not go over so well. I never actually get as far as a third sentence before I give up. I feel bad I can't help Clay out and use some of his stationary. He seems to have too much of it.

Later in the evening when he comes to collect all the unused stationery, I ask him why he has so much. Apparently, he used it to write to his brother every week back when Russell was in the army. I ask if Russell ever wrote back. Clay says he did, but with the way the system worked, he didn't get any of his replies for about three months, then they all came in bunches. I ask how he remembered what Russell was responding to in each letter. Clay says he always made a copy of each letter he sent Russell, so he could go back and reread them when he got Russell's response.

Audrey Wilson

When Clay leaves my room that evening after supper, he doesn't suggest a game of cards or ask if I'd like seconds. He seems preoccupied. There's a sadness about him he didn't have before, but I don't know him well enough to pry.

***

Clay brings the TV into my room so I can watch the news if anything comes on about Kelly, which is probably a mistake because I don't do much but watch the news for the next two days. Clay only takes it into his den to help him get to sleep. Even then, he leaves it on all night and says he'll let me know if he hears anything. I don't know what time he usually wakes up, but I know that each morning when I open my eyes the TV is back in my room and a glass of orange juice is next to my bed. He also leaves the faint smell of fresh-cut grass and cigarette smoke, so even without the TV and juice, I can always tell when he's been in the room. Some people don't like those smells, but I don't mind. I've gotten used to them. They make me feel safe. He makes me feel safe.

There's nothing noteworthy on the news, so I assume they haven't found Kelly's body yet. During commercials, I read one of the cheap mysteries I've found in the nightstand, *Death Never Falls*, which I finish in less than I day. I pick up the old green book next. The first section of poems is about flowers, which bores me. The middle section is filled with poems about death, which depresses me. And the ones towards the end are about love, which depresses me even more.

I flip back to the beginning of the book. There is an inscription on the first page that reads, "To My Darling Clay, Forever yours, Gwen." That's a lot more intriguing than any mystery book.

I skim through the book again, searching for any other secret love notes to Clay. I know I shouldn't snoop, but I'm so bored that I justify it. Even though I don't find any more writing, I do come across a poem that draws me in. It's called

Wrong Girl Gone

If You Were Coming in the Fall and it's written by Emily Dickinson.

If you were coming in the fall,

I'd brush the summer by

With half a smile and half a spurn,

As housewives do a fly.

If I could see you in a year,

I'd wind the months in balls,

And put them each in separate drawers,

Until their time befalls.

If only centuries delayed,

I'd count them on my hand,

Subtracting till my fingers dropped

Into Van Diemen's land.

If certain, when this life was out,

That yours and mine should be,

Audrey Wilson

I'd toss it yonder like a rind,

And taste eternity.

But now, all ignorant of the length

Of time's uncertain wing,

It goads me, like the goblin bee,

That will not state its sting.

I fold the corner of the page and place the book back on the nightstand. Then I spend some time imagining who Gwen is. Maybe she's just the girlfriend he'd mentioned, but this new mystery of Clay's secret long-lost love begins to occupy my mind. I picture her as this beautiful, statuesque woman with curly, flowing red hair and legs a mile long. Then the image starts making me feel a little sick, so I make her short and round with gray hair instead. Whoever she is, my curiosity is undoubtedly piqued. Besides, this is the longest I've ever been without Jerry and I need something to distract me from the ache in my heart.

Chapter Seventeen

Clay follows his mother's instructions and helps me walk a little more each day. I've gotten to the point where I can get to the bathroom and back on my own without my knee buckling, and the brace certainly helps. Winnie is working the overnight shift again, so Clay actually cooks supper from scratch to celebrate my slow recovery. He's ready to bring it up to me, but I say I want to try to make it downstairs. I get to the hallway on my own, with Clay near my side just in case, but when I attempt the first step, my leg buckles out from under me. Before I can even grab the railing, Clay catches me, wrapping his arm around my waist.

"I got you," he says. Then he lifts me up like it's nothing and carries me down the rest of the way. I know I'm married, but a part of me likes him carrying me, even though I shouldn't. The way he makes me feel weightless in his arms, the way the muscles in his shoulders flex to the point where I can feel them through his tee-shirt. Maybe it's because Clay carrying me is the most intimate contact I've had with a man since Carl, but something about it makes me feel cared for. It makes me feel wanted. When we get to the dining table, there's a moment of hesitation before he sets me down, where we make eye contact for a few seconds longer than normal. Until a sudden high-pitched beeping breaks whatever kind of moment we were having.

Audrey Wilson

Clay sets me down in a chair that creaks and goes off to the kitchen to silence the smoke detector. The house smells like burnt corn, although I can't complain. I'm so happy to be out of that bedroom I would have put up with nearly anything. The rest of the home is even homier than my room. Floral patterns and pastel colors fill nearly every corner and family photos hang on the main dining room wall as if they were a page in a photo album. If I had the strength in the lower half of my body, I would have gone over to look at them. I glimpse part of the living room from my chair. There's a fireplace in the corner with a stand of pokers next to it, dusty rose-colored curtains, and a few mismatched lamps. And oak. There's a lot of oak.

My guess about the corn is right. Clay had decided to fix meatloaf, corn, cornbread, and potatoes, but by the time he's finished, the meal has wheedled itself down to just meatloaf, cornbread, and potatoes.

He brings out the last dish, (the cornbread) and takes a seat. "Sorry about the corn," he says, pulling in his chair.

"No, that's fine. I'm not much for vegetables anyway."

"Yeah, neither am I." He takes his napkin out from under his silverware and places it on his lap. "Let me know if the food is too cold or too hot or anything."

I load up my plate with meatloaf and potatoes, then top it off with a piece of cornbread that doesn't even make it to my plate before I take a bite out of it. It's a little dry but good. The meatloaf isn't quite as good as Winnie's, but the potatoes are surprisingly better—rich and creamy. We eat in silence for the first few bites. I watch Clay for a moment. He takes a bite of cornbread, leaving a few crumbs around his mouth. I try to hide my smile. For a second, I feel something I haven't felt in a long time, but I can't place what it is.

"You've got a little…" I point to my mouth.

Clay takes the hint and wipes his own. "Thanks." After a few minutes, Clay stops eating. I can feel him looking over at me. "How did you get that scar on your arm?" he asks, referring to the burn mark I'd gotten from Carl a few years back. It's about the length of a pencil and a little wider than an inch. I shove another piece of cornbread into my face. "Sorry, it's none of my business. I don't know what I'm thinking sometimes." He mumbles his words like it might close the subject faster.

"Carl did it." The words just come out. No piece of cornbread can stop them.

Clay's fork hits the plate. I hadn't meant to cause him to chip any of his dishes. "He what?"

"He did it," I say again, a little taken aback. To be honest, I'm surprised to get this sort of reaction from someone. The first time I told Kelly that Carl hit me, she was beside herself, telling me I had to leave him. But after a few years passed, and I was still married to him, I think she slowly gave up. Occasionally, something would set her off and she'd try again to convince me to leave. Other times, she'd choose her battles, and try not to get too angry when she'd see a new scar.

Mama saw the one on my arm that Clay is looking at when it was fresh, but she didn't ask about it and I didn't tell her. Then I watched as she poured herself a bourbon neat. For the sake of her alcohol intake, I kept the story to myself.

"Was it an accident?" he asks.

"He'll tell you it is."

"I— I don't... I'm really— Jesus..." Clay doesn't seem to know how to react to this piece of information. "I'm sorry," he finally settles on.

In turn, I don't know how to react to him. Thank you? It's okay? It's not your fault? "I'm used to it." I take a bite of meatloaf.

"You mean he hurt you more than once?"

I let out a bitter laugh that I probably should have forced down. "Most of them heal faster than this one. Burns leave the worst scars." I clear my throat and try to recall the story to the best of my ability. "I'd gone to pick up Jerry from preschool. When I got there, his teacher took me off to the side. She said he hadn't talked all week. Not to anyone. Just sat there every day playing with a little plastic airplane. She said they thought he might be autistic. Just what every parent wants to hear, right? When I told this to Carl he jumped right on her bandwagon. He said we needed to get him to a therapist and a special school and all that, but I said no. I didn't want to. I was the one who was around him most of the time and I didn't see those signs at all. I mean, he was always talking to me. I told Carl this, and he lost it. Said Jerry hardly spoke two words to him most days. I'd been in the middle of fixin' supper when he'd started in. He pushed me up against the stove, trying to get me to hold still. I don't think he realized it was on at first. As soon as my skin was pressed against the metal. I just saw red. It hurt so much that I couldn't even feel it hurting at all. I don't really remember what happened next, so I think that was when I passed out. Carl took me to the hospital and the doctors fixed it up, no questions asked. They treated me differently than they normally would have, though. I could tell. I think they knew you could only get burns like that by holding your skin against something hot for longer than someone could usually stand."

"Does it still hurt?" Clay asks.

"Only when I think about it." Clay doesn't laugh. "No. It doesn't hurt. It doesn't feel like anything, to be honest. It went through to the nerves so it's pretty much numb now."

"What about Jerry?"

"I tried to think back on what had happened before that week he stopped talking at school. And I remembered Carl and I had gotten into it bad that Sunday night. I don't remember what the fight was about, but I remember Carl pushing me up against the wall outside of Jerry's room, screaming at me. Jerry opened the door, crying and yelling for him to let me go."

"My God, Joy… Why didn't you leave him sooner?"

I feel defensive all of a sudden. "Well, I didn't have much of a choice. I mean, I was trying to raise Jerry and I didn't have any money or anything. There wasn't anything I could do."

"Are you going back to him?"

I'm not sure I like all these questions. Still, I try to answer as honestly as I can. "I don't know," I say, then change my answer. "No," I tell myself. Clay just happens to be listening. "I'm going back for Jerry, that's all."

"Do you have any idea who might have come after you? I mean, do you think it's possible—"

"Carl wouldn't kill me," I say quickly. "He's all talk."

"Clearly he isn't all talk." Clay nods at my arm. "That man killed your sister. Your twin sister. Maybe he was sent to kill you and thought she was you."

My stomach turns. Just because Clay and John had both suggested the same possibility didn't make it true. "I don't think that's it."

Clay must notice my brisk tone because he seems to back down. "Sorry. It's not my business."

"You're fine," I say dismissively. "I just know he wouldn't try to kill me."

I shove a few bites of potatoes into my mouth and search my mind for a new subject. Something to put Clay in the spotlight instead of me. "That book of poems you have is an interesting read."

He hesitates for a moment before putting a fork full of food into his mouth, but he doesn't look up. After finishing up the last few bites on his plate, he stands. "Do you want anything else?"

"No, I'm still eating." He picks up his plate and takes it into the kitchen. He heard me. I know he heard me.

I put the last bite of meatloaf into my mouth, then pick up my plate and painfully will my legs into the kitchen. "Where do you want these?"

"Just on the counter is fine." He's scraping off the plates into the sink. "You shouldn't be on your feet too much."

"Who's Gwen?" He has no way out now, other than to turn on the garbage disposal. When he reaches for the switch, I quickly block it with my hand. He gives up.

"She was the girlfriend I was telling you about. And my fiancée." He glances away from me, and I know we're about to start another round of that old favorite game called "Anything but Eye Contact."

"You're not together anymore?"

"No." He begins washing the dishes in the sink. "She and Russell have been married three years now."

"She left you for Russell?" He probably didn't want to hear it said back to him, but I can't help my reaction.

"Yeah. She did."

I try to think of something technical to ask. Technical questions are less painful than emotional ones any day. "How long were you two together?"

He turns on the water and proceeds to rinse the plates. "We started dating in high school then broke up for a few years after graduation. She moved to New York for a while to become a singer, but that didn't work out, so she came back here. We got back together soon after that and were going strong for about two years. Then my dad died. I think I was so preoccupied with grief and looking after my mother and Russell that Gwen and I started growing apart. I was scrambling to hold onto her, and I proposed. She said yes. I think out of pity."

"Not the best reason to agree to marry someone."

"It wasn't. She started seeing Russell behind my back."

"Shit. I'm sorry."

"He was young and grieving. I don't think his head was really screwed on right at that time. He was the one who told me about the two of them. Gwen didn't even have the guts to tell me herself. I was pretty hard on Russell for a while after that. We didn't talk much. I was angry, but the two of them seemed happy. I don't know if that made it easier or harder to deal with. But even with her in his life, he was still lost. He moved from job to job, drank too much, couldn't seem to focus, always asking to borrow money…

"One day we got into a terrible fight. I don't even remember how it started, but Gwen was there. She was trying to calm us both down, but we were too heated. I was screaming at him to do something with his life, to quit relying on me for everything he was ashamed to ask our mother for. He'd been toying with the idea of joining the army. He'd first considered it when we were teenagers, and I'd always steered him away from the idea. But that night I practically dared him to do it. I told him to quit screwing around and make something of his life like Dad did. I also said he probably wouldn't go through with it because he was nothing like him.

"I think that's what pushed him to actually do it. He married Gwen before he left. I didn't go to the wedding. I always regretted that…" The water is still running very low. He turns it off. "I went to his going away party to say goodbye the day he left for the army. Before I could get the words out, he took me to the other room and told me he wasn't going to leave without forgiveness from me. The truth was I'd already forgiven him, I just hadn't told him yet." He smiles a little. "I forgave him for what he did. I just didn't forgive myself for pushing him to go."

"Is he still touring?"

"No. He was just gone for two years. Then one night some of his fellow soldiers beat him up real bad, so bad that they discharged him."

"Jesus. Why did they beat him up?"

Clay shrugs. "Because he was Black. Because he was too soft. Who knows? They don't need a reason. He came back with scars and bad PTSD."

"I guess you don't need to go to war to be traumatized."

"You don't. It's a common misconception. Hell, you probably are a victim of it yourself."

"Me?"

"Yeah. After what happened to you in the woods. Maybe even with your husband."

I feel a wave of fear wash over me, followed by a tightening in my chest and churning in my stomach. I always thought if I survived the pain, if I handled it, then I could get through it. But maybe trauma goes deeper than what we can control. Maybe that is PTSD.

"How's Russell doing now?"

"Varies day to day."

There's another one of those familiar silences between us.

He glances at the switch on the wall. "Can I turn on the garbage disposal now?"

I smile at him and he smiles back. "Sure."

***

After supper Clay goes outside to mow the lawn before the sun completely sets. He says Winnie doesn't mind doing it herself, which doesn't surprise me, but he figures it's the least he can do to help her out while he's staying with her.

I watch him from the window. The sun is at that low point in the sky where everything is slowly turning from gold to blue. I don't like that the days keep getting shorter. Kelly used to call the hours of those long summer days "Time Stealers." They were more hours than we knew what to do with when we were little and would give anything to have back now.

I go out the back door onto the screened-in porch, where I take a seat in the nearest lawn chair. The porch is a lot nicer than the one in Jasper. There are no tears in the screen. The smell of mold wafting from the wood is absent. Instead, I smell nothing but fresh-cut grass, hay, and leftover dampness from the last rain. The view is a lot nicer too. I can see for miles. It's half sky, half crops, and all beautiful. There are cicadas chirping all around me. I wish I had a camera. I suddenly feel the need to capture every moment I experience on film, so I'll never forget it. I think that's why Kelly loved photography. She was always determined to hold everything in until there was no more room in her memory for old photographs, so she had no choice but to start putting those memories on film.

Clay stops the lawnmower to wipe his face with a rag. My eyes drift to his arms, right where the short sleeve of his shirt meets his skin. The same arms that carried me. His muscles aren't bulky, but they do fill out his shirt perfectly. When he takes a drink from his water bottle, his muscles flex, and I feel my tongue catch in the back of my throat like a starstruck teenage girl. He notices I'm looking at him and gives me a wave with the towel. I wave back, grateful that he's too far away to see me blush. But the color drains from my face almost instantly as the image of Carl pops into my head. Even if I am leaving him, I'm still married to him now. And having these kinds of feelings for a man who isn't Jerry's father puts a knot in my stomach.

Chapter Eighteen

"Norman Lance," John says in response to my usual opening greeting at the start of our nightly call.

"What?"

"Harrison County Police force, badge number seven-one-four. Norman Lance."

I sit up. "How did you find out? Do you know what he looks like?"

"No. Just his name. Sorry it took me so long. I called the non-emergency number of the force every day and this was the first time they actually answered. I asked if they could give me the name associated with someone's badge number. They seemed suspicious at first, but I said I was a journalist writing an article on the best cops in the county. Ironic, right?"

"What else did they say?"

"I guess he's only part-time due to some recent cutbacks. And get this; he left for a last-minute fishing trip last week and hasn't returned yet."

My heart pounds in my chest. I think back to the fishing equipment in the back of the van. His alibi. "It's him," I say.

"He's still out there, Joy. You gotta look out for yourself."

"Clay's taking good care of me. Thanks for calling them, John. Have you seen Jerry at all?"

"I drove by the house yesterday on my way home from work. He was sitting on the front porch playing with his trucks."

"How did he seem?"

Wrong Girl Gone

"He seemed sad. I pulled over down the street and watched him for a minute. Any car that drove by, he looked up at. He's waiting for you to come home, Joy."

A lump catches in my throat. "Thanks, John. You're a good friend."

After we hang up, I'm just about to write down the few things I now know about Norman Lance to help keep track of my thoughts, when the doorbell rings. Clay's footsteps creak across the house. I hear the front door unlock and open, followed by what sounds like two male voices that aren't Clay's. Something about their tones sound official, and I wonder if they're cops. My heart races.

What if it's him?

What if he knows I'm alive and he found me, the only witness to Kelly's murder? What if he knows I took his badge? I never should have taken his badge. He's going to kill me. Well, first he's going to kill Clay, so I can have another head on my conscience, then he's going to kill me. And then… then Jerry won't have a mother anymore.

The muffled voices downstairs grow a little louder and I catch a few words of their conversation.

"Sorry to bother you this late," one of the men says.

"No trouble at all. Please, have a seat…" says Clay. They move into the kitchen and their voices become too muffled to understand.

It's all I can do not to hobble over to the top of the stairs and listen in, the way Kelly and I used to sit in our closet at the mobile home because it was there that we could most clearly hear whatever "discussion" our parents were having in the other room. But the floors in this house are old and creaky and if I so much as turn over in bed, someone might discover I'm here.

I lay there for a good half hour, helpless, fearfully waiting for the sound of a struggle, or worse, a gunshot. I try not to move. I try not to breathe. Finally, the footsteps start up again, and the voices move toward the door.

"Sorry I couldn't be of more help," I hear Clay say.

"Not a problem. Take it easy," says one of the men. I let out a long breath of relief and reach for the glass of water on the nightstand to wet my dry mouth, and in the process knock the whole glass on the floor. There is a sharp silence downstairs, and I can picture all three of the men looking right up to my bedroom. Looking right at me.

"Damn that cat." Clay's voice cuts the silence. "He'll be sleeping outside tonight if he doesn't watch it."

The silence lingers. I look at the floor. The glass didn't shatter but is now audibly rolling away from the bed. I hold my breath like it will help.

"All right, well…" one of the men says. "We'll call you if we have any follow-up questions."

After the door shuts, Clay's footsteps make their way up the stairs until he finally knocks on my door.

"Come in," I breathe, still trying to slow my heart.

The door opens. He looks from me to the glass and back to me. "Next time maybe you should just throw it across the room. I don't think they heard you."

"What did they want? Did you see their badges?"

Clay walks over to the glass and picks it up. "I did see their badges. They're local, Monroe County. I guess there was a robbery in the area. They're asking around to see if anyone saw or heard anything."

"That was a long conversation for a robbery we didn't know anything about."

"Yeah, well. You know how cops are in these small towns. Just looking for something to do."

"What did they look like?" I can see Norman's face so clearly in my mind. The hook of his nose, his greasy skin, those glasses…

"One was shorter, dark hair. The other was a bigger guy, potbelly, balding."

I let the relief wash over me. Neither sounded like him.

"I think John found him," I say as Clay begins mopping up the spilled water with an old towel. "Same badge number. He left for a fishing trip last week. He's not back yet."

Wrong Girl Gone

Clay stops and looks at me. "Do you think he thinks you're dead?"

"I don't know," I say. "But if he does find out I'm alive, there's nothing stopping him from coming after me."

Chapter Nineteen

The next afternoon, I'm sitting on the floor at the foot of the bed looking out the window, thrilled to have some freedom from my mattress. It looks like someone is standing outside the window, spraying a water hose on the glass. Daytime rain showers always make me think of my daddy. On rainy days in the summertime while Kelly and Mama were out shopping, and we had nothing else to do, he and I would sit at the kitchen table in our trailer and make model airplanes. We didn't talk much, of course, but those memories were still some of the best I had of him. He would build the planes and I would paint. He wouldn't even care if I messed up and got paint on a part of the plane where there wasn't supposed to be any. If it had been *him* painting, he would have mumbled and cursed himself. When I did it, he just smiled and said, "Happens to all of us."

I hobble into the bathroom, brush my teeth, and do my best to fix my hair. Winnie must be home from her shift because I hear her talking to Clay downstairs. I need a few items from the store and even though Clay offered to get them for me, I can't help but feel some fresh air will do me good, so he's taking me on a tour of Boone this afternoon. I pull my hair back tight and remind myself to borrow one of Clay's baseball caps before we leave. I can't look too much like myself, on the off-chance Norman Lance isn't far away. I can't imagine why he'd be in Boone, but like John and Clay have both said, I need to be careful.

Wrong Girl Gone

When I come back into my room, Winnie is laying out some clothes on my now-made bed. I'm not sure how I'll ever be able to repay these kind folks.

"Hey, sugar," she says when she sees me. She holds up two nearly identical blouses, one in blue and one in peach. "I have blue and I have peach. You seem like a blue kind of gal to me."

"You got me pegged."

Winnie helps me put on the blue blouse. Even though my muscles are still sore, I can feel them starting to heal the more I move them. Just stretching them through the sleeves of the blouse feels like waking up after a long nap.

Once I'm done putting on the blouse and matching cropped polyester pants, I pick up one of the baseball caps on Clay's dresser, put it on, and take a look at myself in the mirror. Although it hardly goes with the baseball cap, the outfit makes me look very unlike myself, which can only be a good thing under these circumstances.

"Oh, sugar, you can't wear that hat with that outfit! Here..." She bustles out of the room and returns a minute later with a white sunhat and some sunglasses. "If you're trying to lay low, I can assure you this will do the trick."

I'm not sure how much information Clay has given Winnie about my situation, but she seems more than trustworthy. I thank her and begin to switch hats, but as soon as I take off the cap, Winnie insists on running a brush through my hair. I let her, partly because my hair needs it, and partly because it feels nice to have it brushed. Maybe it's because Mama used to brush our hair when we were little, but it's one of those comforts I don't realize I miss until I feel it again.

"How are you feeling these days, sugar?"

"Better." I choke back the sentiment that has crept into my throat. "I'm still a little sore, but much better than I was."

"That's good to hear. Good lord, it was all I could do not to insist that Clay drive you to the hospital when he first found you. You were such a mess, bless your heart."

Audrey Wilson

The sentimental feeling in my throat vanishes and is replaced with a knot in my stomach. "I thought Clay didn't think I'd make it to the hospital."

"Oh, you'd have made it. He told me you woke up crying when he found you, saying you didn't want to go to the hospital."

The knot tightens. Why would Clay say one thing to me and another to his mother? I want to give him the benefit of the doubt, I really do. But he's making it difficult.

"He's a good man, your son." I try my best to sound casual as I seek out reassurance. "Isn't he?"

"One of the best. Sure, he's made his share of mistakes. We all have. But I love him with all my heart. Both of my sons. You'll have to meet Russell sometime."

Winnie is proving to be no help at all. A mother's love and all that nonsense. I try to push the negative thoughts out of my head and enjoy what's left of the hair brushing.

After she brushes my hair and makes sure I'm ready to go, Winnie leaves to go take a nap. A few minutes later, Clay is at my door.

"Ready to go?"

I do better going down the stairs this time if you count making it halfway down the stairs as better. I think Clay is going to carry me all the way to the car, but he stops at the bottom of the front porch and sets me down gently. Even though it's stopped raining, the dampness has left the air thick with humidity. I never thought I'd miss humidity. "Can you walk the rest of the way?" he asks.

"Yeah." I nod my head and make my way towards the navy pick-up truck. The house is taller than I had guessed and the chipped paint on it is gray. For whatever reason, I'd been expecting white. I walk across the gravel, but the closer I get to the truck, the worse I feel. It's like there's a dark shadow around the truck and I'm being sucked into it. I don't know what's wrong with me. It's just a truck. I stop walking. And as soon as I stop, I see headlights. I see a figure. I taste dirt and blood in my mouth. My palms are burning, my body goes numb, and all I see is white.

There is a sharp blow to both my knees as I hit the gravel. The white slowly fades and I feel a large, warm hand on each of my arms. One of them moves to my back and helps me sit up. The other brushes a piece of hair off my face. My body suddenly feels very heavy, my arms and legs dangling at my sides. The air around me goes from sticky and humid to cool and dry in a matter of seconds, and it takes me a moment to realize it's because I've been carried back inside.

Clay lays me down on the sofa in the living room. He puts a few decorative pillows behind my back to help me sit up. Then he leaves and comes back with a glass of ice water. I take a couple of sips and pretend not to notice Clay sitting across from me, staring at me as if I'm a China doll that might break if he so much as breathes too close to me.

"I'm sorry," he says. "We shouldn't have tried to go out. It was probably too much for you to take in—"

"Why did you tell me I wouldn't have made it to the hospital?" I set my glass down on the table and wait for his response.

Clay sits back, looking at me. "What do you mean?" He picks up a coaster from an end table, lifts my glass, and slides it underneath.

"You told me I wouldn't make it and told your mother that I begged you not to take me. She said I would have made it to the hospital." Clay doesn't say anything. "I never told you not to take me, did I?"

Clay rubs his face. "No, you didn't. I'm sorry," he says. My worst fears are realized. He must have done something wrong if he has to apologize for it. "I'm not proud of that. I probably should have taken you to the hospital. If my mother had insisted and you had been in worse shape, I would have. I swear. But I've done some things that I'm not proud of. If I took you to the hospital, the police would be involved, and I just didn't want things from my past to cause more problems. But it was a selfish decision on my part, and I shouldn't have been arrogant enough to assume agency over your body like that. It wasn't my place to make that decision."

"What kind of things?"

"It doesn't matter now. It's in my past and it doesn't concern you. But please know that you're safe with me. Okay?"

I really have no reason to believe him. Then again, I don't have the greatest track record myself, so there's a big part of me that feels like I have no right to judge someone else's shady past. And the night I told him what happened to me, he did ask me if I wanted to call the police. It was an admirable decision for anyone to put someone else's needs before their own, let alone a stranger. I nod my head.

"I am sorry again." He doesn't meet my eyes, but I can tell by the tremble in his voice that he's sincere. "We don't have to go into town today if it's too much for you."

"No, I'm fine." I'm not going to spend another day inside that room, alone with my thoughts, tearing my bedroom apart for more clues to Clay's past. "Let's go into town."

I start to get up, but Clay stops me. "Wait—" I look up at him. "Can I trust you not to go to the police about me?"

If I decide to not trust him, what am I supposed to do? Go to the police when the man who killed Kelly might be one of them? Turn him and his mother in for helping me, giving me medical care, feeding me, and taking care of me for the past week? At this point, I should probably just take my chances with the man in front of me.

"Yes," I say firmly. "I promise."

I get to the truck just fine the second time. Clay doesn't have to even hold my arm, and I'm proud of myself for that. There's no air conditioning in the truck, so we keep the windows down the whole drive into town, which is okay with me. I can't get enough fresh air.

Downtown Boone is quaint, to say the least. I let my head hang out the window like a dog as we drive around and people-watch. A group of young teenage boys walk down Main Street, smoking cigarettes and marveling at how cool they are. A small group of girls is walking towards them, one of them lingering towards the back of the group, fiddling with her hair, another one adjusting her bra, trying to show off what little cleavage she has. A girl with wavy blonde hair nudges the one fixing her bra as they approach the boys. The girl quickly stops adjusting herself and fluffs her hair a little as they pass. The girls smile and wave, the boys nod and call. One of the boys is being particularly showy by walking across a park bench like a trapeze artist. He's the class clown, the jerky show-off all the girls go for. I see myself in the group right away. I'm the shy one in the back, Kelly is the one adjusting her cleavage, and Carl is the class clown. Maybe we all see ourselves in other people, or maybe I still don't know who I am so I'm constantly trying to figure it out.

We park in front of a hair salon called Curl Up and Dye. If Kelly were here, she would have pulled out her camera and snapped a few pictures of that one. "For the books," she'd say. Clay offers to buy me a haircut if it'll make me feel better. I say that it won't make me feel better, so I guess it's out of the question. He gets it and laughs. I like it when he laughs; when he shows he has a sense of humor. It's tiring being sarcastic enough for the both of us.

We go to Benny's Drug and Sundry first, a dingy but charming place with a little bell that rings when we walk in the door. Well, Clay walks, I shuffle.

"I guess an angel just got his wings," I say, smiling to myself as I think of John.

"Hey there, Grady. Haven't seen you in a while," the man behind the counter says to Clay. He has a big, perfectly trimmed handlebar mustache and wears a green John Deere cap, even though he isn't even standing in the sun. But I guess in my hat and dark glasses, I shouldn't talk.

"Yeah, just been helping out my mom. How are things for you, Benny?" says Clay.

"Not too bad, not too bad..." He lowers his voice some and I catch his hand motioning Clay closer. "Who's your friend?"

"She's my—" he hesitates. "My cousin."

Benny looks between the two of us with a raised eyebrow.

"Yep. First cousins." I slap Clay on the back. "We're practically siblings."

Benny seems to be holding his tongue. I smile and go back to shopping. As Clay and I browse, I hear Benny say to the young clerk, "Is that possible?"

I'm still moving slowly, but I'm doing better than I thought I would. When I walk by the refrigerated section, I glean my reflection in the glass and look down at myself. My shoes are black with dirt. They were white just over a week ago.

"You can't be walking around in shoes like those." Clay stands behind me, looking down at my filthy feet. "We'll get you some new ones today." I'm about to argue that they're fine and he doesn't need to spend any money on me, but he's already moved on with the rest of his shopping.

I pick up a box of tampons and a toothbrush and before Clay can beat me to the register, pay for my items with what little money Kelly has in her wallet. I wait by the door for Clay. He finishes paying and walks over to me.

"I was going to buy your things for you."

"It's all right. I found some money in—" I stop when I notice Benny leaning over the counter to hear our conversation in what he seems to think is a subtle manner. I nod towards the door and we leave Benny's Drug and Sundry. The little bell rings again.

"A lot of angels getting wings today," Clay says as we step outside. It's starting to get cloudy again. The change from cool to warm is more than my body is used to. I suddenly feel lightheaded and lean on Clay for support. "You okay?"

I nod my head and steady myself. Once I'm balanced, he helps me in the direction of the truck. "So where did you say you got the money?"

"Kelly's wallet," I say. He's looking at me, trying to catch my eye. It makes me uncomfortable, and I don't quite know why. "Why?" I suddenly feel a twinge of anger. "Did you think I stole it from you or something?"

"What? No, of course not."

"I know I took the money from Carl, but that was different. I'm not a thief."

He doesn't seem to know what to say. "I wasn't accusing you of stealing. I'm sorry if it seemed that way. I just don't want you to have to use your sister's money, that's all."

I avoid his eyes, the hot flush of shame creeping into my face. "What am I supposed to use? I don't have anything."

"Joy, listen to me." He takes a step closer to me. "Whatever you need, I'll pay for. It's no trouble, honest. You're my guest."

"Your guest?" I repeat. "You really shouldn't call strays you take in off the street *guests*. The only reason I'm here, the only reason I'm even alive is because of you. Out of all the people who may have driven past me, you were the one who stopped." There are tears in my eyes, even though I'm not quite sure why. I just know Clay doesn't deserve this. I'm a burden to him. I can't handle being a burden. "If you knew me, you'd know I don't deserve this. I don't deserve to be here. And because of you, I am. And there's no way I'll ever be able to repay you and I can't live with that."

I'm breathing like I just ran a mile. I'm ready for Clay to walk away from me. But he doesn't. He reaches his hand up, hesitates for a second, then gently wipes a tear from my cheek. "You don't have anything to repay me for."

I'm trying to figure out how to react when I decide to just give in to my emotions and put my arms around him. He doesn't let go. He doesn't flinch. He pats my hair and holds me. And that's all I need.

***

Miss Littlefoot's Fine Family Dining is where Clay takes me for lunch. With a name like Miss Littlefoot, I just have to ask the waitress how it got its name. She doesn't know where the name came from, so she asks the manager. The manager says the woman who opened the restaurant in 1954 had one foot that was considerably smaller than the other. She never tried to hide it and limped on it with pride, so people started calling her Miss Littlefoot. When she finally realized her dream of opening her own restaurant, Miss Littlefoot couldn't think of any name more fitting. I think it's a neat little story. If I'd been a waitress at a diner called Miss Littlefoot, the first thing I would have done when I applied for the job was ask where the name came from.

Our waitress rolls her eyes after the manager finishes the story. "You ready to order?" she asks once the manager has left.

"I'll have the cheeseburger with just ketchup, onion, and relish, please." I fold the menu and set it on the table.

She stares at me. "Relish?"

"Yeah," I say.

"That stuff you put on hot dogs?"

"Yeah."

"On a cheeseburger?"

"Yes," I say. "On a cheeseburger." She stares at me for a moment longer, then shakes her head and writes it down.

"I'll have the same," says Clay. He smiles at me and turns his menu over to the waitress. She shakes her head and jots down the orders, then leaves.

Clay and I enjoy our food, mostly in silence. Silence makes me uncomfortable with many people, but not him. The longest silence with Clay feels like the best conversation with anyone else. In our silence, I can hear the distant voices of a news station coming from the old TV over the bar. I'm about to down my last fry when I hear someone say, "Jerry Larson." I drop the fry on my plate and whirl my head around.

Clay stops eating too. "What's wrong?"

My eyes are fixated on the television screen. There are headlines written in red in a banner running across the bottom of the screen, but I'm not looking at that. I'm watching my husband carry my son out of the Silver Bell

Wrong Girl Gone

Motel. Even though the footage is probably a week old, it's new to me. I stand up and walk over to the TV, the words pulling me in like a magnet, the screen hypnotizing me.

A woman's voice speaks over the footage. "Following up on last week's story of five-year-old Jerry Larson, who was discovered alone in a room at the Silver Bell Motel in Ashville. According to hotel records, the boy's mother, twenty-two-year-old Joy Larson, checked in with Jerry last week and hasn't been seen since. Police quickly contacted Carl Larson, father of Jerry and husband of Joy, who arrived at the motel only minutes later to retrieve his son. Knowing his wife to be mentally unstable, Carl had filed a kidnapping report against her upon discovering she and his son were both missing."

Mentally unstable?

On the screen, Carl stands in front of our car at the Silver Bell Motel, holding Jerry, whose face is blurred out. "I came home from work and my son was gone. My wife was gone. The two most important people in the world to me had just vanished. I didn't know what I was going to do. Now, I thank God that I have my son. I just wish I had my wife back too."

As Carl breaks down, the TV cuts to the reporter in the studio. "Just a week after young Jerry was retrieved by his father, the Larson family receives heartbreaking news. The police have just discovered the body of a woman on the edge of the Kawanee River near Boone, Alabama, about three-hundred and fifty miles east of Jasper, Mississippi." On the screen, the police and paramedics pull Kelly's body out of the river. "The twenty-two-year-old Caucasian female with dirty blonde hair, brown eyes, and a petite frame has been identified by her driver's license as Joy Larson, Jasper resident, wife of Carl Larson and mother of Jerry Larson." Of course. Kelly must have picked up my wallet at the hotel after I'd gone out to get food that night. "She was found face-down in the mud, covered in cuts and bruises, her extremities swollen from the rising tide. Carl Larson will be taken in for questioning, but as of right now the police have no leads on a suspect. Up next, traffic…"

I turn to Clay, trying hard to believe that everyone in the diner is not staring at me. My heart races. My body has been discovered by the edge of the Kawanee river.

But I wasn't.

"They think she's me."

Chapter Twenty

Clay assures me that there is nothing I can do right now besides keep a low profile and keep getting stronger. I know he's right and try not to think about how my mama would react if she saw it on the news. I can only hope that she's isolated enough from the world to not turn on the TV and discover that one of her babies is dead.

I also can't stop myself from thinking that Kelly's killer is out there somewhere. *Norman Lance.* Why her? Was it ever supposed to be her? No. He had been following *me.* I was the one he was after. But why? I know it's not Carl. He wouldn't try to have me killed. He's an abuser, a self-centered alcoholic, and sure, he might be pissed about the money, but he loves me. He loves Jerry. And he knows Jerry loves me. Why kill me if there's a chance I might come back to him? He needs me. He needs the power he has over me.

Once I've calmed down a bit, Clay takes me to a few clothing stores where I pick out some basic items, not even half a week's worth. Still, it's better than nothing. Then we go to a shoe store to replace my muddy sneakers. I try on a bunch and finally find a pair that fit. They're just like my old ones, but navy. If I'd found them in white, I would have gotten those instead. I'm not much for change like Kelly was. She was the adventurous one. The one who had the guts to move away from her hometown when she turned eighteen to go to college. The one who wasn't afraid to live on her own and who had the intelligence to say "no" even when "yes" was the favored answer. I don't even like buying shoes that aren't a safe color like white.

I look out the window of the store while Clay pays for the shoes. A few drops of rain hit the glass, but my eyes are fixed past them. I see him before anything else, like a bee to the brightest flower, and something inside me dies. His glasses are foggy and covered in water droplets. He's wearing the same olive-green jacket and carrying an umbrella. His face appears wet, but it isn't. It's just greasy. He has the same mustache, the same big, crooked nose, and the same two hands he tightened around my sister's neck. I can see him carrying that heavy black bag and holding the crowbar to the sky just before bringing it down on me. I can see his beady black eyes as the lightning struck above us in the middle of those woods. I knew then that if I ever saw those eyes again, I would recognize them in a second. And now here I am. And I can't take my eyes off him. I can't move. I can't breathe. All I can do is watch.

"Joy?" Clay says.

"It's him," I manage. "It's Norman Lance." I can't bring myself to look at Clay, but I don't need to. He follows my gaze to Norman Lance. Before I can find the strength to speak again, Clay steps in front of me, shielding me from the window. It's only then that I realize my whole body is trembling. He puts his hands on my arms. "It's okay," he says softly. "We'll just hang out here for a few minutes until he's gone, okay?"

This is where I'm supposed to nod my head or utter a few words, but I can't. I'm frozen, feeling every eye in the shoe store on the back of my head.

"Sorry," Clay says to the customers. "She's not feeling well."

"Washroom's in the back," a curly-haired, heavyset blonde employee says.

"Thanks." Clay gently guides me to the bathroom in the back of the store. The two of us barely fit. I glance around the bathroom. The walls are aqua green and there is a frame of tea-stained artificial flowers around the mirror over the sink. It's supposed to be cheerful, but all the decor does is make me feel sick.

After a few deep breaths I'm finally able to speak. "We're going to lose him," I say.

"Isn't that the idea?"

I shake my head. "What if he's headed back to Jasper?" I swallow hard. "What if Jerry's next?"

Clay runs his hand through his hair. "We need a plan." I can tell he's itching to pace back and forth, confined by the small space. "We'll go out, get in the truck, and follow him. Just you and me. That's it." He looks at me with such strength and determination that I can't breathe for a moment. He doesn't want anything from me. It isn't often that someone doesn't want anything from me. He wants to do something for me. He wants to *help* me. "Are you ready?" he asks.

I nod my head.

"How's she feeling?" the same woman asks as soon as we come out of the bathroom.

"She's fine. Thanks."

Clay goes outside first and takes a look around, then motions for me to follow him. We walk through the rain down the sidewalk towards the truck, Clay's arm wrapped around me. It's hard enough to see through the rain normally, let alone behind my sunglasses. We're only half a block away from the truck when I spot him again, standing at a newspaper stand, thumbing through the stack. His eyes. His nose. His glasses. His skin… He's so cautious. So careful. So gentle in the way he selects his paper and closes the little rusted glass door. To my right is Curl Up and Dye. I pull Clay into the beauty shop.

A smiling hairdresser approaches us. "Do you have an appointment?"

"Uh, no. Just getting out of the rain for a sec," says Clay. The woman's smile fades, but she lets us stay. We take a seat for a few minutes. I'm almost certain that Norman would have no reason to come into a beauty shop, but my nerves still get the better of me. Clay pats my arm, which is resting on my jiggling leg. "I'm going to step outside."

I nod and Clay goes out the door. A few minutes later, he returns, even more soaked than when we first came in. "We're good."

The hairdresser looks over at us. "You sure? The rain's coming down even harder now."

It's a good point. But we're not hiding from the rain.

I look on the shelf behind the counter. "Are those for sale?" I ask, pointing to the boxes of hair dye.

"The do-it-yourself kits?" she says. "Yeah, four ninety-five each."

"I'll take two boxes, medium-brown." I reach into my pocket for money, but Clay is a step ahead of me. He puts down the cash and picks up the boxes.

We beeline towards Clay's truck. Once we're inside, he starts the engine and backs out. "I saw him get into his van just around the corner. We can still tail him." Clay turns onto the street. Sure enough, a white van is sitting at the stoplight ahead of us. We keep our distance as we follow him. For over ten minutes, neither of us speaks. I look over at Clay. His fingers won't stop moving. He keeps readjusting them on the steering wheel like he's trying to find a comfortable position for them, but there isn't one.

The van pulls into a gas station just outside of town. "Stay down," Clay says. There's enough legroom in the front seat for me to fit my whole body in, so I do just that. We pull into the parking lot and park out of the way of traffic. Clay doesn't say anything more to me. He gets out of the truck and walks up to the station As I wait for him, I do my best to ignore the throbbing pain in my injured knee. When that doesn't work, I wonder if Clay has any aspirin and open the glove box above my head, feeling around for a pill bottle to ease my pain. I feel paper, I feel napkins, and then I feel something cold, hard, and heavy. My heart skips a beat as I wrap my hand around the object and lift it out of the glovebox. My heart races even faster as I stare at the gun in my hand.

Wrong Girl Gone

I lift myself up enough to see out the window, and spot Clay exiting the gas station with a bag of groceries. I shove the gun back into the glovebox, push some napkins on top of it, and shut it just as Clay opens the door. He gets in, turns on the engine, and drives looking straight ahead the whole time as if I'm not even there.

My left foot is starting to go numb and tingle. There isn't much space to move in, so I can't even shake it to keep it from falling asleep. "Can I come up now?" I ask, like a little girl asking if it's okay to come out of her room after a time-out.

"You better stay down there," he says.

"Are we still following him?" Clay nods, his eyes still straight ahead.

I rest my head against the glove box and try not to think about the gun. "Clay, what are we doing?"

"We're tracking him down. Keeping tabs on him."

"But then what? If we don't find a way to turn him in, what are we supposed to do?"

"I don't know. And neither do you. And sometimes that's just the way it is. Sometimes you just follow your gut."

We sit there in silence for a moment and I realize something about Clay right then. "You know, I sometimes wonder if you're trying to run away just as much as I am."

"What's that supposed to mean?"

I don't really mean anything, but his quick reaction makes me feel like I should. "Nothing." We're both quiet then, although I can't stop thinking about what's in the glove box next to my head. "Clay, why is there a gun in your glovebox?"

Clay glances over at me. It's the first time he's taken his eyes off the road since the gas station. "Protection," he says. "If it helps, there aren't any bullets in it."

"I don't know if a gun without bullets will do you much good."

"No one else has to know."

After almost twenty more minutes of driving, Clay finally says, "All right. I think it's safe for you to come back up."

Audrey Wilson

I climb back into my seat and buckle up. It's stopped raining and what little sun is left in the sky is shining through the clouds ahead of us. We're right in between those two worlds, where everything behind you is turning blue and gray and everything ahead of you is pink and gold. It's the kind of divider you only see after a rainstorm.

With one hand on the wheel, Clay reaches into his pocket and takes out a pack of Camels. He pulls out two cigarettes and lights them both in his mouth. Then he hands one to me. It helps some. I look at the leftover drops of water racing their way across the window and think about how Jerry and I used to place bets on which one would win. What I wouldn't give to be with him right now, watching raindrops chase one another, instead of chasing the man who killed my sister.

Chapter Twenty-One

Clay and I keep our eyes forward, not taking them off the van's RTZ 540 license plate. There are a couple of times when cars cut between the two of us, but Clay always manages to catch up to him again, despite actually going the speed limit. A few times we let him get far enough ahead that we're out of view, so we don't raise suspicion, but we never lose him.

It's almost dark as we follow him off the highway onto an exit with a sign that reads *Green Pine Hotel this exit*. A few miles later, he pulls into the parking lot of the Green Pine Hotel. It looks like a log cabin in the middle of the woods, with only a handful of cars out front and a satellite dish on the roof. We drive right on past it and park the truck on a nearby side street.

Clay turns to me. "Do you think we should call the police?"

"I don't think we should yet. He doesn't know we're following him, right? If he is headed to Jasper, he can get there in just a few hours. I don't want to lose him. But I want to make sure Jerry's safe."

Clay nods. "We should get a room here. We can keep an eye out and get right back on his trail when he leaves first thing in the morning."

"Yeah. Once we're closer to Jasper, we can call the Jackson police. It's the county just east of Jasper. I'm hoping the police force there will believe us. They helped John before when some homophobic assholes vandalized his car. They have a little more sensitivity than the cops in Jasper."

We make our way across the parking lot towards the front desk. I glimpse the man up ahead, twirling a key in his hand as he heads for his room. We stop between two cars. Clay turns his body towards me, blocking me entirely from view. I glance around Clay just enough to see the man heading upstairs to the second level of rooms. When we're sure we're out of sight, we make our way to the front desk, Clay's arm still wrapped around me. The thought occurs to me that anyone who sees us probably assumes we were a couple, which is fine with me. It's a decent cover.

"He's in room seventeen upstairs," Clay whispers to me. "We'll get a room on the main floor just in case."

We approach the front desk. "Hi," says a tall, skinny man behind the counter.

"Hi," says Clay. "One room. Please."

"You want upper or lower?"

"Lower," I say.

He checks his computer. "Sorry, guys. I spoke too soon. Only got uppers."

I share a glance with Clay. "Are you sure?" I ask the man.

"Yep. Lowers are booked." Although the thought of spending the night within fifty yards of the man who killed my sister turns my stomach, it's the only choice we have.

"Fine," Clay says. "That's fine."

The guy asks us if we have any luggage. When we say we don't, aside from a few shopping bags and Clay's messenger tote, he smiles and nods like he knows exactly what we're up to. I wish our reasons for being there were so simple.

Clay goes up the stairs first to make sure the coast is clear. He comes back down a moment later to get me, and we both go up the narrow staircase together.

"Did you see him at all?" I whisper to Clay.

"No," he says. "I think he's in his room." He fumbles with the key to our room, which seems to be sticking.

Wrong Girl Gone

"Here—" I gently take the key out of his hand and try it myself. With a little wiggle, I get it open.

He looks a little flustered. "Thanks." He quickly opens the door and lets me in first.

We turn on the few 1960s lamps to brighten up the place. It helps some. Clay goes into the bathroom to wash up and I turn on the TV in the corner of the room. Judging by the rabbit ears on it, I doubt we'll get much reception, but it's worth a shot.

The air conditioner in the room is making my damp shirt feel even colder. "Don't come out, I'm going to change," I warn him, taking off my shirt.

Clay pops his head out of the bathroom. "Did you say something?"

I grab my shirt off the bed and pull it up to my chest. "I said I was changing."

Clay shuts his eyes the moment he sees me. "Sorry," he mumbles and goes back into the bathroom.

I dump the bag of clothes Clay bought me out on the red and green comforter that looks like a lit-up Christmas tree. Out of the pile, I choose a pair of large, checkered pajama pants, a maroon tee-shirt, and a cream sweater to wrap around me. Even though the baggy clothes make me feel even smaller than usual, I don't care. They're comfortable. Like my own little protective cocoon.

After I'm done changing, I sit down on the side of the bed closest to the telephone and farthest from the door. I stare at the phone for a second before picking it up. My first thought is to call Jerry. I always call Jerry when I go away. Even if it was just for one night to visit Kelly, or if I was staying at Mama's trailer because she'd passed out drunk, I'd still call him just before bed. This time I know the circumstances are different, but it's all I can do not to dial the number. Instead, I call John and let him know where we are, that we're safe.

Audrey Wilson

After talking to John, I hang up the phone and look up to see Clay standing expectantly by the bathroom door. "You ready?"

"For what?"

"Your hair."

"Oh, right."

Clay looks at the phone. "Sorry, were you on the phone?"

"I was just calling John to let him know we're safe."

He's quiet for a second before he says, "He's going to be okay." I know he's not talking about John.

I catch the lump in my throat before it can surface. "I just wish I could hear his voice."

"Why don't you call him?"

"I can't. Carl can't know anything. Right now, he thinks I'm dead."

He looks from me to the phone. "Give me the phone," he says.

"Why?"

He picks up the phone and sits down next to me on the bed. "I'm going to call him for you. What's the number?" I tell him the number. It starts to ring, and he holds the phone between us, so I can hear too. We listen for a couple of rings. I hold my finger over the button on the phone, ready to press it if Carl should answer. But he doesn't. Instead, the sweetest voice in the world comes through the earpiece.

"Larson residence, Jerry speaking," he says through a yawn. I can't even feel my pulse, my heart is beating so fast.

"Hi, Jerry," says Clay. "This is Bob Crane." He cringes at the words as they come out of his mouth. I guess *Hogan's Heroes* is on his mind.

"Daddy!" Jerry calls away from the phone. "Bob Crane is calling for you!"

I hear Carl's voice too. It sounds distant and distracted. "Bob Crane, huh?" Carl laughs. "Just hang up, Jer. Damn prank callers…"

"Sorry, but my daddy says I hafta hang up now." And then there's a click. And then he's gone.

Wrong Girl Gone

I replay his voice in my head twice before I can speak. "Thanks," I say.

"Of course." I guess I must look spacey or dazed for a moment because Clay asks, "You all right?"

"He sounded different," I say. "He sounded sadder."

"I'm sure he's sadder. You're not there." I don't respond. Clay doesn't seem to know what to say, so he just pats me on the back and gets off the bed. "You better start on your hair before it gets too late. We should try to get some sleep before tomorrow."

I stand in the bathroom for a good ten minutes with the scissors in my hand, trying to decide where to start. I need to look different. I need to look unrecognizable. But I don't want more change. My hair has always been the same. Always a few inches longer than my shoulder line. Always thin. Always blonde. The dirty kind of blonde that men find unattractive. Even if I've never liked my hair, I still have trouble cutting it off.

"Clay," I call to the other room.

He appears in the doorway. "Yeah?"

"I can't do this." I hand him the scissors and sit down on the toilet lid. "Just cut it off." I close my eyes.

"It isn't going to hurt," he says, reassuring me like I would have done with Jerry. I keep them shut anyway. As he cuts, I start to relax. My neck begins to feel longer and my head lighter with each snip.

"You want to see what it looks like before the dye goes on?" he asks when he's finished.

"No, just finish it up. I trust you."

He grins. "Well, that's your first mistake right there."

The coloring process isn't as nerve-wracking as the cutting. It's almost relaxing. He takes his time putting on the dye and working it through each section of hair. There's a tenderness in his hands that I hadn't expected. After a few minutes of massaging my scalp, I begin to wonder if he's doing so more than necessary to help me relax. If he is, it's working. I sink deeper into his touch with every movement.

144

Audrey Wilson

Struggling to stay awake, I open my eyes to find him looking at me. He quickly looks away, so I close my eyes again, but I know I'll never forget that look. I've never seen him look at me that way before. Caring, but concerned, like he's trying to figure me out. There's the smallest hint of a smile on his mouth and a shimmer of mystery in his eye. And suddenly I feel like crying. Because I'm pretty sure no one has ever looked at me quite like that before.

I take a breath and try to clear my head. There's no reason to invite emotions like these into my life right now. All they've ever done is complicate things. Besides, I'm still married to Carl. Thinking about Clay in any way other than a kind stranger who's helping me would be wrong. And yet all I want to do in this moment is look into his brown eyes again and have them look at me.

Clay clears his throat before he speaks. "You're almost done. Then it just has to set for thirty minutes before we rinse." The way he says it makes me wonder if he'd been a beautician in another life. I suddenly let out a laugh at the image that comes to mind. "What's so funny?"

I shake my head and try to compose myself. "It's nothing."

He isn't going to let me get away without a response that easily. "Tell me." He grins. "Come on."

"I was just thinking," I say through my laughter, "that you would have made a wonderful beautician in another life. I can just picture you with a little floral smock and highlights."

For that, I get a squirt on the cheek from the bottle of dye. It's an unfair shot. I have no form of defense. I think fast and grab a handful of pink potpourri from a basket on the sink and toss it in his face. He reaches for the basket and, before I can stop him, picks up the whole thing and tosses all of its contents in my face. I sit there for a moment, covered in hair dye and dried roses, letting the shock sink in.

"Oh," I'm looking right at him, holding back my grin, and shaking my head. "Oh, you are so dead."

Wrong Girl Gone

He squeezes past me and runs out of the bathroom. I follow after him, spitting out petals. He climbs over the bed and for a second, we're opposite each other. With each move I make, he does the reverse, dodging me. Finally, he breaks the pattern, heading for the corner by the TV. He searches around for a weapon and grabs the closest thing to one, which is one of the antennas on top of the TV, and points it at me like a sword. Empty-handed, I have no choice but to make a run around to the other side of the bed, but Clay stops me. His grip on me isn't so great, and he falls over onto the bed, taking me with him.

I can't stop laughing. I can't remember the last time I laughed like this. Even though my cheeks and stomach hurt, it feels so good. Clay's face is flushed, and his eyes squinted, making me laugh even more. Finally, the laughter slows, and we try to catch our breath.

"Your hair," he says, still laughing and looking at the mess of hair dye on the comforter.

"It's temporary." I'm still smiling. "I think it'll be okay." Clay and I look at each other. He's still smiling too. The blush on his face is dissolving but the smile is still there. We just lay there, looking at each other. I can't tell if it's just my imagination, but after a moment it seems like his smile has changed. I'm suddenly very aware of my heartbeat. I can hear Clay's too. He reaches a hand to my cheek and moves a strand of dye-covered hair off my face. Then he gently rubs the remnant of dye off my skin. I close my eyes for a moment, sinking into the caress. His hand stays where it is even once I'm sure the dye is gone. When I open my eyes, his smile has faded, and his eyes are tracing the outline of my face.

"What is it?" I ask.

He shakes his head, but still doesn't remove his hand. "Nothing," he says. "You're just... So different than anyone I've ever met."

"In what way?"

"I don't know. I just... I feel like I've known you for a very long time."

Audrey Wilson

I reach my hand up to my face and place it on top of his, feeling the warmth of his palm on my skin. Our faces are just inches apart, but it somehow feels too far. I let our gazes hold longer than I should. I can't seem to help myself. I can't remember ever feeling like this with Carl. Maybe this is how love's supposed to feel. My eyes wander to Clay's lips. I feel the urge to kiss him.

Instantly, I feel sick and guilty. How the hell can I laugh and desire when my sister is gone, my marriage ruined, and my son is hundreds of miles away from me in the hands of Carl? Whatever feeling I'd had a moment ago with Clay immediately goes sour. I sit up quickly and try to pretend nothing happened.

"You okay?" Clay asks.

"Yep." My tone is harsh and short, even though I don't mean for it to be.

"You sure?" Before he can sit up, I'm on my feet moving away from the bed.

"We'd better finish up with my hair. It's getting late." I rub my arms, even though I'm no longer cold, and go back to the bathroom.

I sit there on the toilet while Clay finishes dying my hair in silence, feeling so guilty I can hardly breathe. I blame Carl for that brick of guilt. He's the only person that can make me go from feeling so happy one moment to so lousy the next. He has that effect on people, especially me. I feel bad, like I'm somehow being unfaithful to him. He's cheated on me multiple times, and yet the idea of even being attracted to another man is sending my conscience into a state of complete anguish.

Jerry was a little over a year when I found out about the first affair. The first affair I knew about, at least. Carl had started coming home late, smelling of beer and dime-store perfume. When I confronted him about it, he tried to convince me I was paranoid. At nineteen, I was convinced easily and locked my suspicions away. But then I heard him whispering on the phone one day and listened in on the

147

conversation. I discovered that the two of them planned on getting together the next evening.

That next foggy December night, I decided to follow him home from work like the paranoid wife I was, hoping he'd prove me wrong. Of course, he didn't.

They met at a shitty motel on the edge of town. I watched her from the car as she got off the bus. She was tall and thin with long, dark hair. She looked like a model. He kissed her when he saw her and led her to their room.

I may have fantasized about other men—I no longer considered that cheating after I found Carl's collection of *Playboys* in his sock drawer—but I had never actually cheated on my husband, just as I had naively assumed that he had never actually cheated on me. But that moment was all it took. It was in that moment that I wished for the first time since I met Carl that I had fucked someone else.

They didn't have a chance to do anything in that shitty room at the Starlight Motel before I stole the room key from the front desk and opened the door. I don't know what I said. All I remember about the incident was the pain in my throat from yelling so much. The police showed up eventually because of all the yelling and Carl had to escort me home like I was the crazy one.

When we were back at the house, I had him at my mercy for a change. In some sick way, I think he liked it. He liked it because he knew that no matter how mad I was, I wasn't going to leave him. With that in mind, he humored me and answered every question I asked.

What was her name?

"Her name's Rachel Warner," he said.

What did she do for a living?

"She's an actress," he said.

I said for a living.

"She's a receptionist in a dentist's office."

How old was she?

"Twenty-five."

Oh, going for someone older, huh?

Audrey Wilson

"No, baby, you're the only girl for me."

Obviously not. Why'd you do it?

"I don't know what I was thinking, baby. It was a stupid, stupid thing to do—"

Damn right.

"And I promise, I swear to God I'll never do it again."

For the record, he did it again.

"It didn't mean a thing to me, darlin'. Please don't leave me. I love you."

It ended with him down on one knee, holding onto my hands for dear life. I should have left him then, but I didn't. The second time was right after Jerry's third birthday. Between work and Jerry and life in general, I had no energy to be paranoid. I knew what he was up to and I let him go on. Because when I so much as mentioned my suspicions, it turned into a fight that left me black and blue. I got off easy with Rachel Warner. Maybe I was stronger then.

Now, sitting here in this pine green hotel bathroom with Clay makes me wish I'd confronted Carl more about his other liaisons. I think the weaker I became, the stronger he grew, feeding off the fear. Maybe if I'd stayed strong, there would have been nothing to feed off.

I get a lot of dyed water in my mouth when I have my head under the faucet in the bathtub. I wonder what it must be like to go to a salon to have your hair dyed. I used to think it was a waste of money but every time I bump the back of my head on that tarnished gold faucet, I can't help but think it might be worth it.

Clay hands me a towel and I dry off my hair. I catch a glimpse of the color before I wrap it up and begin to get very nervous about how dark it is. Clay offers to comb my hair after we're done washing it, but I politely decline. I can't risk feeling anything else tonight. I have to limit any more intimate situations with Clay.

I walk out of the bathroom after combing my hair to find Clay turning down the bed in his boxers and tee-shirt and feel my stomach flip.

Wrong Girl Gone

He tosses down a pillow and takes a step back. "I was just getting it ready for you. I'm sleeping in the chair."

"You can take the bed," I offer. "It's the least I can do for you."

"You're not sleeping in the chair."

He pulls a crocheted blanket and one of the pillows from the bed. Then he pulls the matching footstool in front of the chair and climbs into the makeshift bed. I wish I had a picture of what this six-foot-tall, one-hundred-eighty-pound man looked like in this chair that looks like it was built for someone under the age of ten.

"Clay, this is ridiculous. You can sleep in the bed—"

"I told you, you're not sleeping in the chair."

"—too." He looks at me. "With me. It's fine. Really," I say. "I want you to." So much for limiting intimate contact. "Not sleep with me. Just, in the same bed. Not that you're not, or I wouldn't—" I can't seem to stop myself from talking. The words are just spilling out. "Jesus. Just shut me up anytime." Clay averts his eyes, appearing to be at a loss for words. I'll gladly give him some of mine. "Well, good night." I climb into bed and turn off the light as quickly as possible. Then I just lay there, listening to the chair squeak as Clay settles himself into it. I wait for the sound of his snoring, but it doesn't come.

Chapter Twenty-Two

I'm in a dark parking lot behind what appears to be a school. The only source of light is a single streetlamp in the center of the lot. I can see yellow markings on the ground. They're much too big to be actual parking spaces, so I just assume they're for cars the giants' drive. I walk up to the streetlamp and realize that it's also too big to be a regular streetlamp. The light isn't bright enough either. It's slowly dimming, and I know I only have a few more moments before it goes out completely and I'm left in the dark. I begin to run across the blacktop. The farther I get from the light, the colder and the darker it gets. I'm not wearing any shoes, so there's no noise when my feet hit the ground.

I reach the edge of the blacktop and slow to a stop. The sky has gotten a little lighter. It's still black, but now it's a transparent black. Like there's a little child with a flashlight on the other side of the sky, shining a light through it. I can see grass on the ground a few feet ahead of me, but I don't want to move toward it. The blacktop has grown warm under my feet, and I know the grass is going to be colder. The blacktop feels soft too. It's getting very soft and even more comfortable. I'm starting to get extremely tired. I wonder if lying down on the blacktop will be as comfortable as lying down on a bed, so I try it. As soon as my head touches the ground, the school bell rings. I open my eyes and see about fifty kids running out of a door on the other side of the parking lot. They're talking loudly and running around, playing games and laughing. A large rubber ball rolls towards me and gently bumps my foot. I stand and pick it up. The streetlamp is much brighter now, and I can see most of the lot. I look around for the owner of the ball and suddenly see Kelly standing a little ways in front of me, staring.

"What are you waiting for?" she says. She's only eight. "Throw it away."

I look down at the ball. It's not a ball anymore. It's a small head wrapped in a bloody handkerchief. The head's eyes are closed. It's sleeping.

"It'll wake up," I say. "You can't wake it up before it's ready."

"Just get rid of it," she says, getting on a small bike. "It's not worth saving." She rides off on the bike. I look back down at the head. It's a girl, I think. I stare at it for a moment before realizing it's me. I open my mouth, and so does the head. I close it, and so does the head. I close my eyes and open them, and the head opens hers. When we blink, we blink at the same time, a game of copycat I don't understand.

The bell rings again. I look up from the head and see that all the kids are already gone. I look back down at the head. I wish I knew what to do with her. She's very fragile so I can't leave her outside. Mrs. Walsh probably won't let me bring her into class. I could hide her in my locker, but she might cry and then we'd both get caught. I decide to not go back to school. Then things start to change and I'm sitting in the front seat of Clay's truck on the floor and the head is gone.

Clay's driving the truck.

"We're wasting a lot of time, you know," he says. "You never should have let it die." He's talking about the head.

"Did we give it a name? It's always harder to get over something dying when you give it a name."

"You named it Kelly," he says.

"We should bury it."

"You already did. It's in the trunk." I climb into the backseat and open the trunk from the inside. It's full of dirt, so I start digging. My hand finds something, and I pull it out.

It's not Kelly. It's me, just like it was before. We buried me by mistake. I hold the head in my arms. My eyes are hot and I'm crying a little.

"He's gone," Clay says. "Joy, he's gone."

I want him to stop calling it, *he*. "It's me," I tell him. "I'm still here."

"Joy." I open my eyes. "Wake up." The lamp on the nightstand is on and I can see from the amount of light coming through the window that it's early. "We have to go."

"Go where?" Clay's throwing what few belongings we have into his bag. "What are you doing?" I pull the clock around to check the time. It's seven thirty-three.

"He's gone. That son of a bitch already checked out."

I wake up a little faster after that. "Shit." I get out of bed and pull on my jeans. My bladder feels like it's about to burst so I hobble to the bathroom. I've grown accustomed to my body's usual morning stiffness since the incident, but I'm beginning to wonder if it will ever return to normal. "How did you find out?" I ask through the door.

"I went down to the vending machines to get some coffee and figured I'd ask the guy at the front desk to let me know when the man in room seventeen checked out. He said he checked out a half-hour ago."

My heart sinks. "A half-hour ago?" I flush, wash, and come back out.

"Just get your stuff," Clay says. "If we leave now, we can still catch up to him."

We get in the car and bolt out of the parking lot. Clay is sweating and breathing heavily. He glances over at me. "You okay?"

I haven't said anything since we left, half my mind still asleep. "I'm fine."

He looks back to the road, then back at me again. "You're bleeding," he says.

"What?" I reach my hand up to a tingly spot on my cheek. When I look at my fingers, I see they have blood on them.

153

Wrong Girl Gone

"Here." Clay takes a handkerchief out of his pocket and hands it to me. I press it to the scratch on my cheek. "What happened to you?"

"I probably did it in my sleep." I pull down the visor and look in the mirror. It doesn't hurt, really. And once I clean up the blood, it's barely noticeable. "My nails are lethal. Kelly refused to share a bed with me when we were young."

"I'm glad I slept in the chair." Clay stares straight ahead, stepping on the gas.

I pull the handkerchief away from my face and look at it. Red staining white. I suddenly feel nauseous. "Clay, if he checked out half an hour ago, how are we gonna catch up to him? We don't even know where he's headed."

"The man at the front desk said he asked for directions to Jasper."

***

We leave the radio on the whole time, listening to the news. Even going twenty miles over the speed limit, I feel like we'll never catch up to him.

"Do you know how badly I wished I could trade places with Kelly when we were little?" I gaze out the window, watching the yellow lines on the road beside me jump in and out of view. "Not just because I'd seen *The Parent Trap* over a dozen times, but because she was the one doing everything right. I hated the fact that I was the 'other sister.' The screwup. The one who was always relying on those around her and never safe to leave on her own. I can't blame my daddy for leaving. I wouldn't want to be the one that had to raise me. I always wished I could trade lives with Kelly." Clay doesn't respond. He just keeps driving. I force the tears to stay in my eyes. "I'm still wishing that today."

"Don't do this." His tone is oddly sharp.

"What?" He doesn't say anything. "Don't do what?"

"Don't wish that it was you instead of her. I get it, believe me, I do." I think of Russell, Clay's Kelly. I imagine Clay has

154

wished on more than one occasion that he could take away Russell's pain and suffering. No matter how much the people we love hurt us, we'll still do anything to ease their pain. "But your life matters too, Joy. Neither of you was more important than the other."

I feel a swell of defensiveness rise up inside me. "Of course, she was more important. She was more important to me."

"You don't think you were as important to her?"

"No." I swallow hard because I know it's true.

"You were."

"You don't know that. You don't know anything about me." I pretend there aren't tears falling from my eyes. "It should have been me."

"It shouldn't have been either of you."

In two jerky motions, I wipe each side of my face and keep my eyes firmly out the window.

After a few minutes of silence, I hear Clay mutter, "Shit."

"What is it?"

As soon as I ask, I hear the whirr of a siren in the distance. I look out the back window and catch a glimpse of flashing red and blue. Clay's eyes shoot to the rearview mirror and back to the road, sweat beginning to bead at his temples. He turns on his blinkers and slows to a stop on the side of the road, the cop car following close behind us. Clay keeps his hands firmly around the wheel as if he's frozen to it, his eyes glued to the rearview mirror.

"It's gonna be okay," I say as we wait for the officer to approach the truck. "We were speeding, but that's it. He doesn't have any other reason—"

"He doesn't need a reason," Clay says sharply.

The officer approaches Clay's open window, his right hand hovering over his gun. "You have any idea how fast you were going?"

"I'm sorry, officer."

As quickly as Clay starts to loosen his grip on the wheel, the officer tightens his around his gun. "You keep your hands right there where I can see them," he says. "Where you running off to?" The officer looks over at me, then glances into the back seat. "You running from something, boy?"

Clay shakes his head. "No, sir."

The officer switches his gaze back to me. "And who's this? Don't tell me she's your sister."

I hold up my left hand, pointing to the band of gold on my ring finger. "I'm his wife."

"Oh, are you now?" He looks back at Clay. "Got yourself a pretty young lady there, don't you? And this isn't a bad vehicle either. Is it yours? Or did you steal it, and that's why you're running?"

"Do you want to see my license and registration?" Clay lifts his trembling right hand off the wheel, and that's just enough. The officer draws his gun.

"I said keep your hands where I can see them!"

"I was just—"

"Get the fuck out of the car!" The officer reaches in and unlocks the door, then swings it open. "Hands up, where I can see them!"

As soon as Clay is out of his seat, the officer turns him around and pushes him against the truck, keeping his arms in the air. I catch a glimpse of Clay's eyes, sad and scared, but also worn like he's been through this before.

"Are you concealing any drugs or weapons, boy?" He pats Clay up and down. My eyes flash to the glove box as the officer kicks Clay's legs apart. If he finds that gun, that's it. If he finds that gun, Clay is as good as dead.

"Please," I croak. "I'm sick. I'm pregnant." The officer stops frisking Clay and looks over at me. "I was bleeding buckets this morning. My husband was just trying to get me to the hospital as fast as possible, so we don't lose the baby."

For a second, I can't tell if he's buying it. He just stares at me, his face grimacing in either disgust or suspicion. Then I see him glance down to the blood-stained handkerchief in my lap. He looks at Clay.

"Your lady telling the truth, boy?"

Clay nods. "Yes, sir. I'm very worried about her."

The officer looks from Clay to me. "I'm still gonna need to write you a ticket for how fast you were going." He lowers his gun and fumbles for his pad of paper. "Don't move, or you'll be under arrest. You hear me?" Clay nods.

As the officer scribbles the ticket, Clay and I exchange glances. I like to think we have a whole conversation with that look. The officer tears the ticket off his pad and hands it to me through the window. Then he puts his gun to Clay's back again. "Get back in your vehicle. Keep your hands up."

Clay does as he's told and places his hands safely back on the wheel as soon as he's in the car. He doesn't even buckle because that could be mistaken for reaching for a weapon. The officer lowers his gun and puts it in his holster. "Go on," he says. Clay carefully starts the engine. The officer leans over to him, practically spitting in his face. "I catch you speeding through here again, believe me, I won't be afraid to use this." He pats his gun before finally taking a step back and letting us drive on until those blue and red lights are far behind us.

I have no words, so I revert to the few I know best. "Clay, I'm so sorry."

"Not your fault," he says, his jaw tight.

"You were speeding because of me."

"I was the one who sped."

"Has that happened to you before?" Clay nods. "That's awful."

Clay glances from the road to the speedometer, not going a mile over the limit. "That's Alabama."

***

We stop only once on the road and that's to buy gas, just after we cross the border into Mississippi. While I wait in the car for Clay to pay, my head reels with thoughts of what my sister's killer is going to do once he gets to Jasper. If he's working for Carl, and he already got the money back at the hotel room, why has he waited around this long? Is he hiding out? If he isn't working *for* Carl, maybe he just works *with* Carl. Maybe Carl owes him money and is too cheap to pay him back. Or maybe Carl just owes him too much. Maybe he came after the money because it's rightfully his, and Kelly got in his way. Maybe she was just collateral.

It's early afternoon when we pass the sign that reads *Welcome to Jasper!* It's so surreal coming back. It feels both like I never left, and like I'm visiting a place I've never been before. As I look up and down the side streets, searching for familiarity, I come to realize Jasper doesn't look much different than I remember it. Of course, it isn't going to have changed much in the brief time I've been gone. It's still worn, still tired, and still smells like sewage after a hard rain. We drive over the train tracks, past the drug store, past Hank's Diner, into my neighborhood, and just down the street from my house. There's no sign of a white van, and no car in the driveway, which means Carl is at work and Jerry is most likely at school.

"We must have beat him here," Clay says.

"If he was even coming here. He could be anywhere in Jasper." He could be hiding out around any corner, waiting to wreak more havoc on the people I love. That's when it strikes me. Even if I don't get Jerry back today, I can still come one step closer to figuring out who the man I'm married to really is. That's how I found the money in the first place, isn't it? Snooping? Of course, if Carl is a suspect of my murder, the police have probably already searched the house. But they don't know it like I know it. "Maybe I can do a quick once-over of the house, see if I can find something— anything that can point us in the right direction."

"Do you want me to go in first?" Clay offers.

I shake my head. "No. I need to do this on my own."

I open the door and get out of the truck. As I cross the street, I wrap my sweater around my body, trying to cover the chill that comes over me as I walk up the driveway like I've done a hundred thousand times before. I slide in through the back porch and find the spare key under the second potted plant from the door, same as always. Only that plant wasn't dead when I left like it is now.

The house is empty and dark. I look around the kitchen. It's worse than I've ever seen it before. There are piles of dirty dishes in the sink that are probably growing God knows what. The counters look like they haven't been wiped off since I'd done it last, so little colonies of crumbs have gathered in between the tiles, and in true Carl fashion, the trash can is filled to the brim with bottles.

I go into the living room and up the stairs, two at a time. I suddenly have this horrible fear that I'm going to open the door to Jerry's room and find him lying there on his back in bed with his eyes open, but the room is empty. No one is home, not even me. Because this isn't my home anymore. This is a place I once lived. And the only thing I care about isn't there either.

I start my search in our bedroom, careful not to disturb anything. I rummage through the sock drawers, thumb through his *Playboys*, and try as hard as I can to suppress the déjà vu that blurs my vision. After I check the closet, I make my way to the bathroom. I open up the medicine cabinet and look closely at each pill bottle, checking them for God knows what, but nothing is out of the ordinary. I shut the cabinet and am about to start in on the drawers when I hear a car horn honking down the street over and over again.

I practically ride the railing trying to get down the stairs so fast. The living room curtain is parted just enough for me to look outside without moving it. Carl is holding Jerry by the arm and flipping off the guy in a familiar pickup truck, who's barreling past the house, honking. I catch eyes with Clay, my heart throbbing, then run into the kitchen and through the back door. My hands shake as I slip the key into the lock and turn it, then return it to the base of the potted plant. I run around to the front of the house where I peer around the corner.

"Fucking negros driving around here, acting like they own the neighborhood..." I hear Carl mumble as he approaches the front door. When Carl and I were still living under the same roof, I picked my battles with him. A remark like that would have been worth it.

Jerry is crying and playing the "my legs don't work" game I know so well. He's also wearing an oversized jean jacket with the sleeves rolled up. My jean jacket. A sudden warmth fills my body. "Daddy, let go of my arm!"

"Stop that crying. Shut up!" He jerks Jerry up onto the front porch by his arm and the warm feeling is instantly gone. I want to strangle Carl right then and there.

"You're hurting me!" He cries even louder.

"You want the neighbors to see what a spoiled little brat looks like? Huh?"

"I want Mama! I want my mama!" Jerry cries.

"Yeah, well your mama's not here right now. And my whole day is fucked because of you. You know that? Sick my ass. You were faking it. Good little actor, aren't you?"

"I... threw... up..." The words come out between sobs.

"Yeah, right. You're going to be sorry, you just—" I lose the rest of their conversation as the door slams shut. I run away from the house as fast as I can, even though it's all I can do not to turn back, bang down the front door, grab Jerry and take him far away from the man I'm married to. But I don't. Because as far as Carl is concerned, I'm dead. So instead, I run. I run until I see the tail end of Clay's truck sticking out at the end of the street and climb inside. As soon as the door is shut, Clay hits the gas. It's not until we're out of the neighborhood that I look down to see my hand clasped in Clay's.

Chapter Twenty-Three

We drive around Jasper for a good forty-five minutes, scanning every side street for that white van. But it's not there. He was heading to Jasper. We're in Jasper, and he's not here. We can't call the police now because what would we even say? We have no proof. We have no killer. I wonder if I'm going to have to spend the rest of my life looking down every side street for a white van. Knowing Jerry's safe at this moment isn't enough. I need to be able to keep him safe every moment of every day.

"I want to visit my mama," I say to Carl after our third pass down Main Street.

"Does she know about Kelly?"

"I doubt it."

"What about the news?"

"She never watches the news. I think she prefers to block out anything negative that she can't fix."

"I can't say I blame her." He glances over at me. "It's better that it comes from you."

He's right, of course. I know I should be the one to tell her. I just don't know if I have the strength.

I walk up to the door of Mama's trailer and knock three times.

Wrong Girl Gone

I hear her voice on the other side of the door. "Who's there?"

"Mama?"

She cracks the door open and looks at me through the screen. Her eyes widen and she looks like she might be sick. "Joy? Oh, good lord—" She pushes open the screen and throws her arms around me. "Oh lord... Joy..." She's sobbing uncontrollably. Maybe she had been watching the news. I look over at Clay. He's standing by the truck and looks down at the ground when I meet his eyes.

"It's okay. Mama, it's okay." I pat her back. Then I realize I'm crying too and quickly wipe my face.

"Jesus. Where have you been? Are you okay? Oh, God..."

"I'm okay, Mama. Really."

"Carl says he's been keeping an eye on the news for me. He hasn't seen anything, hasn't heard from you."

A knot forms in my stomach. I know Carl has been watching the news. I know the authorities have been in touch with him about my whereabouts. He's either keeping my "death" a secret from Mama to protect her, or he has some other reason to hide it.

She glances over at the truck and then at Clay. "Who's that?"

"Sorry, this is Clay Grady. He's been helping me. Clay, this is my mother, Alice."

She composes herself. "Hello, Clay."

"Hello, Alice. Good to meet you."

Mama leads us inside the trailer. We take seats in the living room while she puts on some tea. The sofa used to be a lime green, now it's turning a brownish shade of olive. It's a lot squishier than it used to be too. I can easily feel the springs in my back. She finishes boiling the water and sits down in the chair across from me. "What happened," she says. It isn't a question. "And what did you do to your hair? Are you on the run now or something?"

162

Audrey Wilson

I take a breath and begin to recount the story I've grown so used to telling. "That night after I talked to you on the phone, Jerry and I checked into a hotel to get some sleep. In the middle of the night..." I know I should, but I just can't bring myself to tell her the truth. I can't tell her that her daughter, the *good* daughter, is gone and never coming back. "A man broke into the room. I think he... drugged me or knocked me out somehow because the next thing I remembered was waking up in a black, plastic bag. I started struggling around and I got the bag open. I saw that we were in the woods, somewhere deep in the woods... I fought as hard as I could to get away..." I look down at my own hands. They're practically pruney from sweating so much. "He beat me and left me for dead. The next time I woke up it was daylight. I crawled through the woods and finally made it to the highway. And that's where Clay found me. He took me to his house where he and his mother helped me get better. I started walking again..."

"You couldn't walk? Jesus, Joy, why didn't you go to the hospital?" She catches Clay's eyes and gives him a glare—the lion protecting her cub.

Him not taking me to the hospital is already a sore spot for me, and Clay knows it. But my protective instincts kick in too. "Clay's mother's a county nurse. It was better for her to come to us than to go forty miles away to the hospital. So, then, yesterday we went into town and we saw him."

"You saw the man?"

"Yeah. And we followed him. And that led us back here."

"You're saying this man that did this to you is here in Jasper?"

"We haven't seen him yet, but we think he might be. That's why I changed my hair. Figured it was best to look less like myself."

"Oh my God... Well, haven't you gone to the police?"

Clay jumps in. "No. No. We're not going to the police."

"I'm talking to Joy." Mama can shoot pretty good sometimes. She just doesn't always hit the right person.

163

Wrong Girl Gone

"He's just as involved as I am," I tell her. "Let him talk."

Clay looks a little rattled but starts again anyway. "We think this man might be a cop. Besides, he knows who Kelly is—"

"Kelly?" Mama's eyes light up. "When did you see Kelly?"

"Joy. I meant Joy." Clay quickly tries to get in the rest of his words. "He knows who Joy is and right now, he thinks she's dead. If we can keep it that way, then we can at least get Jerry and make sure he's safe."

The boiling kettle of water lets out a whistle and Mama leaves to pour the tea. I give Clay a small smile, then follow Mama into the kitchen. "That man seems to know a lot about you."

I open the cabinet and take out three cups with roses around the outside and little chips on the brim. "That man saved my life."

"You don't know how scared I was." I look at her while she gets out the tea bags. She's crying again, although she hides it better this time. "I thought I'd never see you again."

"But I'm okay now." I put my hand on her back. "I'm here and everything's going to be okay."

"There are no guarantees, Joy. I'm not going to have you play the hero and risk your life just so you can do something yourself. You're worth too much to me."

I've finally done it. I might have failed when I was eight and packed my little red suitcase, but I've succeeded this time. I ran away till people missed me and now that I'm back they seem to appreciate me more than they did before. It's not as fun as I thought it'd be.

"It's not about doing something myself," I say. "It's about keeping you and Jerry safe."

"I know, I know... I just want you to take care of yourself." She stops dipping the tea bags in the water and looks at me. Her eyes are red and watery. The way she locks eyes with me is rare. I never see that look when she's drinking, and I've only seen it a few times when she's been sober. It's the kind of look you give someone that you don't even mean to give. When you're looking into them, not at them, and you're really seeing them. "You remind me so much of your father."

I remember the folded little piece of paper in my back pocket. "Really?"

"Yeah. You really do."

I'm suddenly feeling hopeful. "I found him, Mama."

She seems puzzled. "Found who?"

"Daddy." My mind is buzzing. I feel high off my own excitement. Even if I can't bring myself to tell her the awful news I need to, maybe this can be the news I bear. "I found his address. Kelly…" My buzz fades with my next lie, but it's worth it for a moment of happiness with Mama. "She gave it to me when I talked to her on the phone a while back." She doesn't give me a response as quickly as I hope she will, so I go on. "He lives in Raycene. Raycene, Mama! That's just a few hours from here, right?"

"It is." She's dipping her teabag again, even though her tea is black as coffee.

"Aren't you surprised? Or happy or sad or—"

"I know where he lives, Joy."

I don't get it. "You—You already know where he lives?"

"Of course. He moved there after we divorced."

I feel like I'm eleven all over again. "He said he was going to Oregon to live with Uncle Charlie."

"He was afraid if you knew how close he really was, you and Kelly would come looking for him. He asked me not to tell you where he was. He said he didn't want to bother us."

Kelly did know how close he was. She probably went snooping around in Mama's stuff one day until she found his address. She'd been in touch with him. Maybe she'd even visited him. The thought made me resent her in the painful way that only comes from being angry at a dead person. "But he never bothered us."

"Of course he didn't! But I couldn't force him to realize that. Him leaving was hell on me, on you, on Kelly… He kept thinking something was wrong with him, that he didn't deserve us. I couldn't convince him otherwise. But, Jesus, I wish I'd tried harder."

I wait till she catches her breath before I speak again. "You could have at least told us."

"He didn't want you looking for him, Joy!"

"Isn't that for us to decide? He's our father!"

"I'm only trying to do what he asked."

"No, you've just been able to push everything down over the years. That's the difference between us. You've always had your bottle to turn to, but me, I had to deal with whatever came up. Escaping life is a lot quicker solution than actually dealing with it."

There has never been a time I've hated myself more than I do in this moment. Her face is what gets me the most. Shell-shocked and broken. I can't take it. I leave.

Clay is standing on the front porch, smoking a cigarette. I know he's heard everything. I know how easy it is to hear yelling through those tin can walls. I'm sobbing. I can't stop myself. It just keeps coming. Clay stands next to me, although doesn't do anything to console me. I feel sick. I feel dizzy. I feel like I'm trapped inside one of my own twisted nightmares and can't scream loud enough to wake myself up. I feel cold.

"My sweater's in the trailer," I say. "I can't— I can't go back in there." Clay doesn't say anything. He just shifts back and forth like he wants to say something. "I want to go." I walk over to the truck and start to get in.

Clay doesn't budge. "I think you should go back in there."

"What?"

"You need to go back in there and talk to her."

I shut the door and walk back over to Clay. "Didn't you hear what just went on in there?"

"Yeah. I did. And that's why I'm saying you should go back in there. It's not healthy to leave things like that."

"Healthy? You're not my therapist or *social worker* or whatever you want to call it. You have no idea what my family is like."

"Maybe I don't, but I know you'll regret it if you don't go back in there."

I storm over to the truck, caught in the crossroads of fuming and tears. "She can call me if she wants." I climb in and shut the door.

Clay puts his cigarette out in the dirt and gets in the truck. It hurts to keep the tears down, but somehow, I manage. I stare out the window as we drive out of the trailer park, hating myself for that cold front that comes up whenever I'm too weak to face whatever is in front of me. My memory bottle.

Chapter Twenty-Four

I don't particularly want to stay at the same motel where I found my husband fucking Rachel Warner, but the Starlight is the only motel far enough from Jasper that I don't think I'll be seen and close enough that we might still be able to track down Norman Lance. It's all I can do not to camp out in Clay's truck in front of our house to keep an eye on Jerry, but Clay reminds me that we'll just look conspicuous and Carl might call the cops. He assures me that we'll make sure to do another drive by the house tonight to check in on Jerry. I feel mildly reassured, but mostly just anxious.

The Starlight Motel is the kind of motel you picture when someone says, "by the hour." The kind that your husband cheats on you at. And it hasn't changed a bit since the last time I was there. The room we're staying in isn't the same one, although it looks so similar it might as well have been. It's still dark, with the same floral wallpaper and matching maroon carpet. Only this one has two queen beds instead of one. Clay turns on the TV and switches the channel from *The Brady Bunch* to the news.

I set my bags down on the bed and try to push the memory of me screaming into Carl's awestruck face and Rachel yelling for us to stop with her legs curled up to her chest, out of my head.

"There's no alarm clock," Clay notes, jolting me back to the present. I check the nightstand. He's right. "I'm going to see if they have one at the front desk."

I take off my bag and Clay's jacket, which he draped over my shoulders in the car. I pick up the phone and dial John's number. A man answers, but it doesn't sound like John.

"John?"

"No, this is Paul. Who's calling?" he says.

I have no idea who Paul is. "Can I speak to John?"

"Who is it?" A voice in the background says. *That* is John.

"She won't give her name." There's a soft thud, some rattling, and John is on the other line.

"Joy, is that you?" He's whispering and I feel the urge to whisper too.

"Yeah, who was that?"

"No one." I hear a door close and he stops whispering. "Where are you? Are you all right?"

"I'm at the Starlight—"

"I'll be right there."

"No. Wait—John?"

"Don't try to talk me out of seeing you, Joy."

"I'm not. Can you just drive by my house and let me know if you see a white van or anything strange there? Just check in on Jerry?"

"On it." Before I can say "thank you" there's a click. I'm about to hang up the phone when Clay comes in, holding an outdated alarm clock. "John's coming over."

"Now?"

"Apparently." Clay gets in the shower while I lay down on the bed and try not to fall asleep. I can't close my eyes without seeing Norman standing over me in the woods with the crowbar. I see the lightning shoot through the sky behind his head, and in the flash of white, Norman's face turns into Carl's.

The knock on the door makes me jolt in fear, but it's only John. He looks the same as he always has. Short blond hair. Tan skin. Thick black glasses. Khakis and a floral Hawaiian shirt. Clay is still in the shower as I welcome John inside and let him pull me into a hug. Just being in his presence calms me down.

"No white van," he says, sitting down on the bed. "I could see Jerry and Carl sitting in the living room watching TV. Nothing out of the ordinary."

"Thank you." I can feel him looking at me, waiting for me to speak as I sit down on the bed beside him. When I do, my voice quivers. I can't bring myself to say his name. "That man." John lowers his head, and I know he must feel as helpless as I do. "We let him get away. We should have just called the police—"

"Joy, he *is* the police."

"We could have called a different district—"

"Either way, it's a lot harder to try to prove a cop guilty than a civilian." John pushes his glasses back up on his nose.

The water turns off in the bathroom. John glances over at the bathroom door and lowers his voice to a whisper. "So, he's just... in this for the long haul, huh?"

"Yeah. He's really been great."

"He doesn't... you know."

I feel my guard ready to come up. "He doesn't what?"

John seems to be searching for the right words. "Expect anything in return?"

I don't like feeling annoyed at John, but in this moment, I can't help it. "No. We're just friends." I decide to change the subject. "But on that note, who's Paul?" Clay emerges from the bathroom right when I ask my question.

"Just... no one," John says quickly as he stands and nods at Clay.

"Sorry." I get to my feet. "John, this is Clay. Clay, John."

"Hi," Clay reaches out his hand. John shakes it and nods. After the introduction, a painfully awkward silence creeps into the room. John looks from Clay to me and down to the floor.

Clay glances between the two of us. "Do you want me to leave? I didn't mean to interrupt."

I turn to John. "Would you like him to leave?"

"No, no… It's fine," John says. He rubs his hands together nervously.

I lean in very close to John so only he can hear my words. "He won't say anything. He's not like that. It's okay if you want to talk in front of him."

John glances over at Clay. "Okay." He lifts his glasses and rubs his face with a handkerchief. "I'm sorry, Clay, I don't mean to be so…. What's the word…? Paranoid, I guess. It's just hard for me to have any privacy in this town. Everyone knows everything, or at least they think they do. I try to keep parts of my life as private as I can."

"Really, I can leave, if you want," Clay says again.

"No," John says. He puts on an accepting smile. "It's fine." He turns back to me. "I met Paul through Victor at work. Paul is his cousin; he just moved here. We had a blind date over at Tortelli's a few weeks ago and things just kind of took off from there. I'm sorry I didn't tell you about him sooner, but you've been dealing with so much. I really like him, Joy. I do."

"John, that's great." I pat him on the knee. "I'm so happy for you."

"Thanks, Joy. I am happy. For once." He laughs sadly.

I feel my eyes starting to grow heavy and put on a pot of coffee for the three of us. After a little while, the conversation shifts away from John's good news and back to Norman.

"Maybe he's back in Harrison County?" John suggests as we discuss his possible whereabouts.

"He asked the hotel clerk for directions to Jasper when he checked out this morning." Clay takes a sip of coffee.

"I just… I have a feeling that he's here." Call it my woman's intuition, but it's true. This man has spent two weeks away from the force. He's not finished here yet. "I think he's in Jasper somewhere."

"Even if it's too late for us to track him down, maybe we can find out why he did this," says Clay.

"The money," says John. "It has to be the money."

Wrong Girl Gone

I take a long breath. "I feel like it's something more though. It wasn't enough money to kill someone over."

"Any amount of money can be enough to kill someone over," says John, his love of crime shows fully visible. "If we can get some evidence... I mean, he might not even be the brains behind this." John leans in towards me, his eyes filled with concern. "I know this isn't something you want to think about, but we can't rule out the possibility that Carl—"

"I never said he might not be involved," I say defensively. "But he's not a killer."

John puts up his hands. "I know, I know. But if we're able to find the link to Carl, we might be able to find Norman."

I nod my head. "I thought the same thing. I snuck into the house earlier."

John raises his eyebrows. "You did *what?*"

"They weren't home. I couldn't find anything, but they came back before I could look too much."

John finishes off his cup of coffee. "Until we find some evidence, you've just gotta keep laying low."

I'm staring not at John or Clay, but straight ahead, out the small opening of the curtain covering the window. "I just want my son back."

Chapter Twenty-Five

When I wake up, the room is dark, save for a small, yellow glow coming from the bathroom where we left the light on. Clay is asleep in the other queen bed, breathing quietly.

The alarm clock Clay brought back to the room reads 4:42. I should go back to sleep, but my mind is reeling from a nightmare I can't remember. All I can see in the forefront of my mind is that white van. What if it's parked outside my house right now? What if he's walking up to the back door, ready to break inside and do unspeakable things to my child? What if he's heading for the mobile home park? What if he's driving down John's street, looking for his house number? This time of day would be the ideal time for him to do it, any of it. Before dawn, while this sleepy little town is still asleep. I'll just do a drive-by. I'll just check in on them. I'll just look for any sign of *him*.

I get out of bed and pull on my clothes and Clay's jacket. Then I dig around his bag for his keys, hoping he won't mind me borrowing his truck under these circumstances. Once I find them, I quietly shut the door on my way out of the room. I get to Clay's truck and am about to climb in when I realize I don't have my driver's license. I have Kelly's. I open the door and get in. Should I get pulled over, I'll just pretend to be Kelly. With the whole state of Mississippi thinking she's me, it's only fair. I start the car and head into Jasper. There's no one else on the road, and I feel like I'm the only person in the world who's awake.

Wrong Girl Gone

The sky is turning a deep blue by the time I get to our house. All the lights are off inside and there's no white van in sight. I sit in Clay's truck for a good ten minutes, just staring at the house in a trance. It's the strangest feeling in the world to be sitting outside your home, looking in. I feel like a ghost. Like I'm trapped in this sort of purgatory where I'm only allowed to watch my life from afar, not actually live it. Joy is dead, after all.

The sun is just beginning to crest over the horizon, and I take that as my cue to leave. I start the engine back up and am about to head out to the trailer park to check on Mama when I realize the gas light is on. My stomach drops. There's a gas station just down the street from the Starlight, so I figure that's my safest bet. If Clay's awake, I can pick him up and we can go to the trailer park for a check-in together. When I pull into the station, I do a quick scan of the parking lot, no white van. I pull on a gray baseball cap I find in the back seat and keep my head down as I pump the gas and make my way inside to pay.

When I walk through the door, I'm hit with a blast of cold air, along with the smell of stale pecan rolls and coffee strong enough to wake the dead. I quickly glance around to see if the coast is clear so I can grab a few coffees for Clay and me. The only other person in the gas station is the girl behind the counter.

"Good morning," she says in a feigned pleasant voice. Even without looking up from her magazine, I still recognize her right away. Her name is Lana Walsh. She babysat Jerry a couple of times until she ran up our phone bill calling her boyfriend so much. Carl saw the bill and thought I was having an affair with Frank Harper at 590-6340, a discussion that left a good-sized bruise on my throat and a week without a voice.

"Morning," I mumble, keeping my hat pulled down over my head and going straight for the coffee at the back of the shop. They have large cups for sixty-nine cents, so I grab two coffees and two bear claws. I head for the checkout. There's a book display next to the register, with three brand new copies of *A Time to Kill* sitting on the top shelf, waiting to be bought. I think of Clay and grin.

I turn my back to Lana as she rings me up, keeping my eyes out the window. It's barely light out, but I can see enough to feel my heart drop five stories when I see him. There's a man in a green jacket with glasses walking through the parking lot, away from that white van. I turn away from his line of sight and head to the back of the store.

"Forget something?" Lana asks.

"Yeah. Forgot," I mutter. I keep my head down, pretending to look for something on the bottom shelf of the refrigerator. The little bell above the door rings and the man enters. I kneel down like I'm trying to take a closer look at the item on the bottom shelf, which happens to be a case of Miller Lite, Carl's beer of choice. It's just the three of us, and it isn't a big gas station. I know he must have seen me. Even if he hasn't recognized me, he's still seen me. Hopefully, to him, I'm already dead.

I glance over my right shoulder, trying to balance on the balls of my feet. The man stops at a stand of chips at the end of my aisle and picks up a bag, crinkling it absentmindedly as he makes his way down the aisle beside mine. The crinkling grows louder the farther down the aisle he gets, slowly moving closer to me. I pray he doesn't get close enough to hear my heart beating, or that if he does, his crinkling drowns it out. When I stand, I narrowly avoid fainting from a head rush, and swiftly move toward the front of the store. I almost walk right out the door, but figure I'll look even more conspicuous if I don't make my purchase, so I walk back up to the counter.

"The way you ran back there I thought maybe you lost your keys," she says as she finishes ringing me up. "Anything else?"

"No," I mumble. Then I remember the truck. "And gas on pump four," I whisper.

"What was that?"

Wrong Girl Gone

"Gas on pump four," I repeat a little louder, my face burning.

"Nine forty-six," Lana says. I can feel her eyes scanning my face as I search for the money. "Joy?"

That's when the crinkling noise stops, and I feel his eyes searing into the back of my head. I don't say anything. I just pretend not to hear her, the same way I pretend not to hear Norman Lance take two steps towards the register.

"Sorry," she says in the awkward silence. "You kind of look like this lady I knew named Joy. I used to babysit her kid once in a while."

"I'm not from around here," I say with a hoarse voice. I'm ready to steal the gas and coffee if I don't find the cash in the next three seconds. I feel around my pockets and my heart nearly stops when I feel the metal of his badge in my back pocket.

"Oh, really? Lucky. Where you from?" She's chewing her gum loudly. I think I'm going to have to start lying through my teeth when I feel paper in my pocket behind the badge and pull out a ten-dollar bill Clay had given me yesterday.

"Sorry, I've really got to get going." I toss the money on the counter and grab the bag and coffees.

"Hey, don't you want your change?" she calls, but I'm already out the door. A few seconds later, that little bell above the door rings again. I catch a glimpse of that horrible white van in the parking lot and resist the urge to throw up. I'm headed for the truck when I realize my hands are too full to reach for the keys. I see the hotel a hundred yards away and walk straight towards it. I'll be safe there. I'll be safe with Clay. The heat from the coffee is burning through the cups and nearly blistering my hands, but I keep walking. And that man keeps walking right behind me.

A little bit of coffee sloshes out from underneath the lid and onto my hand. As painful as it is, I just bite my lip and ignore it. He's getting closer to me now; I can feel it. Before any more coffee can burn my hand, he's pinning me up against the brick wall of the car wash, just out of sight of the gas station. I drop one of the coffees as he covers my mouth with his black glove.

"Where you going, Joy? Huh? You're always running, aren't you?" My first thought as I fight to breathe is that I should have forgiven Mama yesterday in case I die today. Then I think about how the hell I am going to get out of this because I'm not dying behind a gas station outside of Jasper at six in the morning after coming as far as I have.

I try to make a noise but anything I say is muffled by his hand. And even if my lungs were free to scream, no one is around to hear it. That's when I realize I'm still holding one of the cups of coffee. And I can tell by the weight that it's at least half full.

"Look, I don't want to hurt you." He leans in close, hissing in my face. He's even uglier up close, those beady eyes practically twitching as he speaks. "You're running, but I don't want to hurt you. Stop running," he says. "It won't get you anywhere." I throw the cup and its contents into his face. His glasses fly off and land on the ground and he lets out a yell. He doesn't let go, but it's enough of a distraction to allow me to kick him hard between the legs and run. I run past the dumpsters, through the rest of the parking lot, and into a field of corn, and I keep running until I can't anymore. My bad knee gives out and I collapse onto the ground among the cornstalks, sobbing uncontrollably. I want to go home. I want to hold Jerry. I want to stand there in my kitchen with a smile on my face and take all Carl's shit and manipulation, just so I can feel normal again. I want to lay crying in my mama's arms while my daddy makes me a cup of hot cider. I want to stay up till five in the morning sharing secrets with Kelly. I want all these things, but I'm so far away from any of them I feel silly for even wanting them in the first place.

In the distance, a stalk of corn snaps. I spin my head around so fast my neck twinges. Without waiting to see what's lurking in the crops, I get up and push through the pain in my knee. I start running again, praying that I'm at least limping in the direction of the hotel.

Wrong Girl Gone

Finally, I see a break in the wall of corn and burst out of the field, right into the hotel parking lot. Before I can sprint across it to our room, two arms grab me and pull me back. The moment I scream, his hand covers my mouth. His strength overpowers me, and as hard as I try to kick, I'm nothing but a bird in his grasp as he drags me back into the cornfield.

He pulls me into a clearing and pushes me down into the dirt. I turn onto my stomach and make a lame attempt to claw away. That's when I feel the bottom of his boot press down on my back, forcing me into the ground like an insect. He kneels beside me and turns me over, then sits sideways on my chest like you would a park bench, pushing the air out of my lungs.

"Why do you keep running?" he says. "You think you're going to turn me in to the police?" He leans in, inches from my face. "I am the police. Who do you think they're going to believe, huh?" He whips out a switchblade knife and holds it against my neck. I can feel my veins throbbing just beneath the blade and wonder how much I'm going to bleed. He tightens his grip around my throat and presses the knife in harder.

"You killed the wrong girl," I choke.

He barked out a short laugh. "I don't think so." I feel the point of his knife on my neck and wonder how hard he has to press to start drawing blood. "If you so much as talk to the police, I'll kill you," he says. "Or maybe I should go after your little boy instead—"

With a metal thud, all of Norman's weight suddenly lands on me like a two-hundred-pound sandbag, and I see Clay standing behind him, holding a shovel. With the second whack, Norman is on the ground beside me, begging for my help with the twitch in his eye. By the third one, straight to the temple, he's out, and the shovel hits the ground in silence. I look up at Clay. His pupils are small, his face ash, and he looks like he may throw up at any minute. He isn't looking at me, instead, he's staring at the body. It's funny how fast someone can go from a man to a body.

"Did he move?" Clay asks, life draining from his voice. "I think I saw him move."

He hasn't moved at all since that final blow. "No," I say.

Clay bends down and check's Norman's pulse. "I think he's dead." He lets himself go limp and falls to his knees in the dirt. "I killed him."

I nod. "Yeah."

"What are we going to do?" Clay asks.

"I don't know."

Neither of us are looking at him or each other. I don't know what we're looking at, or if we're even looking at all. I don't know much of anything in this moment, to be honest.

Clay stands and picks up the shovel. He pushes the metal head into the ground with his foot and digs up some dirt. Then he repeats the act, again and again.

All I can do is stare at the slowly growing pile of dirt. "What if they find him?" Clay doesn't respond. "Do you think they will?"

"Probably. Eventually."

I stand up and grab the shovel from his hands.

"We'll go to the police," I say.

"What would we tell them?"

Going to the police and confessing to the murder of one of their own, even if he is a dirty cop, means risking losing Jerry all over again. And who knows what it means for Clay. A lot of folks around here aren't kind to people like him. Even if it was self-defense, who knows who they would choose to believe between a dead cop, a Black man, and a runaway mother. The odds are hardly in our favor.

"I know." I'm slowly finding my strength again. "We'll go to the river."

Chapter Twenty-Six

We clean up as much as we can and somehow manage to load his body into that haunting omen of a white van, hopefully without any witnesses. Then Clay drives that while I follow behind him in his truck, both of us careful not to go even a mile over the speed limit. We drive for nearly thirty miles until we reach the Jordan River. Even though the Jordan isn't nearly as big as the Kawanee, it will do. We follow a narrow, winding road that leads all the way up to the edge of the river and park the van in the gravel. What may have been a prime fishing and picnicking spot in the summer is now vacant, giving way to trees, overgrown brush, and the rushing rapids of what must be one of the river's deepest stretches.

Clay lifts him out of the back of the van as I check the floor for blood. We'd lined the floor with newspaper, and it looks like that's prevented any from seeping through. Still, if the police find any of his blood in his van, this won't look like the accident we want it to be. While Clay takes his body over to the river to stage the accident, I do a final scrub down of the back of the van with paper towels and rubbing alcohol. Then I walk over to Clay, trying not to think about the last time I was this deep in the woods with a dead body. He's positioned Norman's fishing rod and bait on the rocky ground like it's just been dropped. Clay is about to roll him in when I remember the badge in my pocket.

"Wait—" I pull the badge out of my pocket and put it in his. That's when I feel paper. An envelope full of paper. I pull it out and hold it in front of me. There it is—that familiar envelope of dirty money. I look up at Clay.

"Is that it?" he says.

I nod my head and shove the envelope into my pocket. Then I stand and take a step back. With one shove from Clay, the body is instantly swept up into the rushing water.

We wash off the shovel in the river and burn the bloody newspapers and towels in a small fire pit nearby. As we stand there in silence, watching the orange flames lick away the evidence, I feel oddly like we're holding a vigil for him, a memorial. But it isn't. Because memorials are for people who are good, who have morals, who have souls. People like Kelly. This man doesn't deserve a memorial. He doesn't even deserve a fire built on newspapers stained by his own blood. But he still gets one.

Clay and I do a final once-over of the van to make sure it's clean of evidence before we leave. It is, and that's what's bugging me. There's no evidence. No evidence of what he did to Kelly. It isn't enough for him to be dead. He needs to be caught, too.

I reach my hand up to my head and rip a fist full of hair from my scalp.

Clay is looking at me like I'm crazy. "What are you doing?"

I hop into the van and drop a few strands of my now brown whisps around the vehicle. Then I jump down and turn to Clay. "Did you know that identical twins have the same DNA?"

***

Clay is too shaky to drive after dumping the body, so I have to. I get us back to the hotel before midday, when the roads are just becoming busy with people going about their days of work and monotony, two things I never thought I'd miss until a morning like this came along.

We park Clay's truck in front of the hotel. Before I get out, Clay reaches across my lap and takes the gun out of the glovebox. "We should keep it in the room," he says. "Just in case."

Once we're back in our room, I wring out my clothes in the bathroom sink while Clay washes his in the tub. I obsessively try to scrub the blood off my white shirt, even though I know it'll never fully come out. I look down at the faint, blurred image of my hands beneath the surface of the dark water in the sink. Suddenly, and in a very surreal way, it hits me that this isn't my blood. This blood is collateral. Deep down I know what we did was in self-defense, but it feels like a trade. This killer's blood for Kelly's revenge. I'm suddenly sickened with how cold I feel inside. I watch my hands turn pruney in the water as I tell myself the same thing over and over again. *No one has seen us. No one will know.*

"How did you know to come looking for me in the field?" I ask Clay, desperate for a distraction.

He wrings out his shirt under the water. "I heard you call my name."

I replay the incident in the corn over and over again in my head. Not once do I remember calling for Clay. That's when it hits me then that he must not have been asleep when I left the room. He was awake, and after I left, he was just waiting for me to return safely. And when I didn't, he followed me into the cornfield, just the way I'd followed Kelly into the woods.

"I told him he killed the wrong girl." I stare blankly at my hands in the murky, red water. Clay glances over at me but doesn't speak. "He said he didn't. What do you think he meant?"

Clay shakes his head. "I don't know if he meant anything. I think he's just a sick man."

"What if he didn't kill the wrong girl? What if someone was trying to kill Kelly?"

Audrey Wilson

"What would someone have against her?"

I retrace the memories of Kelly in my mind, trying to find a time when anyone might have wanted her dead. Maybe an ex from a bad breakup? Or a friend with a chip on their shoulder? Or someone from school?

School.

In her freshman year, Kelly started dating one of her professors. One of her *married* professors. Needless to say, it didn't end well. His wife found out and apparently threatened to leave him if he didn't end it, which he did. Kelly was pretty broken up about it. She dropped the class and considered dropping out of school. That time I managed to talk her out of it. I guess she didn't want to give me the chance to talk her out of it this time.

Could it be another situation like that? Or could it be *that*? Maybe Kelly went back to him. Maybe his wife found out again, and she decided to kill the woman who was sleeping with her husband this time. Maybe Kelly didn't quit school because she was giving up. Maybe she quit because she was still running away.

The mood is already too heavy to speak my thoughts aloud, so I let them simmer inside me instead. Clay finishes washing what blood he can out of the tub, dries his hands, and leaves the bathroom, muttering something I can't hear.

I drain the sink, scrub, wash, rinse it out, and repeat. Clay isn't there when I come out of the bathroom. On his bed is a note that says, "Went to get lunch. Back in half an hour. Clay."

I pick up the paper, fold it, and put it in my pocket, right next to Daddy's address.

It's started raining. I hate the way this hotel room feels when it rains. It was raining the night I was there with Carl and Rachel too. Today it's just as damp and cool. I sit at the fake-wood table in a fake-wood chair by the window, feeling like a goldfish on the wrong side of the glass, trapped and suffocating. I feel a pang of loneliness and decide to do what Clay had wanted me to all along. I pick up the phone on the

183

nightstand and dial Mama's number. She answers on the third ring. I don't tell her about what happened, about the cornfield or the blood on the shovel. And I still can't bring myself to tell her about Kelly.

I just say two words, "I'm sorry."

She starts crying and says she's sorry too. Then she talks for quite a while. As a child, I only tended to listen to Mama when I agreed with her. I try to change that this time. Maybe I really am growing up.

Clay walks into the room while I'm still talking to Mama. "I picked up some burgers, extra relish—" he stops immediately when he sees I'm on the phone.

"Is that the man you're with?" she asks disapprovingly. "Are you sharing a room with him?" She gnaws at me for information. And as quickly as I'd forgiven her, I feel myself growing angry again.

"What difference does that make?"

"You are married, Joy. You have a son, for heaven's sake."

I glance at Clay. He's rummaging around in some of the plastic bags pretending, very poorly, not to notice the intensity of my phone conversation. "I'm also an adult. I can make my own decisions about what I feel is right."

I slam down the phone. So much for growing.

"Sorry," Clay says. "I should have left. I didn't mean to intrude."

"No. You're fine. It's not you." I feel like crying and try to hide it.

"Did you tell her about... anything?" he asks, handing me a carry-out container.

I take it and shake my head. "No." I allow myself a breath. "Do you think we're safe staying here?"

Clay picks up his burger, turning it to find the right spot to bite. "We should be for now."

We eat the rest of our lunch in silence. My mind isn't there in the hotel room with Clay. It's thirty miles away, drifting through the murky, blood-soaked rapids of the Jordan River.

Audrey Wilson

***

The next morning, I have a new plan. With that man gone, I finally feel safe being out in the world. I only have to worry about Carl, but then again, I've had to worry about him for years. I feel strong. I feel capable. I feel like a mother who wants her son back.

Jerry will be at kindergarten until three. And I've decided I'm going to pick him up before Carl gets off work. At this point, I don't care if I ever see Carl again, and if I have to go behind his back to retrieve my son, I will. The plan is for Clay to drive me to the grade school and wait in the car, so we don't create suspicion, but he'll be nearby if I need him.

After his shower, Clay emerges from the bathroom while I'm sitting on the edge of the bed tying my sneakers. He walks over to the table and gathers up his wallet and keys. "You almost ready to go?"

I go through the invisible checklist in my head, but I have trouble thinking about anything other than seeing Jerry's beautiful face again. "Hey—" I finish lacing up my shoes and reach into my pocket. "We shouldn't need any money but if we do—" I take a hundred-dollar bill I'd pulled from the envelope and put it in Clay's hand.

"Joy, no—"

"Yes. Take it."

"I don't want any charity."

"It's not charity. I'm just paying you back for everything you've paid for since finding me."

"I can't accept it. But thank you." He takes my wrist and puts the money back in my hand.

"Please? Like you said, at least half of Carl's money is mine, right?"

"Right. It's yours." Clay gives a twitch of a smile, then remains silent as he pulls on his boots and finishes lacing them up.

Wrong Girl Gone

"Are you okay?" I ask. Clay nods, but still doesn't say anything. "What is it?"

He sighs. "Actually, there was something I wanted to talk with you about—" Of course, that's when the phone rings, at the most inopportune time. Clay and I look at the phone then back at each other.

"It might be John," I say. "Did you give anyone the number?"

"Just my mother."

"Mama's boy."

He laughs, breaking the tension slightly, and answers the phone.

"Hello?" he says. A silence follows. I keep busy and try not to listen. Even though there isn't much privacy in the room, I still want to give him as much as possible.

When the silence stretches, I suspect something isn't right. And as soon as I glance at the side of Clay's face, I know it isn't. There is a deadness in his eyes I've never seen before. His lips are gray, his jaw clenched, and I think if I look any closer, I'll see him shaking.

"When?" he says into the phone. I pretend not to hear his voice crack. He waits for an answer, then says, "Okay," a few times before finally slamming down the phone. He stands there for a moment, turning his back to me. He doesn't speak. I'm about to ask him what happened when he begins kicking his bed repeatedly. When he finally stops the mattress is almost off the frame. "Goddammit, Russell," he chokes, giving the bed one more hard jab with his foot. "Goddammit."

That's when I know there is nothing I can say. I just stand there, helplessly waiting for the next thing Clay is going to do or say. His arm outstretched, he holds himself up against the wall, looking down. He hits it with his free fist. When he speaks, his words seem to come in painful spurts and there are tears leaking from his eyes. "Dammit. God DAMMIT!"

I can't take seeing him in this much pain. I really can't. "Clay—"

"Don't." He shakes his head, staring at a spot on the floor I can't see. "Just... don't." He heads to the door, stopping only to toss his keys on the table. Then he walks out the door, leaving it swinging open behind him. I don't know what to do. I don't know what to think. I don't even want to think. I watch out the window as he walks through the parking lot and across the street until he disappears. I grab the keys and follow Clay out of the room.

When I get outside my first instinct is to run after him, chase him down and make him talk through his pain, like Kelly always tried to do with me. I'm the kind of person who pushes away the people who try to get me to open up but I don't want to give Clay a chance to push me away. I don't think I can take it. And if Clay is anything like me, which he is, I know he's the kind to push.

So as hard as it is not to run after his shadow, I let him walk through the pain.

Chapter Twenty-Seven

As hard as it is to have gone this far with him and not have him by my side now, I tell myself that Clay will be okay. That he's one of the strongest people I've ever met. That he'll come back when he's ready. I actually see a lot of myself in him, at least a lot of what I wish I could be. He's courageous in every way I lack. He's gentle in ways I can't seem to channel. And he's more generous than I'll ever be.

I only have an hour before Jerry's class lets out, and even though a big part of me wants to stay at the hotel feeling helpless, I know that's not what Clay would want me to do. So, I drive his truck over to the school. As soon as I have Jerry back in my arms I'll go back to the hotel for Clay, pack up whatever meaningless items we have there, and the three of us will run off together and start a new life. Of course, I know there is no way in hell that's going to happen, but my romantic imagination is all I have to keep me from pulling off the road and sobbing uncontrollably.

I arrive at the school just as recess is ending and hang by the back entrance where the metal fence meets the orange brick wall, just out of view of the two teachers and herd of kindergartners. They line up, two-by-two, waiting to go inside as the teacher, Mrs. Hammond, counts them off. Some of the children giggle, one picks their nose, and the boy in the very back has stepped out of the line and is crouched on the ground, mesmerized by something even smaller than his tiny world.

The boy.

The boy is an angel. A little angel with a halo of blonde hair on his head and a shimmer of curiosity in his eye that I know he'll never grow out of.

"Jerry! Focus!" Mrs. Hammond claps her hands three times fast. It's all I can do to hold my tongue.

Jerry stands to attention and immediately finds his place back in line as Mrs. Hammond and the other teacher lead them through the double doors.

Once they're inside, I open the gate and creep across the lawn to see what my curious little boy had been looking at. A small, green caterpillar is struggling on the concrete in the hot sun. I do just what Jerry would do. I scoop him up, carry him to a nearby bush, and lay him gently on a leaf where he can have another chance. My son has taught me more about compassion in his five, brief years than the world has taught me in twenty-two.

I wait a few minutes, trying to find my courage, then take a deep breath and walk inside the school. The kids have returned to the classroom and the only person left in the hallway is the younger teacher, who's hanging up a child's jacket in a locker.

"Excuse me?" My voice is hoarse, so I clear my throat.

She turns. "Yes?"

"I'm here to pick up my son. I need to take him home early today."

"Just a second."

She goes inside the classroom and a moment later returns with Mrs. Hammond. I've spoken with her a few times before at parent-teacher meetings, but most of what I dislike about her I've learned from Jerry. According to him, she's angry, moves like a robot, and smells like bug spray. Looking at the woman in front of me, his description fits her perfectly.

"May I help you?" she hisses.

Wrong Girl Gone

"It's me, Jo—" I catch myself. "Jerry's aunt. Kelly. Kelly Elliot." I grapple for Kelly's wallet, pull out her driver's license, and hand it to Mrs. Hammond, who eyes the piece of plastic over the rim of her thin glasses.

The younger teacher looks from me to Mrs. Hammond nervously. "You just said you were here to pick up your son."

"My nephew. I meant my nephew. He's like a son to me."

"Your sister's story has been all over the news."

I swallow. "I know. It's been a very difficult time for our family. That's why I'm picking him up today."

Mrs. Hammond shoves the wallet back in my hand. "You're not authorized."

"Excuse me?"

"Only the child's mother or father are authorized to pick them up from school unless otherwise noted."

"No, listen. You must have different rules for unusual circumstances. This is a family emergency."

She turns to the other teacher. "Call Jerry Larson's father and ask him if he authorizes Kelly Elliot to pick up his son."

"No!" I say, much too loudly. "I mean—I already talked with him. He's busy at work, there's no need to bother him. Look, I'd be happy to send an authorized notice later, but right now I really need my s—nephew."

I take a step around them towards the classroom door. I see Jerry through the glass and he sees me too. His eyes get wide, but he doesn't move. Even with my new hair and distraught appearance, I was certain he'd recognize me. "Jerry! Jerry, it's me—It's Kiki—"

Mrs. Hammond immediately steps in between me and the door.

"If you don't leave, I'm going to be forced to call Jerry's father."

"What? No, don't—"

"Jennifer, call Mr. Larson." Mrs. Hammond snips at the young teacher.

"No, please—"

But it's too late. She's already walking down the hall toward the principal's office.

Mrs. Hammond turns to me, her eyebrow raised. "You're leaving me no choice but to call Jerry's legal guardian. There has clearly been a lot going on in your family these past few weeks, Ms. Elliot. We're only looking out for your nephew's safety."

I look from Mrs. Hammond to the classroom. I'm very tempted to push past her, burst into the room, grab Jerry into my arms and run out the door with him. But I don't.

"Wait," I beg. "Please don't call him." Mrs. Hammond eyes me suspiciously. "I don't want to disrupt Jerry's class more than I already have. I'll talk with Carl tonight so he can authorize me to pick him up in the future."

Jennifer is almost out of view down the long hallway. I glance from her to Mrs. Hammond.

"Fine," Mrs. Hammond rolls her eyes. "Jennifer!" Jennifer stops and turns back towards us. "Never you mind." She motions Jennifer back, lowers her voice and narrows her eyes even more than I thought was possible. "I suggest you leave and work this out with his father before you set foot in this school again."

"I will. Sorry for the disturbance." I nod to her and Jennifer, then turn and walk out of the school, feeling even more empty than when I'd entered. Jerry is gone.

He's gone all over again.

✳✳✳

I pull back into the hotel parking lot feeling so defeated, so stupid. I don't know how I thought I could just walk into school and pick up my son the way I'd done a hundred times in the past. Things are different now. I need to get that through my head. I'm not myself anymore. I'm not Kelly. I'm not Joy Larson. I'm not even Joy Elliot. I'm the empty mimic of the beautiful idea of a person who has always been five times the woman I am.

Wrong Girl Gone

As I cross the dark parking lot, I realize our hotel room door is open, and Clay is sitting inside it on the edge of the bed. The curtains have been taken down from the window. The lighting in the room seems strange and oddly white. I walk up to the doorway and realize it's because the lamp closest to the window has been knocked over and is laying on the floor. I speak to Clay from the threshold even though I have no words.

"Hey," I say heavily.

Clay is silent for a long moment. When he speaks, his voice is flat and emotionless. "He killed himself," he says.

"Clay…"

"I killed a man this morning, and this afternoon I find out my only brother took his own life." For a moment, neither of us speaks. "It's my fault he did it."

"It isn't, Clay. God, it isn't."

"He never even got to fight. The army broke him before he had the chance." Silent tears are falling out of his eyes and making wet spots on his pale blue checkered top. "I told him to go. I told him to go join the fucking army. Mom was right. He never should have gone. He wasn't cut out for the military. She was right."

He shakes his head, just barely moving. All I want to do is ease Clay's pain, although it feels like an impossible task. Of all people, I know what it's like to lose your sibling, your best friend.

"I'm sorry," I say. "I should have stayed here with you."

"No," he says, still shaking his head. "No. You should have gone." He turns to face me just slightly, still not meeting my eyes. "Where's Jerry?"

"They said I wasn't his legal guardian so I couldn't have him. He's still Carl's."

"I'm sorry."

"It's not important right now." That's when a glint of white light catches my eye. My whole body tenses when I realize it's a gun. "Clay, what are you doing?"

192

"He never wanted to go." His pain is surfacing in full force. I can see every muscle in Clay's face working to hold it back. The anger clenches on every syllable he speaks. "I told him to join. If I hadn't, he'd be here right now." By the end of his sentence, his voice is breaking even more.

I hadn't expected mine to do the same, but it does, and I have to force it to sound stronger than it is. "You don't know that. He was lost. Maybe that was what he wanted. Maybe joining the army is what gave him a purpose."

"He had a purpose."

"But he didn't think he did. Before he left and after, he didn't think he did. Either way, he could have ended up on the edge."

"You don't know—"

"And neither do you. You don't know." I glance back at the gun, my mind grasping for anything to hold him back, to talk him down. "You don't want to do this. Not today. That's what John says when I'm close to giving up. Not today. And somehow, it's enough." Even though Clay still won't look at me, a part of me feels I'm getting through to him. "Russell wouldn't want this for you. He loved you. You were—" I stop myself before I make the same mistake I've always hated people making. "You *are* his brother."

He looks at me for the first time. His brown eyes are clouded with pain and his skin is worn. He looks more real to me now than ever before.

When he speaks, he looks away again, shaking his head. "Everything—everything I did—it's all for nothing." Even though I'm not completely sure what he means, I still try to listen. He looks down at the gun, running his thumb over it. "It's not empty, you know," he says casually, frightening me even more. "I put a bullet in it."

"Clay, give me the gun." He fiddles with the groove in the handle. "I know it hurts. It hurts like hell." My voice isn't so strong anymore. I know I'm breaking, and I can tell he knows it too. I walk over to the bed and sit down beside him. "You saved my life. You wouldn't let me die. As much as I wanted to, you wouldn't let me give in. Even though I've grown up in the Bible Belt, I've never really been a religious person. But I swear I say a prayer for you every night. And not even prayers from an atheist can thank you enough for what you've done for me."

"I appreciate that, Joy. I really do. I just… I need to be alone right now."

"I can't do that. I'm sorry." I put my hand on his so that we're both holding the gun. "I've already lost my father, my sister, and my son. I've lost three people I love. I'm not going to lose you."

It's the longest minute I've ever had to live through. Clay's eyes stare straight ahead, as though he's mesmerized by a film playing on the wall. Then he raises his arm like it's made of lead and places the gun in my hand.

With my hands shaking, I stand and take out the bullet, put it in my pocket, then hold the piece of cold metal under my jacket. I feel it brush against the bit of skin on my waist, just above my jeans, and shiver.

"I think I need some air," he says, getting to his feet.

For a moment I don't know if I should let him leave the room. But with my fingers grasped so tightly around the gun that the metal is now hot, I nod. He walks past me and out the open door.

While Clay's out, I hang up the curtains and pick up the lamp. Then I use the bathroom and when I come out, Clay is standing in the room, closing the door behind him. He silently locks it, then looks at the curtains and the lamp that's now sitting back on the nightstand in its proper place.

"Joy?" he says.

"Yeah?"

"Thanks for cleaning up."

***

I'm running through a crowd of faceless bodies with only dark holes for eyes. They're not standing still, but they're moving slow enough that it looks like they are. I keep running. It feels like I'm running through water, like my body can only move so fast. I know that if I stop moving, I won't be able to start again. I look up. I realize that the sky isn't really a sky at all. It's a very high black ceiling. The walls are black too, from what I can see of them. The only lights are coming from the bodies themselves. They're all letting off a glow, like they each have a candle inside them. I wonder how long I have before one of them catches fire from the candle because after that happens, it's only a matter of time before they all catch fire, including me. I know there's someone chasing me and I have to find a place to hide. I spot a small, square door in the black wall a little ways ahead of me and run to it for safety.

One of the faceless people stands outside the box, holding the door open for me. He's wearing a ticket box around his neck and a plain, squared cap on his head. I don't have a ticket to give to him, but he lets me in anyway. There's a seat on either side of the box, so I take the one on the left and he closes the door. It's painted all black inside and I have to bend my head to keep it from hitting the ceiling. There's only one small yellow light on the black wall between the two seats, giving off a warm glow. Then the warmth increases and I feel myself begin to sweat. I try to bang on the door, but I suddenly realize it's gone. It's only a black wall now. Just when I think I won't be able to breathe again, a loud cranking sound and the rumbling of an engine shakes the box. Then the box begins to move. The top of it seems to dissolve and I can see the sky again, only this time it really is the sky. The wind is gentle and cool. It's like I'm taking the first breath of my life.

The box slowly moves higher and higher. I start to feel less afraid because I remember I'm only on a Ferris wheel and Ferris wheels can't hurt me. I look over the edge of the box and down at the ground. It's getting more difficult to see the ground the higher up I go. The glowing, faceless people with holes for eyes are now more of a large blur than individual people. I look for the other boxes like mine on the ride, but there are none. Mine is the only one. I reach the top and begin my descent back down the other side. I climb over to the seat across from me to get a better view of the park, moving slowly so I don't rock the box too much. I look over the crowd and that's when I see him. I spot a little red cap among all the faceless people and I know it's Jerry.

As soon as I'm close enough to the ground, I climb out of my box and run after him. He's carrying a basketball in his arms and making his way to the exit of the park. I know that if he leaves, I may never see him again, so I run faster, and faster still. I'm only a few feet from him when I trip and fall to the dirty ground. When I pick myself up, I catch a glimpse of his red hat as he runs through the main exit, a brightly lit arch. I make it to the arch and freeze. There's nothing. Only blackness and a hint of an empty parking lot that I can't fully see. It seems to go on forever and I know I can't cross the line from dirt to concrete to get to Jerry.

Just when I'm about to turn back, our brown station wagon pulls up in front of me. Carl rolls down the window and slings his arm over the edge, revealing a silver gun in his hand. He has a mouth, and a nose, but his eyes are just like the others: black holes.

"You can't even save yourself, Joy," he says. "What makes you think you can save anyone else?"

"Mama!" Jerry cries, and I see him sitting in the passenger's seat, trying to climb over Carl to get to me. "Mama, come back!"

Carl looks at me with his black holes. I know he's looking right at me. I know he's looking right through me. Because I am not here. I am asleep. And I will wake up from this nightmare.

Chapter Twenty-Eight

When I open my eyes, Clay is sitting in the armchair across from the bed, his hands clasped between his legs as if he's waiting for me to wake up. My first thought is that he wants the gun. I reach under the pillow beside me and feel the metal of the gun, right where I'd left it, and my heartbeat slows to a normal pace.

"It's still there," he says. "Don't worry, I'm not going to try anything. Sorry if I scared you yesterday."

The sun is shining through the window in a way that makes it hard to read Clay's face. "It's fine. You don't have to apologize."

"I think we should go see your dad."

My mind is trying hard to connect the dots between yesterday and my dad, but even with coffee, I don't think I could draw the line. "What?"

"Your dad. You said you hadn't seen him in years. You have his address. We can be in Raycene by noon if we leave in the next half hour." He speaks like this is a plan he's been thinking out all morning.

"Clay, now's not the time to go visit the father I haven't seen in ten years."

"Will there ever be a good time?" he says. "If you don't do it soon, you'll never do it, and then one day, you'll regret it." I don't think my regrets are the only ones he's talking about. "Besides, I need a distraction. What else have you got going on today?"

"I need to figure out how to get Jerry back," I say.

"Do you have any ideas?"

I open my mouth to speak but no words come out. "I'm working on it."

"Maybe you need to take a little time. Clear your head."

"I just don't think now is the right time."

Clay looks down. He nods. "You're right. I don't know what I was thinking."

I know what he's thinking. Life is too short to wait for the right time.

***

It takes the two of us just a little over two hours to get to Raycene. Neither Clay nor I speak much the whole way. I look over at him a couple of times, but he keeps his eyes forward. They're shadowed by dark circles and his lips are dry. I want to say something. I really do. I can talk someone out of death, but I can't seem to bring life back to them.

Raycene is even smaller than Jasper if you can believe it. There's one main street, promptly titled Main Street, and several other side streets passing through it, each with names like Hickory, Oak, River, and Wood. All simple. All earthy. We pass Jake's Garage and Gas Station, Little Suzy's Diner, and Mary-Ann's Bed and Breakfast. If I'd have known that was the entire downtown, I would have taken a better look at it.

We make a left on Birch St. and drive until we find the mailbox with "235" hanging on it in rusty metal numbers. The five looks like it's one mild windstorm away from falling off, and the two looks more like a pitiful seven. We park on the street across from his house. There's no car in the driveway and I wonder if he even has one. I never remember him driving. Mama was always the one taking us places that were too far to walk to.

The paneling on the house is coated in a peeling sage green, flecked with small patches of white paint. I can smell the dampness of the slowly rotting wood and there are puddles on the path leading up to the house. It must have rained here too, and from the looks of the house, I doubt it's leakproof. The yard is the only part of the home that isn't falling apart. It's perfectly gardened with beautifully colored flowers. The lawn looks like it was cut only hours ago, and even the trees and bushes are trimmed in uniform. And for a second, in the shadows of this dying neighborhood, I'm given the small ounce of hope that my daddy hasn't lost his passion for gardening.

Clay is just a few steps behind me as I climb the tilted concrete porch. A small orange glow lights up the cracked doorbell. My finger hovers over the button a moment longer than I would like prior to pressing it. There is the soft sound of approaching footsteps before the door opens and then I see him through the torn screen door. He steps forward and squints his deep-set brown eyes through the mesh.

"Joy?"

I can't believe he recognizes me. Even with different hair, even ten years later, though I look just like my twin sister, and even though I'm presumably dead, he still recognizes me. "Yeah, Daddy. It's me."

He pushes open the screen door and stares at me with his mouth open and his lip quivering. I can tell he wants to hug me, but I know he won't. "They said you were gone." His hand is shaking as he runs it over his mouth, looking at me like a ghost. "They said you were…"

He swallows and looks down. It suddenly hits me how painful all this must be for him. I force back my tears. I need to pretend to be strong again. "I'm not. I'm here."

He looks me in the eyes again. "You're here." His voice shakes. "You're here." He steps back. Part of me wants to confront him about leaving. To tell him how much he hurt

199

us when he went away. But seeing him standing there, seeing the tears in his eyes, I can't find the strength to dig into old wounds. I just want him to know I've missed him. That he's still my daddy.

"I hope we didn't come at a bad time," I say.

"Not at all. Please, come in, come in…" He holds the door open and we step inside.

I wonder if Clay thinks it's odd that he doesn't hug me. But I honestly can't remember him ever hugging me. He just didn't touch people. No hugs. No kisses. Not even high fives or handshakes. It isn't a coldness, because if you talked to him for five minutes, you'd see how warm his heart is. I've never asked him why he's like that. In fact, I don't think I ever even thought about it. All my life I've known that's just him. That's just who he is. Kelly thought he might have been abused in some way as a child, but he rarely talked about his past, so we really had no way of knowing. I just know that touching someone or being touched by someone is almost painful for him. It makes me wonder sometimes how Kelly and I were ever conceived.

We walk through the living room to the kitchen. The house is smaller than it looks on the outside and perfectly tidy. Everything is in its place. The gold carpet is freshly vacuumed, the out-of-date furniture is totally dusted, and the windows are perfectly washed. Even his model airplane collection is completely dust-free, each one placed meticulously on the shelves in the living room. Some of them I recognize, some I don't. The one that stands out most to me is sitting in a glass case on the center shelf. It's one of the first we ever made together. I smile when I see it.

"Nice to meet you, sir," Clay says as we take seats at the antique wood table in the kitchen.

"Oh, lord, I'm sorry. Daddy, this is Clay Grady. Clay, this is my father."

Clay holds out his hand to Daddy, who stares at him for a moment, wearing an expression I don't recognize. "Good to meet you, Mr. Grady," he finally says with a smile and a nod. Then he moves over to the counter to prepare some coffee, leaving Clay's hand empty.

Clay glances at me, as if worried he's offended him in some way.

"It's not you," I whisper to him.

Clay and I sit at the kitchen table. Daddy only sits in ten-second increments the whole time. He pours our coffee, then sits. Then he stands, washes his hands, and sits. Then stands, gets out the sugar, wipes off the counter, washes his hands again, and sits. A few seconds later he repeats the whole ritual again when he realizes he's forgotten the cream. By the sixth time he's about to stand, I set my hand on his. He looks at it, then at me, with the eyes of a child afraid of being reprimanded.

"It's okay," I say. "Please sit."

With great effort, he nods his head and stays in his chair. I can tell he's forcing himself not to get up and wash his hands and his uneasiness makes him talk quickly. "Kelly told me you have a son now." *Kelly.* The sound of her name makes my heart twinge.

I smile weakly. "I do. Jerry. He's five now."

He gives a sad smile that fades as quickly as it appears. "And a husband. Carl?" I nod my head. "Does he hurt you?"

I look at Clay, who looks away from me. "What makes you think that?"

"Kelly said he doesn't treat you well sometimes. It worries her."

I choke back the pain in my throat and try my best to be as honest with him as possible. I can't handle any more lies in my life. And as distant as my relationship with my daddy has been, I can't risk making the gap any bigger.

"She's right. He didn't treat me well," I say. "That's why I left him."

Clay seems to feel he's invading upon something and stands.

"Joy, I'm just going to wait outside—Give you some privacy," he says.

"Thanks, Clay." He leaves.

"How did you meet him?" Daddy asks.

"Carl?"

"Clay."

My first reaction is to say it's a long story. But really, it isn't.

"He saved my life."

His eyes widen. "He saved your life?"

I tell him about the man in the white van, about the fight in the woods, about Clay finding me and taking me in for no other reason other than to help. I tell him about everything but Kelly. I just can't let the truth come out of my mouth.

When I've finished, he nods with his brow furrowed and stares at the spot on his cup he's rubbing. "You're okay," he says and stands up to wipe off the table and wash his hands again. "You're okay."

"Yeah. I'm okay."

"And your mother's okay?"

"Yeah, she's okay too."

"And Kelly. Kelly's okay."

I don't say anything and instantly know I should have. He freezes at the counter, holding his white rag over the edge of the sink, his eyes fixed straight ahead. He always heard silence better than words.

"Kelly," he says again before I can think of what to say. "Kelly's okay." He moves his rag in circles over the same spot several times and keeps his focus fixed in the same spot. I know he's heard every word that hasn't been said. When he finally speaks, his voice has changed. And it's so painful to hear.

"You're both so beautiful, so different," he says. "You never looked the same to me."

"We didn't?"

"No. Maybe it's because I knew you both. Maybe to others you looked the same, just not to me." He gives me a watery smile. "And not to your mother."

"You can come back, you know," I say. "I don't care why you left. I don't. Just…" I'm breaking. I'm breaking and falling apart, and no one can fix me. The only one who could have come close would have been Kelly. But until I see her again, I'm broken. "Just come back."

"I can't," he says. "This is where I live."

"Your home is with us in Jasper."

"That's my home. But this is where I live. Some people aren't meant to be around others. I mow lawns and garden for my neighbors for a living, and only look in their eyes for a second when they pay me. I can't be any way but how I am."

"You don't have to change."

He wrings the rag in his hands and tugs at one of its loose threads. "You're so much like me, Joy. And Kelly's just like your mother. I tell the three most amazing women in my life to let me go, to not come after me. Two of them listen."

"But Kelly, she—She must have visited. She wrote you."

"She wrote, but she never visited. I think she saw me as a confidant, someone to confide in."

"What did she say in her letters?"

He winces, like the memory of her pains him. "That she was lonely. That she was frustrated with school. That she was afraid."

Kelly? Afraid? She wasn't afraid of anything. I'm the one who's afraid. Kelly was brave. And yet, for however long she'd held Daddy's address, she'd never even visited him. I've had it not even a few weeks and I did. Granted, I do partly have Clay to thank for that.

"I just can't believe she never came to see you."

"She asked if she could, but I said no. Your mother tried to come see me when the two of you were younger too. I said no then, and she listened. I guess they just thought it was better to let me be. I wasn't trying to play hard to get, I swear." His half-laugh is filled with sadness. "And maybe they were right. But part of me didn't want them to let me be. Part of me wanted them to not listen. You didn't listen.

Wrong Girl Gone

You never did." He doesn't look at me, but I can see his face. He looks hurt, almost angry. For the first time since I'd gotten there, it hits me that I might have made a mistake. Maybe it was out of respect and obedience that Kelly hadn't visited him because she thought he hadn't wanted her to. Maybe I'm not brave after all. Maybe I'm just a bad listener.

"Not once," he says. "Not once did you do as you were told. It was infuriating, to be honest. No matter what other people thought you should do, you always thought you knew better. And sometimes you did." He rubs his head, and I realize that he isn't angry with me. He's helping me put together the puzzle of myself. "Ever since I can remember, I've had the strangest dreams. So vivid, so haunting." His words hit me, and I listen closer. "They didn't always make sense, but I still tried to pay attention to them, to remember every detail I could when I woke, as though there would be an answer to my problems in one of them. And one day, I had a dream that I can still play in my mind like a film. I dreamed that I was standing outside our trailer, looking in the window at you and your sister and mother. The three of you were happy and laughing, and I wanted to join you, so I walked forward and into a glass wall that was shielding the trailer. When I realized that I wasn't meant to go any further, what I felt wasn't sadness. I felt like I understood something that I'd taken years to understand. As much as I loved the three of you—and I still do with all my heart—I knew that it was better for me to leave. It wasn't that anyone wanted me to, it was just that I felt it was for the best."

The tears in his eyes mirror mine.

"I hope you never blamed yourself," he says. "And I hope your sister and mother never did either. I was always a loner. Even though your mother tried to help me think I didn't have to be, my love for the three of you just wasn't enough. I've always felt safest alone, but I've still missed you."

He looks at me and smiles. Despite the tears still falling from his eyes, it's the first time I've seen that smile in eleven years. "You never listened. Just like I never listened to your mother's arguments for why I should stay. You're stubborn and strong. I never thought I'd say I wanted either of my daughters to be like me, but, Joy, I—" His voice cracks and breaks the wall of tears shielding my eyes. "I'm glad you didn't listen."

I reach out my hand, and hover over his for a moment, waiting for his approval. When he doesn't pull away, I take that for what I can and hold his hand. Even though he doesn't hold mine back, he doesn't pull away, and that's all I need. That is enough.

Chapter Twenty-Nine

I think it hurts more to leave my daddy now than all the pain I felt while he was gone. Saying goodbye to him on that cracked front porch as the rain starts to fall reminds me of the person who's been missing from my life. Being in his home, in his life, even if just for a few short hours, makes me feel complete for the first time since I was a child. It's like a patch had covered what I was missing. It's what I want to give to Jerry and to every child with a hole in their heart. Maybe that's what a social worker does. Finds the patch that fits perfectly and puts it over that hole. If it is, I want to do that.

Even though my hole is newly patched, I suddenly feel it wearing off again.

"Hey," Daddy says before Clay and I get in the truck. He pulls a small, white envelope out of his pocket and hands it to me. It has *For Joy* scribbled on the front of it in Kelly's handwriting. "Kelly wanted you to have this. She asked me to hold onto it for her. I don't think she intended for you to read it anytime soon, but she wanted you to have it."

"Why didn't she give it to me herself?"

"Must have been something too hard for her to say."

I nod, swallowing hard. I tuck the letter into my back pocket before giving Daddy a final smile goodbye. It's our equivalent of a hug.

Clay and I hit the brunt of a rainstorm driving back. We listen to the radio mostly, but I want to talk. I need to talk, even though God knows Clay probably has enough on his mind without listening to my analysis of life. When we pass the big wooden sign that reads, *Welcome to Jasper* in big blue letters, I realize I can't keep quiet any longer.

"Thank you," I say.

Clay turns off the radio. "You don't have to thank me."

"I know I don't have to thank you. I *want* to thank you. You've changed my life."

"You've changed mine."

"I have?" I've never thought my life impacted anyone else's. Out of all the mistakes I've made, all the selfish thoughts I've had, that's probably one of the worst.

"More than I think you know." He smiles and, for a moment, his pain fades.

We drive until we come to the hotel, and pull in. The storm has broken, and the clouds have parted to reveal the most brilliant blue and pink and orange sky I've ever seen. It's like a painting I could reach up and touch if only I were tall enough. The parking lot is nearly as empty as it was when we'd left, except for a silver Lexus that's now parked in the closest spot to our hotel room. That isn't the first thing to catch my eye, though. The woman leaning against it is. She's wearing perfectly creased beige slacks on her mile-long legs, and a thin white blouse unbuttoned halfway down. Her caramel-colored, highlighted hair is blowing in the wind like an ad for a high-priced conditioner. I'm not usually one to judge by appearances, but even before she speaks, I really don't like her. Maybe it's jealousy.

Clay and I park two spots away from hers and get out of the truck. I've barely gotten out of the car before she has her arms around Clay, sobbing into his shoulder.

Wrong Girl Gone

"Clay… Oh, God, Clay…" she says. Clay's expression is such a blend of emotions I'm not sure what to make of it. He pats the woman awkwardly on the back and gives me a look that I think I'm supposed to be able to read, but I can't.

"Shh," Clay says, trying to calm her down. "It's okay. It's going to be okay."

"He's dead, Clay. Oh, God… He's dead…" she says. She's Gwen. She's Russell's wife. The woman Clay had loved and the one who broke his heart.

After Clay introduces me, I help move our party inside the hotel where we can have more privacy. She sits on the bed and talks, and talks, and won't stop talking.

"The funeral is Saturday," she says in conclusion to her one-sided conversation. "I don't think I can handle going alone." She wipes her tears on the corner of her tissue, trying to save her heavy makeup.

"Where is it?" Clay says. He's sitting in an armchair in the corner of the room, his face in his hands. He's been sitting that way since Gwen started talking.

"First Baptist in Northchester." She blows her nose. "Your mother's been planning it almost all on her own. We really need you, Clay."

Clay looks up at me. "Will you be all right?"

I had been leaning against the door, staring at Gwen's large hoop earrings, and wondering how she manages to keep them from getting hooked on things. I snap myself out of it. "Of course. Please, Clay, you should go."

I can feel Gwen's eyes surveying me, judging me. I know I've been a bit cold to her since she got here, but I can't help it. I know what she did to Clay. And I've had my heart beaten and bruised and cheated on too many times to forget those hardships very easily.

"I hate to be rude," she says to me. "But would you mind if we had some privacy?"

My eyebrows raise as I look from her to Clay who, with an apology in his voice, says, "Joy, would you—"

"I'm going to take a bath," I head for the bathroom. I close the door all but an inch, which is just enough to see part of Clay and Gwen's reflection in the long mirror on the wall. I turn on the bathwater and lean beside the door.

"I'm sorry," she says. "I shouldn't have barged in on you two like this."

"No, it's fine. Really. It's been rough." Clay sits leaning forward with his fingers intertwined, half-looking out the window.

"Yeah." She tugs at a loose string on the comforter. "Are you and uh, Hope, is it?"

"Joy." He seems slightly irritated. "Her name is Joy."

"Are you and Joy... together?"

He's jiggling his leg but stops when he hears the question. I find myself holding my breath, trying to catch each word through the sound of the water. "I appreciate you coming here, Gwen. I do. But why did you come here? We could have just as easily talked on the phone. I was planning on coming home soon anyway."

There's a pause and Gwen takes the opportunity to smile right into it. "Come sit over here, would you?" She pats the spot on the bed beside her. Clay obliges but sits a little further away from her than she probably preferred. "You're right. It has been rough. It's been... brutal. I can only imagine what you must be feeling." She reaches out her hand and sets it on top of his. "He was your brother."

"He *is* my brother." Clay pulls his hand away and scratches the back of his head like I've seen him do so many times.

"You're right. I guess the real reason I came here was to apologize. I never should have treated you the way I did. My behavior was inexcusable. But I was in a different place then." She moves towards him. "A few months ago, I was looking through one of my old photo albums when I found one of us. Before Russell. Before any of that happened. Before he was in the throes of those goddamn pills and that dark mind of his... I just sat there on my half-empty bed, staring at it for the longest time, and I couldn't help the way I started feeling. I started to remember us. I started remembering how I felt about you. I've never stopped thinking about you, Clay. I've never stopped loving you."

"Don't do that," he says.

"Do what?"

"Don't hurt his memory like you hurt me."

She looks taken aback for a moment before she manages to catch herself. "I wouldn't hurt you again." She leans towards him. "I can hardly stand the pain I'm feeling now, let alone the pain of knowing how much I hurt you." Her voice cracks, and Clay turns to look at her. "Could you do me a favor?" she asks. "Could you just hold me for a minute?"

Clay doesn't say anything. Gwen leans in further, and when she's close enough she kisses him. I shut the door without even thinking of the noise it would make. I sit leaning against the sink cabinet with my knees to my chest, trying to ignore the whirlwind of emotions flooding into me.

A few minutes later, I hear the hotel door shut. I turn off the water and leave the bathroom to find the room empty. Through the window, I see Clay walking Gwen to her car. She hugs him, her whole body leaning against his. Watching them, whatever feeling of jealousy I was having transforms into a wave of sadness. Because there's nothing sadder than being jealous over something that's not even yours.

The phone rings, and I take it as an excuse to pull my eyes away from the window.

"Hello?" I assume I'll hear my mother's or John's voice on the other end, but it's neither.

"Joy? Oh, thank heavens you answered. It's Winnie. Is Clay there?"

"Winnie, hi. He just stepped out for a minute." It hits me that she's just lost her son. No words are going to be enough, but I have to say something. "Winnie, I'm so, so sorry about Russell."

"Thank you, Joy. It's been… unbearable at times. But I'm trying to keep praying that he's in a better place. It kills me

210

that he didn't want to stay here with us, but the only salvation I have is in believing the Lord needed him more than we did."

Never in my life have I been able to believe that everything happens for a reason. That some people are "chosen" by God to die, or others are blessed with His good fortune. On good days, I only believe in God half-heartedly. But even on those good days, I can't fathom that the suffering of a human being, child, or animal is occurring because a man in the sky made it so. To me, that's not a god. That's hell.

At the same time, part of me envies people whose faith transcends that logic. Because those people somehow seem to be able to cope with death by moving forward, unlike me and my mother.

I'm not quite sure what to say, so I stick with what I know how to do best. "Well, I am truly sorry."

"Thank you, Joy. That means a lot. But that's not why I called." Winnie takes a sharp breath. "Joy, it's the police. They're suspicious of Clay. I think they know it was him."

"What was him?"

"The money, Joy. I think they know he took the money."

My heart thumps in my ears. "The money." My mouth has gone dry, so the words come out croaked.

"Didn't Clay tell you? Oh, I was certain he did."

"Yes, sorry. Yeah, he told me about the money."

"The police showed up at the house again last night. I played dumb, but they seemed to have figured out the whole thing. The police said they talked to Walt Segar—it's his store after all—but it doesn't sound like he gave them much of a lead. Either he doesn't know who took the money or he's worried about protecting Clay. If he is protecting Clay, I'm sure it's because he knew Clay wouldn't have taken the money without good reason—three thousand dollars is a lot for a little shop like that, after all. Anyway, the police asked me all sorts of questions about Clay and when I'd seen him last, and I just said he was running an errand for me. But they called me twice today trying to talk with him and I had to make up more excuses. I tried to play dumb, honest I did. But, Joy, I don't think I can do this much longer. It's been horrible enough losing Russell. I can't lose both my sons…" she lets out a quiet sob and a sniffle. "Joy, I—I think he needs to turn himself in." My mind is racing, and I can't put all the pieces together fast enough. "Joy? Are you still there?"

I take my first breath since Winnie started talking. "Yeah, sorry. You're right." I look out the window again. Gwen's car is gone, and Clay is sitting on the curb, his head in his hands. "I'll tell him you said that."

"Oh, please do. And please tell him Aunt Cammy has been staying at the house with me. I don't want him to worry. He'll be back for the funeral Saturday, right?"

I watch Clay stand, run his hand through his hair and rub his neck before turning toward the hotel door.

"Yeah, he will. And I'll be sure to tell him."

"Oh, thank you, sweetie. He's lucky to have you. You take care of yourself, now."

"You too."

The click on the other end of the line is followed seconds later by the click of Clay opening the door. I hang up the phone and try to gather my thoughts.

"Someone call?" Clay says. He takes off the checked, button-up shirt he was wearing and proceeds to hang it up in the closet.

I stare at him, pained when I realize for the first time that I don't know the man standing in front of me. "Your mother."

"Is she okay?"

"She said you should turn yourself in." Clay freezes for a few seconds before he finishes putting away his shirt. "When were you going to tell me that you stole three-thousand dollars from Segar's?"

"I was going to tell you."

"When?"

"Before Russell…. I'm sorry. I shouldn't have kept it from you."

212

"I thought this whole time you were helping me, but... you were just as much on the run as I was. That's why you didn't take me to the hospital, isn't it? You were protecting yourself?"

"There's more to it than that."

"You know what? It doesn't even matter. You don't owe me an explanation."

I head for the door, but Clay intercepts, his brown eyes now piercing mine. "Yes," he says. "I do."

Chapter Thirty

Clay motions for me to sit in the chair. I suspect this is going to be the kind of story you need to sit for, so I oblige. He paces for a few seconds, then sits down on the bed across from me, our knees inches from touching.

"I wish I could say Russell's suicide came as a total shock, but it didn't. Like I'd said, he'd been suffering from PTSD for quite some time." He laces his fingers together in front of him as if trying to keep them from shaking. "A few months ago, I was over at his and Gwen's house for supper, and we got into it pretty bad. Russell hadn't been doing well. Gwen was working two jobs to try to support them both while he was out of work, so the house was getting messier each time I'd visit. Russell was constantly on edge and lashed out often. He suffered from anxiety attacks even when he was doing something simple, like going to the store. It was hard for me to watch. I knew it must have been hard for Gwen too.

"After supper that night, I mentioned that he looked tired. He got defensive, and things just escalated from there. Ever since Gwen, things always seemed to escalate quickly. But the incident in the army tempered my anger a bit. I felt bad for him. I said he needed to get help. I even offered to pay for therapy, but he was too proud. Said he wouldn't accept charity. I respected that, but it also frustrated me. Probably because it's too similar to how I would have been." He lets out a sharp, sad laugh.

Audrey Wilson

"I don't recall a lot of what we said, but I remember the argument ended when I said Dad would be heartbroken if he saw how he was living now. I knew Russell wanted nothing more than to make our father happy. I probably shouldn't have said it, but part of me wanted to light a fire under his ass again. You think I would have learned my lesson, pushing him to join the army. But I guess I didn't. Russell stormed out, got in his truck, and drove off. Gwen tried to stop him, but he wouldn't listen to anyone. So, we let him go.

"Gwen said he'd cool off in an hour or two. It was just her and I in the room. We were hardly ever alone in a room together, I made sure of it. It was just too uncomfortable for both of us. But this time I had no excuse to leave. Neither of us said much. When she spoke, it was to tell me to try not to be so hard on Russell. I couldn't say that she was right, of course, so I just held my tongue, thanked her for supper, and said I'd give him a call tomorrow to see if he was feeling better. Then I left. I got a call from Gwen at two in the morning. Russell had driven his truck into the pharmacy on the square in downtown Northchester. He was a little banged up, but the pharmacy was worse.

"He got a five-hundred-dollar ticket for driving uninsured and racked up another five-thousand in damages. He and Gwen had nowhere near that kind of money. I made decent money at Segar's but most of it went to bills and food, so I didn't have much savings. The man who owned the pharmacy threatened to sue Russell if he didn't pay up in thirty days. Part of me felt he just needed to figure it out for himself, but I still cared about him more than I wanted to admit. I came to a decision late one night when Gwen called me at home. She was sobbing uncontrollably, saying Russell was threatening to kill himself over the money. She put him on the phone, and I managed to talk him down. I told him I'd get him the money. He asked me how, and I told him not to worry about it. I'd get it. He didn't kill himself that night.

"My boss, Walt Segar, was on vacation with his family the following weekend. Walt may have been my boss, but he was

215

also a good friend of mine. The guilt I felt for what I was planning to do to him was unbearable. The night before Walt came home, I took three thousand dollars out of the safe at the shop. Between my mother and I, I figured we could maybe scrape up the other two thousand. At the very least, I hoped the pharmacist would accept at least a partial payment and the rest in installments.

"After I took the money, I threw a brick into the shop from outside the back window to make it look like a break-in. Then I locked up the shop like I always did and left. I knew I'd probably be a prime suspect, so I packed up a few things and headed to our mother's house early the next morning. I stopped at a payphone from the road and called Walt to tell him I was sick with the stomach flu and wouldn't be able to make it in to work that day. He'd already discovered the money was gone and was frantic on the phone. I felt horrible. I played dumb, said I'd counted it the night before and it was all there. He said of course I did; I was the best employee he had. He said he found the brick and called the police. Then he said he hoped I'd feel better soon and told me to get some rest. Then I continued driving to my mother's house. On the way, I spotted what I thought was a dead animal on the side of the road. When I got closer, I saw it was a young woman who was very much alive. And that's when I made another choice in my series of bad decisions."

"I didn't realize you considered helping me a bad decision." My words choke in my throat.

"That's not what I meant. I didn't take you to the hospital, and I should have." He takes my hand. "I'm sorry." Almost as quickly as he'd taken my hand, he lets it go. "You know most of the rest. I brought you to my mother's house and told her about the money. She was afraid for me, of course, but she understood why I did it. We came up with a plan. Once the dust settled with Segar's, she'd offer to pay Russell's damages with the money, claiming that Dad had left it to her. I stupidly thought the lie would work."

"Your mother said the police suspect you. That you should turn yourself in."

He rubs his hand over his head. "She's probably right."

I take a breath. In a lot of ways, the truth isn't nearly as bad as what I thought it might be. I look at Clay, beginning to see him the same way I had when we first met. Still, there's a sadness inside me that I can't shake. "Thank you for sharing that with me. I understand why you did it. And I wish you'd been honest with me from the start, but I get why you didn't take me to the hospital. I don't hold it against you."

"I appreciate that."

I collect my thoughts for a moment, trying to pinpoint the source of my sadness. "Can I ask you something?"

"Sure."

"Why are you still here?" I ask. It's an honest question, and it hurts like hell to get it out.

He looks up at me. "What?"

"You should be with her."

He shakes his head and gets to his feet. "You don't know what the hell you're talking about." He walks out the door before I can say anything else, so I follow him outside. The air is cool and heavy, and the sun is slowly sinking behind the gray of the clouds. I can feel the storm catching back up to us.

"I heard what she said," I call to him. "I'm sorry, I didn't mean to eavesdrop."

Clay laughs. "Sure you didn't."

"Fine. I did. But you should be with her. You love her."

"Well, thank you for telling me what I feel." He walks over to his truck to get something out of the front seat.

"I can tell. It's fine, really. I just don't know what you're still doing here. You should have gone with her."

He pulls his bag out of the truck, shuts the door, and stares at me. "I tell you about everything, about the accident and the money, and she's still what you've focused on?"

"Because she's a big part of that story. I know you care about Russell, but he's not the only thing that motivated you to take that money. Be honest with yourself. Was this all for Russell?"

For a moment, he's silent. He shifts on his feet, looking out at the darkening sky and back at me again. "Not at first."

Even though I'd prepared myself to hear it, that doesn't make it any easier to take. "She needs you," I say. "You should be with her."

"That woman ran off with my brother and left me with the heart she broke. You really think I want her back?"

"You didn't seem to mind when she kissed you." My bitterness is growing, and I hate myself for that.

"Well, it's too bad you shut the door before you saw me pull away from her." He sees the look of shame on my face and controls himself. "I did love her. I don't anymore. I'm not going to again."

"You can't just stop loving someone. It doesn't work that way."

"Oh no? Do you still love Carl?"

I don't say anything. I don't know what to say. So, I push out words I don't agree with, words I think he wants to hear. "Maybe Gwen's changed."

He laughs again. His laugh is empty and bitter and sad all at once. "People like her don't change. People like Carl don't change. People like us, we change for them. And that's no way to live."

I can't do this anymore. I feel like I'm keeping this man here with me, and he's only staying out of guilt. No, he shouldn't have lied to me. Yes, he should have taken me to the hospital, but I also didn't know if I would have wanted him to. And if I were in his place, I probably would have done the same thing, whether or not it was right. Whatever is in his past, I know Clay is good. And I know he deserves so much better. He deserves a life, and as messy as it is, I'm keeping him from his. "You shouldn't stay here," I say.

There's a glint of hurt in his eyes. "What?"

"You shouldn't stay. You should go back home and live your own life."

Audrey Wilson

It seems to take a moment for him to let everything sink in. "Is that what you want?"

No. It isn't what I want. It's what I think he wants; what I think he should want. I know what I really want, but I don't dare say it. Instead, I lie. "Yes." The words hurt my whole body. "You should go."

Clay drops his bag and walks straight over to me. He looks into my eyes, and in his, I see all life, all the passion, and all the fear in the world.

"I may have been running when I left," he says. "But I stayed because of you." At that moment I seem to feel everything and nothing all at once. My mouth is dry. There are no words to express what I'm thinking. His eyes stay fixed on mine, trying to pull something out of me that's intangible. "Do you want me to stay?"

I feel several drops of rain hit my face and arms, like minutes tapping at my skin. I shake my head and look down to hide my tears. Then I watch as Clay's white, dust-stained boots turn on the gravel and walk back to the truck. The raindrops beat down harder, multiplying by the thousands. Lightning fills the dusk sky and with the first clash of thunder, all the thoughts swirling around in my head jolt into place.

Before Clay can make it halfway to his truck, I'm running towards him. I call his name, and he turns around just in time to catch me as I jump into his arms and kiss him. He kisses me back with all the passion I'd seen in his eyes only moments ago. His hands run up my back and into my hair, holding my face as he presses his parted lips against mine. I pull his body closer, wanting so badly to close those inches of space we've had between us since we first met. I kiss him like I've never kissed anyone before. I kiss him like he's the piece of me I've been missing for so many years. I kiss him like I never want to stop.

Before I can let myself fall back into reality, he lifts me into his arms and carries me out of the rain.

Chapter Thirty-One

I wake up the next morning with the sun in my eyes and Clay's arm under my neck. The curtains are open, and I squint in the bright light. I wrap a sheet around my body and get out of bed to close them. Clay is still asleep, snoring lightly. I climb back into bed and lay next to him, still wrapped in the sheet. Part of me believes I'm still in a dream. The other part knows I'm not because for once my world isn't falling apart around me, the way it does in my dreams.

I look over at Clay. He looks so tired, so worn. He looks how I feel, only much more beautiful. It's all I can do not to trace my finger over the muscles in his beautiful broad shoulders. Even before last night, I can't deny the connection I feel with Clay, something I've never felt with Carl. I begin to draw parallels between the recent chain of events in our lives—the money, the sibling, the loss of a sibling.... Each of us running away, our paths crossing, simultaneously, at the most opportune and inopportune times. And last night, our connection went even deeper. It was the first time anyone's ever really made love to me. With Carl, it's never making love. I can think of a hundred other names for it, but that isn't one of them. It's funny. All I can see is beauty in the person lying next to me, which is something I never could have said for Carl.

That's when I suddenly realize that I'm not feeling guilty. Then I immediately feel guilty for not feeling guilty.

Audrey Wilson

I look down at my wedding ring and make to take it off but stop myself. Whatever this is with Clay, I'm still married to Carl. And I'm too tired and dazed from last night to try to figure things out just yet. I do know that Carl wouldn't have liked Clay. Of course, he wouldn't have liked him for sleeping with his wife, but Carl wouldn't have liked him regardless.

Carl will never admit it because admitting it would mean admitting that he was far too much like his father, but he's as racist as he is sexist. The fact that Clay is Black would have been enough for Carl to be seemingly polite to his face, then make some shameless, underhanded, racist remark when Clay wasn't around. Carl would pass it off as being society's fault for making him think that way. I wonder if Mississippi will ever move into 1989. I'm certain Carl won't.

The more I think about Carl, the more I hate him, and the more I regret leaving my wedding ring on. But I still don't take it off. Even turning my attention back to Clay doesn't give me any solace. My nerves are starting to work again, and I can't seem to lay still. The room is chilly for this time of year, probably because the air conditioner has been blowing all night. To warm myself up, I go into the bathroom, turn the water on, undress, and get into the shower. I don't start washing, just let the shooting stream of boiling water hit my skin and steam up the whole room.

When I get out of the shower, I can hear the TV on in the other room and know Clay is up. I'm suddenly afraid to leave the bathroom. My clothes are on the chair just outside the door, and now I really wish I'd brought them in with me. There's a knock on the bathroom door.

I quickly wrap a towel around myself and pretend to be looking for something on the sink. "Yes?"

I keep my head down and stay busy. Clay enters the room and before I can turn, wraps an arm around my waist and kisses me on the head. "Good morning," he says. He smiles his half-smile and hands me my clothes without breaking eye contact. I'm suddenly very tempted to go back to bed and not because I'm tired.

Wrong Girl Gone

After he leaves, I finish getting dressed and work a comb through my newly short hair. When I go into the main room, a man on TV is talking about a tornado that was seen near Tupelo last night and Clay is getting dressed. He pulls his shirt over his head and smiles again when he sees me.

"I thought I'd go out and get us some breakfast," he says. "Did you sleep well?"

I nod and smile, at a loss of what to say. I make myself busy again, this time by picking up some trash around the room. The guilt is slowly beginning to creep up on me, and I'm desperately trying not to let it.

"Joy?"

"Yeah?"

He doesn't answer right away. Instead, he lets the TV keep talking. The mindless jabber is starting to get on my nerves until I hear a few words that sound familiar, even though I know I've never heard them before. I look at the screen and see what Clay has been watching.

"Early this morning the body of a man was found in the Jordan River just on the edge of Hemmer, Mississippi—" I freeze. The reporter stands in a clearing on the edge of a river, talking to the camera while a dozen officers and officials move behind her. "That man has just been identified as forty-nine-year-old Norman Lance, a Harrison County police officer. I'm here with Detective Louise Barrow with the details. Detective Barrow, what conclusions have been drawn about this incident so far?"

The camera zooms out to include Detective Barrow. "Shortly after the body was discovered, our team conducted a thorough search of the area. While we won't know too much until the autopsy, we did find a van and some fishing equipment about three miles upstream that we've traced to Norman Lance. Officers of the Harrison County police force have confirmed that Officer Lance left for a fishing trip two weeks ago. As of right now, it appears Officer Lance fell into the river and drowned while fishing, but we can't make any formal statements until we've collected more evidence."

"I'm Rhonda Reed, reporting live from Hemmer, Mississippi. Diane, back to you." The pandemonium of officers and reporters cuts away to the studio, but my eyes stay wide, the reflection of the television screen glaring into them.

"Does this mean...?"

"It worked." Clay runs his hand through his hair, just like he always does. Everything is just like before. The only thing that's different is what we've been through, both good and bad. Everything else, down to the sheets on the bed, the skin on our bones, and the story we wrote for Norman, is exactly the same. And so far, the story is selling.

***

Most "morning afters" don't include finding out on the morning news that the body of the killer that you and your lover killed only days ago has been discovered. But then again, I don't do this very often, so what do I know.

Clay is leaving this afternoon for Russell's funeral tomorrow, so we don't talk much as I help him pack his things. But with every disposable razor or sock I hand him, I can't seem to shake the feeling that he won't be coming back. That this is where we end, right where we began.

Now that Norman's body has been discovered, the investigation is underway, and it's all I can do not to hold my breath and wait for them to find the hair in the back of his van. Once they do, it will only be a matter of time before they trace my DNA— *Kelly's* DNA— right back to her, the evidence needed to condemn him. Because killing him isn't enough. The world deserves to know what he did to her, what he did to us.

Clay finishes up in the room while I bring his bag out to the truck. John had invited me to stay with him, and for once, I accepted the charity. Paying for the room was getting expensive, although Clay never once mentioned the money. He even refused to let me take over the charge, but I couldn't

223

Wrong Girl Gone

let him keep shelling out the cash when I had a wad of stolen money in my bag.

The day is crisp and clear, the sky so blue it feels like I'm looking at it through indigo stained glass. I feel Clay's hand rubbing my shoulder. "You sure you don't want a ride to John's?"

"He's picking me up after work. Besides, we have the room for the rest of the night, so I might take a nap or something."

I shake off the chilly breeze and try to dismiss the déjà vu that's pulling my mind back to the evening before. We stand in silence for a few minutes, just taking in the autumn air.

"The wake's tonight, the funeral is tomorrow morning. I should be back by Sunday evening," Clay finally says. I nod and look at the ground. "Joy?" He waits for me to look at him and I do. "I am coming back."

"Okay," I say. "I believe you." I know I don't, and he knows too, but we both keep quiet about it. "Clay, the day you found out about Russell... when you were holding the gun..." Clay nods, his face slightly pained. "You said it was all for nothing. Were you talking about the money you stole for Russell?"

"Yeah."

"It's not for nothing. You can still clear his name. You can pay off the damages and payback Walt. Even if it takes time."

He smiles sadly. "Thanks. I'll think about it."

I look down for a moment, then back up at him. "Could I please give you some—"

"Joy, no. Absolutely not."

"Please?"

"We've been over this. I don't want your money. This is my burden. It's my mistake. I need to make it right on my own."

I nod. I'd known he wouldn't take it, but I had to try. It's the least I can do for him.

Audrey Wilson

Clay gives me one last hug before he leaves. Then he kisses my forehead, and we break apart. "I'll be back," he says, holding my face in his hands. "I promise."

I wave with a smile on my face as I watch the dust roll out from under the truck. He turns out of the parking lot, onto the road, and disappears from my life as suddenly as he entered it. A few short weeks ago, I'd opened my eyes, and he was there. Today, I close them, and he's gone. I don't even have something to remember him by, to reassure myself that he was real. The wind blows through my jacket and I decide to go inside to get out of the cold. Even though it probably should have felt bigger, the hotel room feels much smaller without Clay. I sit on the bed we'd been in just the night before. When the memories come back, the pain hits, and I choke on it hard. As quickly as our paths crossed, they're splitting again. And it's more than I can bear.

I wipe my face on my sleeve and flip on the TV to fill the silence. Not that Clay had ever been much of a talker, but I'd still gotten used to his silence. Believe it or not, it was a different kind of silence than the one he left behind.

I straighten up the room a bit as newscasters chat on the television. I'm not paying much attention to the voices on the TV until I hear my name.

"Another piece of evidence has surfaced in the case of Joy Larson," a newscaster announces grimly. "An autopsy this afternoon reveals that Ms. Larson was, unfortunately, not the only murder victim in this case. The young mother was nine weeks pregnant."

Thank God the bed is there because it's the only thing between me and the floor when those words hit my ears. I lean against it for support, sliding down the comforter until I finally land on the carpet.

"Carl Larson, Joy's husband, refused to comment, but we can only imagine the pain he must be going through. Our hearts go out to him and, of course, to Carl and Joy's son, Jerry. Coming up next, gas prices continuing to surge—"

Wrong Girl Gone

I click off the TV and curl my knees up into my chest. My head is spinning, thoughts bouncing off the corners of my mind in a million different directions. My heart hurts. My whole body is numb. Because that's when I finally understand it. That's when everything falls into place.

Chapter Thirty-Two

I call John and tell him I no longer need a ride, that I'll be walking to his house. I need to walk. I need to think. And I have a stop I need to make along the way. I pack up what little belongings I have and check out of the hotel with my mind in a trance.

I'd been so convinced that this was a case of mistaken identity, so certain that one of Carl's sleazy sharks had been after me, that I couldn't wrap my head around the idea that someone had actually been after Kelly. The thought crossed my mind when we dumped Norman's body, but it just didn't seem possible. But now his words ring in my ears. He did kill the right girl.

Kelly was pregnant. That's what she had been trying to tell me that night Jerry and I met her at the hotel. She was going to tell me that she was pregnant with some man's baby and she didn't know what she should do. Maybe he was married, maybe he was her teacher, maybe he was both and it was the same man from before. But whoever he was, in his eyes Kelly and her baby were a problem to be gotten rid of.

But why was he following me? Had Kelly already been running when he tried to track her down? She had all her bags packed when I met with her at the hotel. Maybe he tracked me down in hopes that I would lead him to her. And I did.

Somehow, I knew Carl wasn't trying to kill me. Carl is many things. He is a liar, a cheater, an abusive piece of shit, maybe, but not a killer. Knowing that seems to give me the

Wrong Girl Gone

courage I need to go to the house and get Jerry back, even if it means taking him right from Carl himself.

I've probably walked four miles this afternoon, but by some miracle, my feet don't even hurt. Or if they do, I don't feel it. All I can think about is having Jerry back in my arms. I miss everything about him. I miss his little hands, his blond hair, his big, curious eyes. I even miss his smell. He smells like the anti-tear kids' shampoo I use to wash his hair. That and peanut butter.

It's dark when I arrive in the neighborhood. I stop walking and listen. It's just as quiet as it always was. It's cooler than when Clay and I were here, the kind of night on which I might have bundled Jerry up and taken him for a walk or out for a hot chocolate. All the houses look the same as they always have, yet I feel like I'm only seeing them for the first time.

The closer I get to the house, the more I tell myself it isn't too late, I can still run away. Only I'm sick of running. So, this time I don't run. I walk up to the familiar front door, feeling out of place as I reach up and ring the doorbell. I have a speech ready to go that I replayed on my walk over. It involves such zingers as *You could never love Jerry as much as I do, you fucking asshole,* and *Don't you ever come near me or my son again, shit head.*

But it's gone the moment Carl opens the door. I take in a sharp breath, searching for even five words to string together and spit at him, but nothing comes. All my words are lost when I see his eyes. They aren't at all what I had expected. They aren't fiery or enraged. They aren't drunk and crazy. They're filled with tears.

He stares at me in what can only be described as utter disbelief. "Joy? It can't be…. It's you."

With that, he pulls me into his arms, holding me tighter than I can ever remember him holding me before. My body stiffens and my mind goes blank. We just stand there, in this bizarre, one-sided hug. I have no clue what to think or feel. He'd thought I was dead. He really thought I was dead.

228

Finally, he pulls away, wiping his face. "I'm sorry," he says. "Come in, please." He reaches for my arm and I flinch. He pulls his hand away and holds it up in surrender. "Sorry. Please." He steps back, leaving a clear path into the house. I remind myself of my plan and step over the threshold.

"Where's—" I clear my throat. "Where is he?"

"I put him to bed a little early. He was fussy and tired." He sits down in his easy chair and motions for me to join him in the living room. I take a seat on the couch, still stiff and uncertain. "He's missed you so much, Joy. The other day he even came home saying he'd seen you at school. I didn't know what to make of it, except that he must have missed you so much he was just trying to cope the best way he knew how."

I nod my head, my guard still up. Way up. "I want him back," I say.

Carl leans forward in his chair, a look of concern on his face. "You never lost him, baby. He's always been yours." He reaches his hand out and takes mine. "He's always been ours."

"Why are you being this way?" I feel my eyes filling with tears. "Why are you being so nice to me?"

He pulls his hand away and takes a deep breath. I see a flash of that old anger in his eyes, but it disappears as he exhales. Then he takes a long look at me before finally speaking.

"I'm a changed man, Joy," he says. "I haven't had a drink in five days. I know it's not much, but it's a start. I know I haven't always treated you and Jerry the best. I've lost control, I've lied, I've hurt you... And honestly, I'm so ashamed of all of it. You had every right to take that money. I earned it gambling, which I shouldn't have been doing. I was trying to rack up a big enough amount to buy you a new car or fix up our house... maybe even take you on a vacation. But I should have been honest with you about it. Of course you ran away. I'm surprised you didn't run away sooner."

Wrong Girl Gone

He wipes his eyes, rubbing the bridge of his nose. I've never known him to use crocodile tears before, but I wouldn't put it past him.

"Thinking that you were dead almost killed me. Now, I know, you probably have a long story to tell me about what happened to you, and I want to hear every word. But, right now, I'm just so grateful that you're here. Not only that you're alive, but that you chose to come back to me."

"I didn't come back for you. I came back for Jerry."

Carl hangs his head, nodding slowly. "That's fair." He stands up from his chair and gets down on his knees in front of me. "Joy, please. You have a million reasons to take Jerry and leave me forever. If you want to do that—if you want to go upstairs, get Jerry, and walk out that door—I wouldn't stop you. I would understand completely. But Joy—" He takes my hand again, this time with both of his, and looks up at me. "I love you. I love Jerry. And I promise if you stay with me, things are going to be different. I promise."

I feel like I'm suddenly thrown into a parallel universe with no idea how I got there or how to get out. Before I can speak, I hear the sweetest voice in the whole world call from upstairs, "Daddy?"

I stand up instantly. I can't wait another minute to see him. If any part of what Carl just said is true, he'll understand that. "Jerry?" I walk over to the stairs, and that's when I see him, standing on the top step, holding onto the railing with one hand and his blankie with the other. "Baby, it's me. It's Mama."

"Mama?"

"Yeah, baby, it's me." I wait at the bottom of the stairs, fighting every instinct I have to run up the stairs two at a time and scoop him into my arms.

He looks at me for a moment, trying to figure me out. Then, one step at a time, he walks down the stairs, moving faster the closer he gets to the bottom until he's finally right in front of me. Before he can reach out those tiny hands of his, I wrap my arms around him and hold him close.

"I missed you so much," he says, his voice muffled against my shoulder.

I hold him tighter, soaking up every ounce I can of that shampoo and peanut butter smell. "I missed you too, baby," I say into the crook of his neck. That's when the tears come. I don't have the strength to stop them. "So, so much."

I close my eyes and let myself forget about everything around me, even Carl. Even though I can feel him watching us, I'm not afraid of him. Maybe it's because I have the upper hand for once. Or maybe it's because, in some sick way, this is how we're supposed to be. The three of us. This house. This life.

I've grown up without a father, and with a mother who was physically present but not always mentally. As dysfunctional as my family was, they were still my family. And I would have given anything to have us all under the same roof. Maybe that's what I need to do for Jerry. Maybe this is my chance to start over. Clay is gone, and as much as I want to think he'll come back, a big part of me knows he won't. Our lives are too different. But with Carl... our lives are the same. We've made them the same, whether we should have or not. We're tied by more than just marriage. We're tied by the little boy in my arms. And maybe that's all we need. Maybe that's enough.

More than anything, I want it to be enough.

***

Within hours, I find myself starting to feel like I'm actually home again. Like I've just returned from a trip to a new, more hopeful life. When I check the fridge, there are no beers. The bottles still brim the garbage can, but as far as I can tell, there are no more bottles in the trash than there had been when Clay and I were there. Maybe he is sober. Maybe he is trying.

Part of me wants to test the waters just enough to see how sincere Carl is, but the waters don't seem to be disturbed very easily. He doesn't even say a word when I tell him I need to

231

make a call to John. He just kisses me on the temple and goes upstairs.

"You sure you don't want me to come pick you up?" John asks when I tell him I'm going to stay another night at the hotel.

"I'm sure. I'll try to give you a call tomorrow." I hate lying to John. I know I should tell him where I am, but everything still feels so surreal, and I don't want to lose that feeling just yet.

"Call me if you need anything," he says, and we hang up.

I think Carl wants me to stay up and talk with him and tell him my story, but I just don't have the strength. I tuck Jerry in and tell Carl I want to turn in early. I let him know that I don't feel comfortable sharing a bed with him again yet, so he offers to sleep on the couch.

I lay in my bed feeling like I'm in a hotel, even though I've spent the past several nights in a hotel that was just starting to feel like home. I feel unsure of so many things right now, I don't know where to start. To be honest, I'm not even sure if I'm making the right decision in staying with Carl or if I'm just being guided blindly through the darkness. Either way, I'm here now, so I try to pretend I'm myself, in my home, with my life, even though I feel like a stranger in my own bed.

Chapter Thirty-Three

I thought going back to my life would be difficult, but for some reason, it's much too easy. The day after I get back, I spend about four hours cleaning the house and scrubbing down the kitchen. Before when I was gone even for one night to visit Kelly or work a double, I'd come home to a disaster of a house. Like Carl was literally incapable of cleaning. He does apologize for the mess this time and offers to help. But we clearly have different definitions of clean, so I tell him, no, thank you.

Since the rest of Jasper still thinks Joy is dead, and I haven't exactly told Carl that I'd assisted in the murder of "my" killer, I simply let him know that I want to lie low for a while. That he isn't allowed to tell anyone that I'm home until I figure out how I want to move forward with everything that's happened. I keep most of my story to myself. I just tell him about Kelly and the man in the woods. That a kind stranger helped me after finding me on the side of the road. That Clay was nothing more than that. A kind stranger.

I invite Mama over late that morning while Carl is at work and Jerry is at school. And as painful as it is, I tell her about Kelly, even though part of me feels like she already knew. Still, we cry together. Her heavy sobs break my heart, but we hold each other through it.

Wrong Girl Gone

"Things are never going to be the same, are they?" she cries. We both know they won't.

Part of me is afraid to let Mama leave, but her afternoon shift at the bank will at least help distract her from the pain. Once she's gone, I put on a hoodie, pull up the hood, and dart past Fiona, narrowly avoiding her gaze as she waters her azaleas. Then I walk to John's house to pay him the visit I owe him, hoping that seeing him will help me cope with the pain. Despite the fact that I'm now sharing the pain with Mama, it only hurts more.

When I knock on John's door, a man I don't recognize answers. He's holding a cup of coffee, wearing a red dress robe, and his head is bare except for a brightly colored tattoo on the left side of it. He looks young, too. Younger than John and a bit better looking.

He extends his free hand, an intense smile on his face, as though wanting it to rub off on me. "You must be Joy. I'm Paul."

"Nice to meet you, Paul. John's said only the best things about you." I smile back. I'm glad Paul seems nice. John deserves someone nice.

He welcomes me in and lets John know I'm here. I always feel safe at John's house. Even though it's probably from the forties, it's still one of the newer ones in the area. And it's clean. Not *My Daddy Clean*. But clean.

John comes downstairs wearing jeans, a polo shirt, and his thick, black glasses that are as clean as the house. He walks up and hugs me, squeezing me just tight enough to make me feel loved, but not quite tight enough to break me. I've always loved John's hugs.

He and Paul make me a cup of coffee in the kitchen while I hang around the living room, hoping to catch a glimpse of happiness in my fog as I peer at the two of them through the doorway. John hasn't had the best luck with relationships in his life. He dated a man a few years ago who'd cheated on him and stolen his bicycle. It's a long story that I've heard in detail more than a few times. He tries harder and harder to figure out what he did wrong every time he tells the story. And every time, I assure him he hadn't done anything except own a nice bicycle.

John steps back into the living room and hands me a cup of coffee. "I made up the guest bed for you," he says. "I've got an extra pillow too if you need it."

"Thanks, John. I appreciate that," I hold the handle of my cup tightly but don't take a sip. "But I actually won't be needing to stay over anymore." John lowers his cup, looking at me. "I... I'm staying at home. With Jerry. And Carl."

I rarely see John angry, but right then fire flashes in his eyes. Paul, who's standing in the doorway sipping his coffee, seems to note the tension in the room because he promptly excuses himself to take a shower.

John leads me to the couch where we both sit. "You know I'm not one to judge," he says. "But, Joy, what the hell are you doing?"

Even though I really don't have a valid excuse, aside from Jerry, I do my best to explain my current mindset, including everything that's happened over the past few days. He sits there, letting his coffee turn cold, nodding through most of my story, only looking at me for half. When I tell him we were the ones responsible for the death of Norman Lance, John frowns.

"You get rid of any evidence? Any shred of anything they'd be able to trace?" John says when I finish.

"I left some of my hair behind in his van."

"Same DNA as Kelly."

"Yeah."

John nods his head for a moment, taking it all in. "But even with everything that's happened... Why do you wanna stay with Carl?"

"Jerry deserves a normal childhood. He deserves both his parents. I spent too much of my life resenting my daddy for leaving us, resenting my mama for keeping him from me. I don't want that for my son. I don't him to grow up without a father or blame me for leaving him. I want to make his life better than mine."

John takes off his glasses and rubs his eyes, then puts them back on and looks at me, his arms on his knees and his hands limp between his legs. "I remember so many days of you and me sitting here in this living room.... The horror stories you'd tell me about Carl. It took all my strength to stop myself from going over there and hurting that man so badly...." He stands up and walks over to the window as he talks. "You know me. I find a spider crawling across my counter and I pick him up with a piece of paper and put him outside. But I couldn't help myself with him. He brings out the worst in people. He always has. Brought out the worst in you too. I think you just learned how to hide it after a while. You deserve better."

"I'm going to stay with him, John. I've made up my mind."

"Why? Why not Clay?"

"Clay isn't real. He's just an idea."

"He seemed pretty real to me."

"Our lives are just too different. Besides, Carl isn't the worst person in the world. And he's trying. He's quit drinking, he's being nice to me. And Clay and I are no saints. We killed Norman."

"That was self-defense. He would have killed you. He killed Kelly. Clay did the right thing. We do that. We fight and we hurt, and we kill, and we do things we never would have thought of doing before. I would have done the exact same thing he did. We do that for the people we love."

The words hit my ears and ring them like a bell. "What? No," I say quickly. "He doesn't feel that way."

"Just because one man in your life says he loves you, then beats you till you're black and blue, doesn't mean they all will."

"Clay doesn't love me. And if he does, he shouldn't. I'm not worth it."

"Sweetie," John tilts my chin toward him. "If you're not worth it, why are so many wonderful people in your life coming out of the woodwork to help you at a time like this? Saying you're not worth it pretty much puts everything we've all done in the dumpster, doesn't it?" He waits for me to answer, but I don't. I feel so much younger than I am. Twenty-two seemed like a lifetime away when I was sixteen. Now it feels exactly the same as a thousand yesterdays ago. Sitting here on the sofa, I'm just a kid. "But it's none of my business," he says. "It's your life. If Carl is what you want and what you feel you deserve, then I want you to be happy."

I nod, but the action feels detached from my mind. "You know what I wish sometimes?" I say. "I wish I'd never changed my name to Larson. I always liked Elliot better."

"Joy Elliot. I like it," he smiles at me. For a moment, I feel light. "You gave up a lot for him, didn't you?"

"Yeah. Everything. From my virginity to my identity to my whole life." I suddenly feel very heavy again. Guilt will do that to you. "I slept with Clay," I say finally.

John takes a deep breath. "Yeah. I gathered."

"I cheated on Carl. I promised myself so many times I'd never do the same things to him he'd done to me. I promised myself that."

"Yeah, but how can you punish yourself for doing the exact same thing he did to you?"

"Because I need to be better than that. He and I are trying to start a new life. I don't want the past to repeat itself. I don't want Clay to be my Rachel."

"Rachel?"

"Rachel Warner. She was the first one Carl cheated on me with. That I knew about, anyway." I finish off the last swig of my coffee.

"Wait, wait—Rachel Warner?" he repeats, looking at me like I've just cursed God himself.

"Yeah?" He's making me nervous.

"Joy, Rachel Warner is dead."

"What? When did she die?"

Wrong Girl Gone

"A few years ago, before you and I met. It was a huge deal in Jasper. I don't know how you couldn't have heard about it." John's eyes light up and he looks a bit crazed. "I think I still have the newspaper article." He gets up and runs up the stairs. I hardly ever read the paper but seeing everything that's been going on around me lately makes me think I need to start. We always get it, every Sunday, and Carl reads it from the first page to the last. Then he'll inform me of the biggest news of the week. Usually, the most exciting story consists of an old lady who wins Bingo champion for the third time in a month or a little boy who gets a medal for rescuing a cat from a tree. Jasper isn't exactly hopping with the thrilling news of crimes or murder.

John comes downstairs with a page from the paper crinkling in his hand. I've never been so thankful for his hoarding tendencies. I skim the article as John talks.

"She was found in her home over in Carlisle. They said she bled to death, and at first, it looked like she'd tried to give herself an abortion. Then they found bruises. It happened on Christmas Day, 1985," John says, pointing to the paper.

"How did I not hear about this?"

John shrugs. "How many people do you talk to in this town?"

I try to think back to Christmas of 1985. Jerry was just over a year, and I hadn't gone back to work yet. Carl preferred me to stay home and we weren't as strapped for cash. Sure, I talked with Fiona once in a while, or occasionally the checker when I went to the store, but aside from Carl and Mama, I didn't talk to many folks. I do recall overhearing a conversation in a grocery store about a poor girl who had turned up dead in her home, but I never caught her name. I never knew it was her. The death of the woman Carl had an affair with was the kind of news that would have been worth mentioning over the breakfast table the day it appeared in the paper.

"Carl was with us all day that Christmas," I say, convincing myself more than John.

"Just because he has an alibi doesn't mean he's innocent."

I nearly knock the coffee table over as I stand. "It's not possible," I say. "Carl may be a lot of things, but he's not a killer."

"How do you know? How do you know he wasn't trying to kill you?"

"Kelly was pregnant. Okay? She probably had an affair with one of her professors like she did in the past and got herself into trouble. When the guy's marriage was threatened, he hired someone to off her."

"I know you want to stay loyal to Carl and make this work, but don't you think this is just a little too coincidental? Do you know whose baby it was that Kelly was carrying?"

"What are you saying?"

"Carl had affairs. So did Kelly. What if—"

"Don't you dare." It's the first time I'm ever, truly furious with John. My heart pounds in my ears, the back of my throat burning. "Don't you dare finish that sentence."

I turn and storm out of the house, ignoring John's pleas, ignoring Paul's eyes that follow me blankly down the driveway, ignoring any thoughts I have about Carl being a killer. When I know I'm far enough away that they can no longer see me, I sit down on the curb and try to get my legs to stop shaking so I can walk the rest of the way home.

Jerry still has two hours left of school, and Carl won't be home until at least six. With my head pounding and my mind whirling, all I want to do is lay down. But no sooner do I walk through the front door does the phone start ringing. I let the machine pick up, and John's voice fills the empty silence in the house.

"Joy? Are you there?" He pauses. "If you're there, please pick up the phone. I just want to talk. Please?" He pauses again. "Okay, well... Give me a call when you can. Thanks."

As soon as he hangs up, I press the erase button. Not just because I'm mad, but because I know how Carl will react hearing a message from John on the machine. At least I know how Old Carl would react. Maybe New Carl is different, but I don't want to risk finding out.

I take an aspirin with a glass of water and massage my temples, but nothing seems to help. So, I decide to do something I never would have done when living with Old Carl. I go upstairs, set my alarm, and lay down on the bed. With the streams of the afternoon sun peeking through the window, I'm almost positive I won't be able to sleep. But I guess I surprise even myself sometimes because within minutes I'm out cold.

Chapter Thirty-Four

I'm walking through the side streets of Jasper. It's either dawn or twilight, I can't quite make out which. The air is so still, it feels like I'm indoors. I continue walking down the middle of the street. Normally, I'd be worried about cars, but there don't seem to be any cars for miles.

As I approach our home, I stop at the end of the driveway. There's a light on in our living room, which is strange because I didn't think anyone was home. A shadow passes over the window and a moment later, I hear strange noises coming from the house. Something tells me I shouldn't go inside. I walk up to the side of the house and attempt to peer in through the window, but the curtain obscures my view. Still, the noises are getting louder. It sounds like moaning, crying. Something isn't right. I need to go inside. I need to see what's wrong.

I barge through the front door and that's when I see them: Carl and Kelly are on the floor of our living room, entangled. I can't see Kelly's face, but I can tell they're both completely naked. I scream, and Carl looks up at me. He grins but doesn't stop what he's doing. I want to run forward and pull him off her, but I can't seem to move. He keeps staring at me, smiling. I scream again, but he just smiles wider. I'm finally able to get a good look at Kelly's face. Her eyes are lifeless, her jaw swinging loosely. She's dead. He's fucking her… and she's dead.

Wrong Girl Gone

I try to run at him, but I'm still frozen. I try to scream, but this time all that comes out is hot air. I am paralyzed. I am helpless. All I can do is watch.

***

My eyes shoot open like window blinds. I swing my arm through the air, disoriented by the darkness, until I find my alarm clock and turn it towards me: 6:47 PM. I forgot to pick up Jerry from school and Carl is going to be home any minute if he isn't already. I throw my legs over the side of the bed and drunkenly make my way out of the room and downstairs.

In the kitchen, Jerry is sitting at the table and Carl is cooking something at the stove. I shuffle into the doorway, staring at them stupidly.

"What's going on?" I mumble.

Carl turns to me. "Hey! Look who's up." I can't tell if his voice is sincere or dripping with sarcasm.

"Mama was tired," Jerry says.

"I can see that."

I feel tears brimming in my eyes. "I'm sorry." I'm sobbing now. "I'm so sorry. I set the alarm; I swear—"

"Baby, why are you crying?" Carl walks over to me.

"I forgot to pick up Jerry from school. I didn't start supper—"

Carl laughs. Not in a mean way, just like he's genuinely surprised by what I'm saying. "Baby, it's okay." He rests his hand on my cheek. "I came home early and saw you resting, so I turned off the alarm and took it upon myself to pick up Jerry so you could sleep. You've been through a lot, I bet you were exhausted."

I try to take a breath between sobs. He puts his arms around me, pulling me close. Jerry hops up from his chair and comes over to join the hug.

"Don't cry, Mama. Everything's going to be okay. Daddy's making spaghetti."

Audrey Wilson

I let myself be held by the two boys in my life, holding onto the idea that maybe everything is going to be okay.

***

After supper, I put in a load of laundry while Carl watches TV and Jerry plays with his cars on the living room floor. Finally, everything is starting to feel normal. Everything except that dream reeling in my head and the conversation with John replaying in my ears. Those things outweigh any feeling of normalcy I have.

"Five more minutes, baby. Then you need to brush your teeth and get ready for bed," I say to Jerry on my way upstairs with the laundry. As I pass the kitchen, I see the small TV on the counter is on and make to turn it off, when I catch a glimpse of the news headline.

DNA of Joy Larson found in deceased man's van, linking him to her death.

I keep my eyes on the screen and turn the volume down just in case Carl can hear it from the living room. The images they're showing are unrelated, so I must have missed the main story, but I still see enough. Our plan worked. It actually worked. It's all I can do not to call Clay, but then I realize that I don't even have his number. I couldn't call him if I wanted to. And I do want to, so badly. He would have known exactly how to respond to the news about Rachel Warner. I try to imagine what he'd say. Would he have agreed with John and thought everything just seemed too coincidental? Or would he tell me I was thinking about it too much and that Carl wasn't a killer? I have a hard time knowing if what I thought he would say is just what I would have wanted him to say.

Before my hand can touch the dial on the TV, I feel two hands on my waist and scream. I quickly shut off the TV and turn towards Carl.

"Jesus, baby. You okay?"

"Yeah, sorry. You just startled me."

243

Wrong Girl Gone

He looks down his nose at me, half a grin on his face. I can't tell if his expression is playful or suspicious. When I speak, I do my best to sound casual, hoping to tip Carl's mood fully over to playful.

I push the basket of laundry at him, smiling flirtatiously. "Since you're here."

He looks down at the basket and for a moment I think I've made a mistake. Then he smiles. "All right, all right.... I'll help."

We go up to the bedroom, dump the clean clothes on the bed and begin folding. I separate Jerry's underwear from Carl's while he begins sorting socks. We stand there in silence for a moment before he speaks again.

"I really missed you, you know," he says. I smile, suddenly oddly uncomfortable. "Can I ask you something?"

"What is it?"

He rubs his face. "That guy you said helped you out when you were injured…"

I feel my heart begin to race again. "What about him?"

"Anything ever happen between you two?" he says. "I just… I don't want to be made to look like a fool, Joy. You understand?"

I shake my head. "Of course nothing happened."

"Swear it," he says. "Swear on my life."

"I swear."

"Swear on Jerry's life."

I hesitate. Even though deep down I know words don't have that kind of power, I'm still superstitious. "Carl, you know I hate doing that—"

"Swear on his life, Joy."

I discreetly cross my fingers at my side and look into Carl's eyes without blinking. "I swear."

He lets out a long breath. "Good. I know I've made some mistakes in the past, but I hope you know that's all they were. Mistakes."

"Yeah," I say. "I know."

Carl walks around behind me and puts his arms around my waist. "That's my girl," he says, kissing my neck. "You know, it has been a while…"

He kisses it more, pulling the collar of my t-shirt off to the side to kiss my shoulder. I feel my body stiffen, as much as I try to relax. This is what I want. I want to start a new life with him. I want a stable home life for Jerry. I want Carl to dote on me and desire me the way he did when we were first together. And yet, as much as I want to enjoy it, his touch only makes me squirm.

"Maybe we can hold off on the physical stuff for a while," I whisper. He's in the middle of kissing my neck when I speak, and I can feel his jaw clench against my skin.

"If that's what you want," he says. "I just figured you'd miss what you haven't had in so long."

He slides his hand under my shirt, caressing the skin around my waist. I feel like I'm being tested, like he's checking if I really have been faithful to him these past few weeks.

"Carl, please—"

"Mama, I brushed my teeth!" Jerry calls from the other room.

I swallow. "I'll be there in a minute, baby."

Before I can walk to the door, Carl grabs my wrist. "Hurry back," he says. I nod and leave the room.

Jerry is sitting on the floor of his room, surrounded by several toys. Within reach are his Etch-A-Sketch, a Slinky, a model DeLorean complete with a mini-Doc Brown, a broken Transformer, and one of his favorites, his primary-colored toy voice recorder. It's no surprise that he's tinkering with it then, taking the last few seconds before bed to play. I love that about him—his endless imagination and sense of wonder. I pray he never loses it.

"That's all for tonight, folks!" he says into his little microphone. "See you next week!"

"Sounds like you had a good show tonight," I say.

Wrong Girl Gone

"Can I interview you tomorrow?" he says as I lead him into bed and tuck him in.

"What would you interview me about?"

"Everything that happened. Your adventure."

I let out a breath. "I don't know if Mama's ready to talk about that yet, baby."

"Oh," he says. "Maybe another time?"

"We'll see." I kiss him on the forehead and brush his hair off his face. There's a knot in my stomach and I wonder if there's one in his too. "Baby, can I ask you a question?" He nods his head. "That night in the hotel room, when we were with Kiki and I went to get dinner…" I swallow hard. "Do you remember what happened?"

Jerry looks down at the Hot Wheels car in his hands. "There was a knock at the door and Kiki answered it. A man pushed through the door and I got scared and hid under the bed. Just like when Daddy's drunk."

The very thought of Jerry being in the same room as that horrible man sends shivers down my spine, but I try to push past it. "Did he see you?"

"I don't think so."

"Then what happened?"

"There was a lot of noise. She tried to yell for help. I didn't know what to do. Then it stopped and everything got quiet. But I just stayed under the bed." He looks carefully at his car and I can tell he's trying not to cry. "I'm sorry."

"Baby, you have nothing to be sorry for. You did the right thing, staying under the bed."

He looks up at me. "Yeah?"

"Yeah."

He nods and looks back at his car. "Mama?"

"Hmm?"

"I miss Kiki."

"I know," I say. "I miss her too."

"We didn't spend enough time together when she visited last. Why did she have to leave so soon?"

"I think she just had to get back home quickly."

246

"Not because she was mad at Daddy?"

"What do you mean, she was mad at Daddy?"

"They had a fight the night before she left. When you were working."

I think back to that night. I'd had to pick up an overnight shift at the diner last time Kelly was visiting and she left abruptly the next morning. "Did you hear them fighting?"

Jerry nods his head and I suddenly get the feeling there's something he doesn't want to tell me. But he always tells me everything.

"Baby, what happened?"

"I don't want Daddy to get in trouble."

I glance at the door to make sure Carl isn't nearby. Then I lower my voice. "He's not going to get in trouble," I whisper. "Tell me what happened."

"I'd been sleeping, and I heard noises downstairs, so I tip-toed to see what was happening. Kiki was saying Daddy was drunk again and she started to leave but then Daddy grabbed her and pulled her down."

"Pulled her down where?"

"He pulled her onto the couch, and he had his hand over her mouth. I think he was just trying to get her to stay."

My mouth has gone dry. "What happened next?" Jerry looks away, silent.

"I don't remember," he says.

"Please try, baby."

"Daddy bumped the table and knocked over the lamp. Kiki tried to leave again but he pulled her back and that's when I ran back to my room. I covered my ears, but I still heard the noises."

"What noises?"

"Just thump, thump, thump noises. I think he just didn't want her to leave."

I pull my son into my arms, so he won't see the tears in my eyes. I rub the back of his head firmly with my hand, so he won't feel my fingers trembling. I even try to slow my heart rate, so he won't feel it pounding in my chest, but it's an impossible task.

"Did Daddy do something bad?" Jerry whispers into my shoulder.

I kiss him on the head. "We can talk about it more tomorrow. Okay, baby? No matter what, you have nothing to worry about."

Jerry nods and I lay his head down on the pillow, giving him a final kiss goodnight before turning off the light and heading for the door. I've barely walked three steps when my bare foot kicks something hard and plastic. Instantaneously, there's a muffled crackling, and a recording of Jerry's voice fills the room.

"We will be right back after a short bathroom break!"

I stumble around in the darkness, looking for the tape recorder.

"Did you break it?" Jerry says.

"No, I got it—" I pick up the tape recorder and search for the stop button. Before I can press it, I hear Carl's voice, very faintly, coming through the speaker.

"You were supposed to come back as soon as it was done."

I immediately press *stop*, frozen.

"Mama, what is it?"

"Nothing, baby. You get some sleep, okay? I'm just going to take your recorder and make sure I didn't break it. Goodnight, baby."

"Goodnight, Mama."

I shut the door as quietly as I can and make my way down the hall into the bathroom, shutting and locking the door behind me. I turn on the water in the sink and press *rewind* on the recorder for a few seconds, then hit *play*. I turn the volume down as low as possible, press it to my ear, and listen.

"Good afternoon, ladies and gents," Jerry's voice says. "My name is Jerry Larson, and I will be your host for today. We're going to start off our show with a word from our sponsor, Pop-Tarts." He changes his voice into a high-pitched falsetto. "Hi, I'm Pop-Tarts. Buy me because I'm delicious and made with real fruit." He brings his voice back to normal, and I hear the phone ring faintly in the background. "Now, we will be right back after a short bathroom break."

With a soft thud, he leaves the room. All I hear is static coming through the speaker. Then the phone rings again, and I hear Carl's voice answer it. His voice gets closer, and I know he's standing in the hall just outside Jerry's room. When he speaks, it's in a whisper.

"Jesus, Norman, what the hell is wrong with you? You were supposed to come back as soon as it was done." My heart stops and my ears hang on every word, pressing the recorder's speaker even closer to my ear. "Did you get to her before she talked to Joy?" There is a pause. "You think so? What do you mean, *you think so?* The whole fucking point was to get to her before she told Joy. If it's her sister's word against mine, we know who she'd believe. Besides, she won't get rid of the thing herself so she's leaving me no choice. You think I want to do this?" Another pause. "Just—" he lowers his voice. "Don't hurt Joy. Got it? Now get back here with the money and I'll give you your share."

Jerry's voice calls for his dad from a thousand miles away.

"Call me when it's done," Carl says quickly and hangs up the phone.

"Daddy, who are you talking to?"

"Telemarketer," Carl mumbles. "Clean up some of this mess, will you? It's a pigsty in here." Carl's voice fades as he leaves the room.

Jerry picks up the microphone again and speaks into it. "Aaaaand, we're back!" I press stop because I've heard all I need to hear. My body feels like iron, my eyes like glass. I don't think I'll ever be able to breathe again. With slippery palms, I hold onto the voice recorder like it's keeping me alive. I try to find comfort in knowing that I had been right about one thing: Carl never intended to kill me. In his own sick, twisted way, he does love me. He loves Jerry. It was never us he was after. It was always her. It was always Kelly.

Wrong Girl Gone

I remember my dream and what my daddy had said about his own dreams. That they were always so vivid, he felt like they were trying to tell him something. It doesn't take much to see that mine were trying to tell me something today. And as I connect the dots, for the first time since I got home, I really, truly hate Carl. And I hate myself almost as much for thinking for one second that he could have been anything more than the scum he's always been.

There is a knock on the bathroom door that nearly gives me a stroke. "Baby, you okay?"

I turn off the running water. "Just a second," I squeak, my voice abnormally high-pitched. I lamely hide the recorder behind my back and open the door. "Hey, sorry. I was just cleaning up."

"What's that behind your back?"

"Oh. This?" I hold the recorder in front of me. "I stepped on it when I was putting Jerry to bed and just wanted to make sure I didn't break it."

"Why'd you bring it into the bathroom?"

"Better lighting," I say. "Jerry was trying to sleep, so I didn't want to bother him by turning on the lights."

"Well, let me take a look at it—" He reaches for the recorder, but I pull it away.

"No," I say, too quickly. "I checked. It's fine. I'm just going to put it back in his room and then we can... get to bed." I try to say it suggestively enough to distract him, but not suggestively enough that I'm promising anything. As I put the recorder back in Jerry's room, I swiftly eject the tape and hide it in the back of his sock drawer until I know there's a time that I can safely retrieve it.

That time, I decide, is going to be tonight.

Chapter Thirty-Five

When Carl comes into the bedroom after saying goodnight to Jerry, I tell him that I'm really tired and just want to sleep. It's the only tried and true way I've ever usually been able to get out of sex. I say "usually" because I've experienced times Carl wouldn't take "no" for an answer. And apparently, Kelly has too. The thought is enough to churn my stomach, but I thank God that saying I was tired worked this time. When he leans over and kisses me on the cheek with stubble on his chin, I have to bite my tongue to keep from screaming. Instead, I just let out a calm breath that I turn into quiet snores.

Rain starts hitting the windows just as Carl drifts off to sleep. My heart thumps in my throat as I wait for the steady sounds of his snoring to fill the room. They start out as heavy breaths. When he finally starts to sound like a grizzly bear in deep hibernation, I lift the covers off and pull my trembling body out of bed.

I fumble around silently in the dark, holding my breath the whole time. I pull on the same jeans I've been wearing for the past week and gather the few items I can. Mostly dirty clothes I've acquired during my adventure with Clay because those are easy to grab. As I start to zip my bag, Carl makes a particularly loud snort, causing my fingers to slip and my knees to almost give out. He rolls over and is completely silent for five painstaking seconds before the grizzly bear snores start again. I hold the bag tightly and tiptoe out of the room, playing hopscotch around the creaky floorboards.

When I finally close the bedroom door behind me, I let out a breath. I probably shouldn't let myself breathe yet, but I know I might pass out if I don't. I step into the bathroom and splash my face with cold water to keep from fainting. Then I creep into Jerry's room. Before waking him, I gather a few clothes and toys I know are his favorites and stuff those into my bag too. Then I walk over to his bed and gently rub his shoulder to wake him. His eyes flutter open and he yawns. "What time is it?"

"It's really early, honey. I need you to be very quiet, okay? We're going on another adventure."

"Like the last adventure we went on?"

"Better."

I scoop him into my arms, then go over to his sock drawer and reach my hand to the back of it, feeling around for the hard plastic of the tape. But I don't feel it. I open the drawer wider, my left arm going numb from Jerry's weight and my right shaking and sweaty as it searches for the evidence that's no longer there.

"Baby, did you take a tape out of your sock drawer?"

"What tape?"

"From your tape recorder. Did you take it out?"

"No," he fusses.

I feel tears coming and fight them down. I carry Jerry out of the room and down the stairs in the dark. Because now I have a new goal. Get the hell out of this house.

"Come on, baby, put on your shoes quick—"

"Forget something?" The hall light flips on and there stands Carl, waving the tape in his hand like he's preparing to do a magic trick and make it disappear. "Where you running off to this time, Joy?"

I shake my head, searching for words I'll never find.

Carl walks over to us. Instinct overcomes me and I step in front of Jerry, shielding him. "You hurt me so bad, baby. One little hiccup in our relationship and you're ready to run out the door again. We're never going to make this work if you don't talk to me. If you don't trust me." He holds up a bottle of newly opened Jack Daniels and I wonder if he was keeping it in our bedroom. "See this?" he says. "You did this to me. One fucking week of sobriety and you did this to me." He takes a long swig and wipes the remaining drops of alcohol off his chin. "I want you to know that."

"Jerry, go upstairs."

Without a word, he runs upstairs. I take a step towards the staircase just in case Carl tries to go after him. But he doesn't. He just takes another drink before stepping towards me.

"I would never, ever hurt him," he says, his voice shaking. "I'm not even going to hurt you. That's all behind me."

And yet my body is still a canvas of bruises and scars. Bruises and scars that Carl was capable of giving me even from hundreds of miles away.

He holds the tape again, his hand shaking. "Jesus Christ, Joy, you didn't even give me a chance to explain."

"Fine," I say, trying to buy time. "Explain."

He takes another drink, a slave to the poison in his hand. My eyes dart to the tape, racking my brain for a way to get it, get Jerry, and get out.

"I fucked up," he says simply. The smell of alcohol on his breath is growing stronger with every swig, and I have to fight the urge to vomit. "But I don't think you know the full story. You remember the last time she came to visit? And you had to work that overnight shift?"

"Yes." You're goddamn right I remember it. Jerry's story has been playing like a video in my head since he told it to me.

"Well, I was just being a good host, trying to entertain her. We were having some wine and she started crying about how she didn't want to go back to school. She was real upset, so I was trying to comfort her, give her words of encouragement, you know… Well, the next thing I know, she's throwing herself at me. It was probably the alcohol talking, but she would not let me be. I tried to tell her no. I swear to God, I did. But…. And you're not going to want to hear this…"

"I think I can take it."

He takes a deep breath. "She said if I didn't have sex with her, she'd tell you I raped her."

Although I can still smell the Jack Daniels, this time it's his words that make me want to vomit. "Did she now?" I hold my cool, but inside I feel a twinge of uncertainty, which I hate myself for. "So, you had to kill her?"

"Baby, she got pregnant. What the hell was I supposed to do? She was going to tell you that I raped her. Probably because she felt so guilty about the damn thing. I tried to talk some sense into her, but she wouldn't have it. She's always been out to get me. I should have known she'd pull something like this. But, Joy, you have to believe me…. When Norman said he'd left you for dead in those woods, I almost killed him. I swear to God, he wasn't to lay a finger on you." My eyes almost shift to the tape, Carl's voice ringing in my ears. *Don't hurt Joy…* "But my whole world fell apart when I thought you were dead. It was all I could do to keep a stiff lip for Jerry, telling him that his mom would be home any day now, trying to give both of us hope."

"If you really didn't want anything to happen to me," I say, steadying my voice, "why did you send a killer after me?"

"He wasn't after you! He was after Kelly!" He says, like his argument makes perfect sense. "Listen, I know, I should have told you what happened from the beginning, but…." His eyes fill with tears, and this time I'm certain they're fake. He takes my hand in his, bringing me that much closer to the tape. "Baby, I couldn't lose you."

"Fine," I say. My eyes flash to the tape again. "What happened with Rachel Warner?"

Carl groans and rubs his face again. "Nothing. She was nothing. She meant nothing to me."

"So you killed her?"

He takes my hand again, more urgently this time, and moves in close to me. "Joy, listen to me. I know it was wrong.

I know what I did to Kelly was wrong. But don't you get it?" He looks at me with a strange sort of passion in his eyes. I can't tell if it's determination or insanity. Then again Carl often walks a thin line between the two. In some sick, twisted way, it's the same look that made me fall in love with him. As much as I hate to admit it, I used to love the drama of our relationship. I loved the forbidden passion we shared. I loved those secret make-out sessions under the bridge by the railroad tracks. And that same love has caused me to lose so much. I'm not going to let it take another goddamn thing from me.

He takes my hand and runs his thumb over my skin. As much as it pains me, I let him. Because my hand is running over something too. It's running over the bullet from Clay's gun, forgotten in my pocket. It may not be enough to be a weapon, but it's more than enough to be a reminder. And so, I pull the trigger.

"Okay," I say.

"Okay?" His eyes brighten with relief.

I grab the tape from Carl's hand and run out the front door, leaving him somewhere between falling over and grabbing my arm. But he misses. Thank God he misses, because I need as much of a head start as I can get.

Chapter Thirty-Six

I don't think I've ever run so hard in my entire life. I didn't think my bad knee would allow me to run this fast, but somehow it does. I feel like the Flash, running down the street so fast that I probably look like a blur to anyone watching. Maybe this is what adrenaline does to you. It turns you into a superhero.

I can't hear Carl's footsteps, but I can hear his breathing. He must not be far behind me, but I don't dare look. I pray that someone will see us and call for help, but it's probably too late or too early for anyone to care.

With my heart throbbing, I take a sharp right before Fig Street, heading straight for the woods. I can't recall the last time Carl ran, and I can only hope that he's not in good enough shape to catch up to me. Moments after I take off in the new direction, I hear him yelling something at me in the distance. It sounds like something along the lines of, "Get the fuck back here!"

Once I'm in the midst of the trees, heading down a small hill, I zig-zag a bit, hoping to lose him. But he's close. I can tell when he yells again, and I can actually make out what he's saying.

"Joy! Goddamn it—Stop fucking running!"

But I don't stop running. I don't think I'll ever stop running.

My world jolts to a halt as I trip on a root, the cassette flying from my hand. As soon as my knees hit the ground, I pull myself back up, my eyes darting around frantically for the tape. In my frenzy, I catch my first glimpse of Carl's outline in the distance. He's farther behind me than I thought, but still moving towards me as fast as he can through the trees. My eyes shoot back to the ground, searching for a glimpse of the white tape in the black soil. I spot it at the base of a tree in front of me and dive for it, grabbing it as I run past.

"Joy! Get the fuck back here!" He's closer now. But I won't let him catch me. I run as hard as my damaged body will let me, pushing through the pain.

All the trees in the woods look exactly the same. The leaves, the branches, everything. I feel like I'm running in circles, steadily becoming disoriented in the darkness. My heart hurts and my legs feel like they're no longer a part of my body, but still, I keep running. I run for Jerry. I run for Kelly. And I run for myself.

I shift right, then make a sharp left. There's a clearing somewhere up ahead. I can see the moonlight illuminating the branches and leaves behind the trees. And suddenly I know exactly where I am.

When I finally burst out of the woods, I'm met with the train tracks that run through Jasper. Finally oriented, I head east towards the train tunnel. Our old stomping grounds.

With a rustle and a thump, I hear Carl emerge from the woods behind me. I steal a quick glance as I run alongside the tracks. Carl is on the ground, but he's getting up quickly. And then he's running again.

"Joy, please!" he calls. "I just want to talk with you!"

I see the tunnel up ahead, crumbling with stone beneath the road above it. I take a breath as if I'm about to go underwater, hop onto the tracks, and run inside the tunnel. "Joy!" Carl calls. His voice echoes, and I know he's in the tunnel too. In the hint of moonlight, I can see our little make-out nook. It's smaller than I remember, and only reinforces how stupid we were, thinking that was a prime spot for necking.

Wrong Girl Gone

I emerge from the tunnel and hop off the tracks, heading for the woods again. If I can make it the mile, I'll eventually run right to John's. I know I'll be safe there. And we'll go get Jerry, and then he'll be safe too.

As I duck back into the woods, it takes me a few seconds to realize I no longer hear Carl's breathing or yells behind me. I slow to a stop and turn around. No Carl.

I suddenly feel like I'm in a horror movie, and the killer is going to jump out from behind a tree with a huge knife and stab me to death. I back up into a large tree trunk and try to look in all directions at once. I hold the cassette tightly in my hand, even though it's hardly a weapon. I listen for Carl's voice, but for a moment all I hear is silence. Then he calls my name.

"Joy!" I spin my head around, but his voice is distant. "Joy, please!" he calls.

And that's when I hear it. The faint, low train whistle blowing in the distance.

"Joy! God, help me!" His loud cry is slightly echoed, and I know he's still in the tunnel.

The whistle blows again, louder this time. Closer. My heart pounds even faster than it had when I was running. I should keep running. I should run to John. I should run to Jerry. I should just keep running.

And when the whistle blows a third time, I do.

I run back to that fucking tunnel. Because Carl isn't going to die like this. Whether he deserves to or not, it isn't going to end this way. He's going to be tried. He's going to pay for what he did. The world deserves to know who he really is, what he's capable of.

I can see the train's light illuminating its path, speeding towards the tunnel. When I run back inside, Carl looks almost stunned to see me. "You came back."

He's kneeling, his steel-toed boot caught in the metal of the tracks. I run over to him and grab the edges of his foot, trying to wiggle it free. But his boots are too solid to move in the grip of the metal, and the tracks are acting as an iron clamp. The light is getting brighter, the roar louder, the train closer. "Just take it off!" I yell.

"I tried but I can't get my goddamn foot out!"

We both pull on it with all our might, but it won't budge. I glance up to see the train barreling down on us. Carl cranks his head so he can see it too. The horn blows frantically, a warning we can't heed. He looks at me, then at the make out nook.

"Carl—"

Before I can finish, he shoves me with all the strength he seems to have. I stumble backwards, falling into the nook seconds before the train hits. Seconds before the force of a hurricane storms past me with a roar so loud I think I may never hear again. Seconds before I could have died. Seconds before he's gone.

Chapter Thirty-Seven

You know that feeling when you suddenly realize you're dreaming and that realization wakes you up? I wait for that realization indefinitely inside the hospital, but it never comes. Apparently, I went into shock after the train hit. I have no recollection of the police and ambulances showing up, and I only vaguely remember being brought to the hospital. A doctor examines me and asks me a series of questions, then two officers come in and ask me another series of questions. But all I want to do is hold Jerry in my arms and sleep.

"I know it's hard for you to talk about this right now, but the fresher the memory is in your head, the better," one of the officers says to me. I tell them what I can remember, but I feel lifeless explaining it. I haven't even cried yet. I know I'm supposed to. I just feel too numb.

The second officer says something, but whatever it is doesn't register.

"Kelly?" she says. I don't correct her, just turn to face her. "Do you know why he was chasing you?" I immediately search my pocket for the tape, but it's gone. I stammer that he'd wanted to hurt me and that he wanted it back, but I must not be making much sense. She looks at me with pity, then says they're going to let me get some rest tonight and will talk to me more later this week. They just ask me to wait a little longer to retrieve Carl's things. Maybe this makes me a bad person, but I don't want his things. I just want everything to be normal. Still, I nod, my mind foggy.

Mama had gone over to the house with the police to pick up Jerry and they're going to be at the hospital soon to pick me up. I instruct her not to call me Joy until I can think clearly again. Right now, everyone thinks I'm Kelly and I'm more than okay not being myself for a while.

I watch for Mama out the window of the hospital lobby. A few cars pass by on the highway. An officer gets out of his squad car carrying a cup of coffee. It all looks normal, even though I feel anything but. All I can think about is Carl pushing me out of the way. He was so unwell, so unhealthy, that all I can pray is that maybe this is how it's supposed to end. Maybe it's the end of suffering for both of us.

I watch as our car pulls off the highway and into the hospital parking lot. There's a woman driving and a small boy in the front seat.

Almost on cue, I feel the tears beginning to come. I push open the glass door and walk outside into the brisk fall air. Jerry climbs out of his seat and out of the car before my mama can even get herself out, his blue windbreaker falling off his shoulder. He doesn't even bother to shut the door; he just runs as fast as he can towards me.

He doesn't speak, just runs. I know he would have called "Mama!" at the top of his lungs if he hadn't been instructed to not do so.

I run forward and scoop him up in my arms, sobbing into his tiny shoulder. I kiss him until my lips are dry; I spin him around and let his legs dangle outward. This life, this wonderful innocent child in my arms, is what has kept me going. He's what wakes me up every day, what makes me put one foot in front of the other. He's rescued me more times than I've ever rescued him. He is my lifesaver. He is my son.

When my body can't take it anymore, I kneel with him on the ground, still holding him in my arms. Mama comes over after a minute and holds us both. Clay suddenly appears in the front of my mind, and I cry even harder. I cry because I wouldn't be here without him, and I cry because I may never be with him again.

Jerry doesn't ask where Carl is, but I dread him doing so. How do you tell your five-year-old that their father is gone and not coming back?

"Ms. Elliot?" An officer with salt and pepper hair and a matching mustache approaches me with a small bin. I hand Jerry back to Mama and take the bin from the officer. In it is what remains of Carl's belongings: A mostly shredded wallet and his wedding ring. I don't even want to think about what the train did to the rest of him.

"Thanks," I say.

"Are you feeling well enough to be the temporary guardian of your nephew tonight? We'll help you arrange a meeting with an attorney in the morning to help take care of the rest."

"I can take him." I've stopped crying, but I'm sure my face looks like shit.

"It's going to be all right, miss," he says. I nod my head. The officer looks over at Mama and Jerry. "He's a real trooper, huh?"

"He's my grandson," Mama says, smiling through her tears.

He holds out his hand to her. "Officer Boyd."

She shakes it. "Alice," she says. Something about the sight warms my heart just the slightest.

I use the washroom before we leave the hospital, and as I'm zipping up my pants, I feel something crinkle in the back pocket. I reach in and pull out a small wad of papers; the note from Clay saying he was going to get lunch, my daddy's address, and a folded envelope with *For Joy* written on it. Kelly's letter. I haven't opened it. I emerge from the stall and open it with weary hands.

Dear Joy,

Audrey Wilson

I never thought there would be anything I couldn't tell you. Now there is, and I know I'm a coward for keeping it from you. I've felt for a long time that you should leave Carl. I've tried to be supportive, but it hurt my heart to see the way he treats you. You deserve the world, and I don't feel like he's come close to giving it to you. Still, I've tried to keep my opinions to myself (as much as I can. We are Elliots, aren't we?), for your sake and for Jerry's.

Carl's abuse goes so much deeper than I realized. When I visited last month, and you had to work late, he attacked me. I couldn't get away, as hard as I fought. Now I'm pregnant, and I know it's Carl's. He is capable of more than you even know. And I'm sorry that it took this horrific act to make me realize just how dangerous he is.

I know I should have told you, instead of running like I did, but I didn't. Now I fear for yours and Jerry's safety more than I ever have before. I didn't tell you because I was afraid of him, but also because I was afraid of where your loyalties might lie. I wouldn't blame you for questioning me. I know I haven't exactly had a clean track record in the past. But I hope that you'll believe me over him when it comes to this. I hope you'll do what's right for you and Jerry.

Wrong Girl Gone

Maybe I shouldn't be telling you any of this. Maybe I won't even send this letter to you. Maybe I just need to write it down, so I know I'm telling the truth.

Carl is unwell. I know we're all a little unwell, but his sickness is hurting you. It hurt me. It will hurt Jerry. I only want what's best for you, Joy. You're my family. You're my sister. I only want you to be happy, whatever that is for you.

Love Always,

Kelly

I read the letter twice and sob at the same parts both times. I wipe my tears on my sleeve, despite the convenient paper towels right next to me. I could turn Kelly's letter over to the police. I could let them give it to the media. I could let all of Jasper see who Carl really is. Part of me wants to, so, so badly. Part of me wants to show them what he's capable of. To silence everyone in town who saw him day to day, smiling and laughing, as I stood beside him, a thick coat of concealer covering the bruises he'd left on me the night before. Part of me wants that. But the part of me that loves my son more than anything outweighs it.

To hand over Kelly's letter would be to bring everything out into the open. It would no longer look like Carl's pregnant wife was killed by Norman Lance. It would mean Jerry growing up with everyone in a hundred-mile radius

264

knowing his father wasn't only a drunk, but a killer and a rapist. It would mean Kelly's letter would be in tomorrow's newspapers. The letter that she didn't even know if she wanted to send me.

"Kelly," Mama calls from the waiting room, holding Jerry in her arms. I can tell the name is painful for her to say. "You ready to go? I think someone's tired."

"Yeah, I'm coming."

I look down at the letter, remembering the train coming at Carl and me. I remember the white light and the threatening horn blaring through the night. I remember the look on his face right before he pushed me off of him. I remember him saving my life. A confession won't bring Kelly back, the same way killing, and framing Norman didn't bring her back. At this point, all it would do is throw us into that dreaded spotlight. Telling the police who I really am would only expose the truth of the monster Carl was. Even though he may not understand the true horrors of what his father was capable of, Jerry already knows enough. He doesn't need everyone else knowing too. Maybe this is how Carl's story was supposed to end, with Kelly's truth in my hands and his memory left on the tracks.

I fold the letter and tuck it back into my pocket, saving us both from the oncoming train.

Chapter Thirty-Eight

Back at the house, while Mama sleeps in my bed, I lay in Jerry's, holding him in my arms. I've slept off and on for the past two hours, but now that dawn is approaching, I don't think I'll be able to sleep anymore. A faint blue glow from the sky is coming through the window, waking all the birds. I pull on my jeans, go downstairs and out on the front porch. I take a seat on the chipped white wood swing and pull my sweater tightly around me. The neighborhood is still dim, just on the verge of daylight. That's when I see what can only be a dream.

A navy pick-up truck pulls up down the street and parks. A person emerges from the truck, walking down the street towards our house. When they get closer, I think my eyes are deceiving me. When I see his face, I know my faith isn't completely gone. All dressed in black like Johnny Cash, he walks up to the house, until he's standing at the bottom of the porch. I walk down the steps and stop when we're standing a yard apart. It all feels so surreal, I can't shake the feeling that I'm dreaming.

"You're up early," Clay says, his voice hoarse and weak.

As the sky lightens, I can see the wear on his skin and under his eyes. I know that kind of wear. It can only be brought on by two things: pain or love. The line between the two is not as easily defined as I once thought it was.

"I didn't think you'd come back," I say, like I'm letting out my first breath of air.

266

Something inside him seems to buckle right then. He lets his strength go and his shoulders drop, the weight of the world lifting from his back. He moves forward and pulls me into his arms, holding me like I'm his lifeline. "I'll always come back."

***

Each day after Carl's death seems to become brighter and more open than the last, like a flower blossoming a little wider with each rain. And every day that I look in the mirror, I find myself growing fonder of what I see.

When all is said and done with the lawyers, I'm left with the house and custody of Jerry. The money I get from selling the house combined with Carl's gambling money should be enough to get me on my feet and pay for my first semester of classes in social work. It's going to be a long road, but I don't have anywhere else I need to be.

Clay invited me to stay with him in Northchester while I get settled with school and a job. He'd informed me that the Northchester Community College offers a social work associates' program, so I figure that's a good place to start. I'll keep my identity as Kelly until I'm settled in Northchester. Then, maybe one day, I can go back to being Joy. But not yet. Right now, I'm still too uncertain of who Joy is, but at least I have time to figure it out.

The hardest part about moving is going to be leaving Mama. But somehow, I know we'll be closer than before, even closer than when we lived under the same roof. I'm also not as worried about her as I used to be. She hasn't had a drink since I told her about Kelly. It seems odd to me, that such a painful event could stop her like that. I guess she wanted to stop filling up her memory bottles and move forward after all.

I pay one last visit to John before leaving. At the very least, I owe him an apology for not listening to him about Carl.

Wrong Girl Gone

"I sure as hell didn't want to be right," he says.

"I know. But you were. And I should have listened to you."

John shrugs. "I'm just glad it's over. You'd suffered for a long time."

We hug good-bye and make plans to have him visit next weekend. I'd invited Mama for that weekend, but she's apparently preoccupied with a date with Officer Boyd.

Clay helps me pack up everything I don't want to leave in the house. As I carry out one of the last boxes to Clay's truck, I glance at the "For Sale" sign with a big "SOLD" label over it in my front lawn. I thought seeing it there would make me feel nostalgic or regretful in some way, but it doesn't. This isn't my home. I could call any of the other places I've stayed these past few months home, but not this one. If this town holds too many memories for me, then this house holds ten times more than that.

I'm handing Clay a box of my clothes when Fiona walks up to me.

"We hate to see you go, Joy."

"It's actually Kelly. I'm Joy's twin sister."

Fiona eyes me up and down suspiciously. "Right," she says, finally. "Your sister's been through a lot. I didn't mean to eavesdrop, but that man she was married to was no good. I was one more fight away from calling the cops on that bastard."

With those words, my eyes fill with tears. I'm sniffling pathetically when Fiona gives me a hug. "Wherever you're headed, be sure to take care of yourself. And surround yourself with people who will do the same, you hear?"

I nod and wipe my face, going back into the house to retrieve the last box. I almost pause before walking back outside, to give myself one last moment with the empty house. But the truth is, I don't want one. I want to move on.

"Is that everything?" Clay asks as I hand him the box marked *Jerry's Toys*.

"That's it." I lean against the truck and survey the neighborhood.

"Are you going to miss it here?"

I shake my head, squinting my eyes in the sunlight. "No. I think what I'm going to miss most is what I thought I wanted when I lived here. I wanted to get out of this town, but I never seemed to have the guts to actually do it."

"You're doing it now." There is a brief silence between us. "I talked to Walt," Clay says. "I guess he told the police he wanted to drop the charges. He didn't say, but we both know that he knows it was me. He said that my job is waiting for me, and it's still mine as long as the money turns up. I worked out a payment plan with the pharmacy, and I should be able to come up with what I owe Walt eventually. Clear Russell's name, like you said."

"That reminds me. I have something for you." I reach into my purse and pull out an envelope with Clay's name scribbled on it. I hand it to Clay, who looks at me suspiciously as he opens it.

"I can't accept this."

"It's three-thousand, not a dollar more. You can give Walt his money back and use this for the damages."

"Joy, I told you, I really can't—"

"Please. I want to. You have done more for me than any stranger ever would have. Let me thank you. It's not charity. It's a loan."

He looks down at the envelope, then up at me. "You promise you'll let me pay you back?"

"Promise." I push the envelope into his hand, and watch his fingers shake as they tighten around it.

"I don't know what to say."

"You don't have to say anything."

After a moment, he looks back up at me. "Thank you," he says, and hugs me tight. "I actually have something for you too."

"Please don't tell me it's an envelope of money."

Wrong Girl Gone

He grins and reaches into the front seat of his truck and takes out an old book. It's one of the few old books I would probably recognize. "I found this in the dresser back at home. You'd folded a corner of one of the pages."

"I'm sorry. I shouldn't have—" Before I can open the book to fix it, he stops me.

"It's okay," he says. "I did the same thing." His smile looks like it holds all the answers in the world. He reaches up a hand and strokes my cheek. For a moment, I close my eyes and hold onto the moment as tightly as I can. "I'll be right behind you." He brushes a strand of my now light brown hair out of my eyes and walks over to his truck.

With every feeling I can imagine swirling around inside me, I look at the house one last time, waiting for fond memories to come flooding back to me. But they don't. It wasn't a home. It was a shell I once lived in. Now all that's left inside it are memories from another time.

I see Jerry sitting in the grass playing with his DeLorean. He hasn't played with anything else since I took him to see *Back to the Future 2* last weekend. "Jerry, honey, time to go," I call.

"Okay!" he calls back.

I get behind the wheel of my pathetic brown station wagon I never thought I'd miss, shut the door, and open the book. The first page with the folded corner is the one I'd marked; *If You Were Coming in The Fall* by Emily Dickinson. I read it again and smile to myself. Then I flip through until I come across the page Clay had marked. It's a poem by Christopher Brennan called *Because She Would Ask Me Why I Loved Her.*

If questioning would make us wise

No eyes would ever gaze in eyes;

If all our tale were told in speech

270

Audrey Wilson

No mouths would wander each to each.

Were spirits free from mortal mesh

And love not bound in hearts of flesh

No aching breasts would yearn to meet

And find their ecstasy complete.

For who is there that lives and knows

The secret powers by which he grows?

Were knowledge all, what were our need

To thrill and faint and sweetly bleed?

Then seek not, sweet, the "If" and "Why"

I love you now until I die.

For I must love because I live

And life in me is what you give.

    Since I've met him, Clay hasn't been much of a talker, but when he does have something to say, he says so much.

Wrong Girl Gone

Jerry opens the car door and climbs into the back seat. I close the book and set it in an open box on the floor of the backseat, right beside my daddy's old harmonica that I still need to learn how to play.

"What's that?" he asks.

"It's a book of poems."

"What's it about?"

I think about his question longer than I expect to. "What happiness is like."

He's holding his DeLorean in his lap and looking at me with those angel blue eyes of his, which I decide are nothing like his father's. "Why do you need a book to tell you what it's like?"

I laugh and a few of the tears fall out of my eyes. Jerry doesn't seem to know why I'm laughing, but he smiles too. "I don't," I say. "Are you happy?" He nods his head. "Then that's all we need."

I start the car and turn on the radio. I catch Clay's eyes in the rearview mirror, and he waves to me. I smile to myself and drive down the street and out of the neighborhood, leaving my tired memories behind me. Finally, our paths are no longer crossing. We're both headed in the same direction; we're both going forward. There's nowhere to go but forward.

I drive through town, past Hank's Diner, past the trailer park, until I make it to the highway, Clay a short distance behind me. I know I can't outrun my past, no matter how many miles I put on my tires, but I'm not trying to. Everything that had happened to me in my lifetime is what made me what I am, and a new name doesn't change that.

Two months ago, I would have given my soul to be somebody else. To live any other kind of life. Now I wouldn't trade what I have for anything. The pain is still there, of course, but it's a different kind of pain. I will miss my sister forever, and I will think about her every day, but the pain from her loss isn't as powerful as the strength she's given me.

Audrey Wilson

I hope that's what Kelly would have wanted for me, because I've only ever wanted that for her.

As I turn the corner onto Highway 80, I take comfort in knowing that I no longer feel the need to check over my shoulder every five minutes to make sure my shadow is still behind me. I don't feel a cloud of dread in the pit of my stomach that won't go away. I don't even give a second glance to the dilapidated green and white sign that reads *You Are Now Leaving Jasper* because this time I'm not running away. I don't need to anymore.

I'm right where I want to be.

Acknowledgements

There are so many people in my life who have helped make my dream of writing this book a reality. I am grateful to have been educated by the mentors and teachers above me, inspired by those around me, and supported and loved by those beside me.

I would not be where I am today without the love of my dear friends. For Rachel, with whom the best stories are always born. For Will, my brother from another mother. For Shaina, my favorite audiobook narrator. For Brittany, who is always there for me. For Alyson, who has been by my side since first grade. For Hannah, who has always fueled my creativity. For Maggie, my creative other. And for Becca, my number one fan who will always read anything I let her.

For Dreaming Big Publications, for taking a chance on *Wrong Girl Gone* and allowing me to grow with them as a writer. And for Kristi, who has been with me for every step of the publishing process. Thank you for never losing faith in me, and in Joy.

For my grandparents, Bryant and Sharon Keeling, and my uncle and aunt, Keith and Margie Keeling, who have always supported me and encouraged me to pursue my dreams. I'd like to thank them for all they've done for me and the wisdom they've shared.

For my grandmas, Joanne Reynolds Keeling and Shirley Wilson, two of the most compassionate women I've known,

Audrey Wilson

whose generosity has always reminded me to be kind to others.

I'd like to thank my cousin Kara Keeling and her husband Scott Pollard for inspiring me through their love of literature and dedication to their writing; my cousin Kent Keeling and his wife Marie-Claude Laplante for their support; and my aunt Carol Baffa and her partner Joe Loughlin for always sharing their stories with me.

There's no question that I would not be where I am today without the unconditional love and support of my parents; my mother, Sharon Keeling Wilson, who has taught me to be kind and compassionate, and who I have gone to time and time again for advice, and my father, Richard Wilson, whose thoughtfulness, hard work, and creativity I always admire, and who I look up to every day.

I would like to thank my partner in life, love, crime, and fiction, Danny Quinlan. Not a day goes by that he doesn't support me and my passion for writing, always reminding me that I can do anything I set my mind to.

And, finally, I'd like to thank Joy Elliot for giving a voice to all the women fighting the same fight she did. You are strong. You are brave. You are not alone.

Author's Note

One in four women experiences domestic abuse, an appalling statistic. Joy Elliot may be fictional, but her experience with domestic abuse is very real. When the idea of *Wrong Girl Gone* came to me when I was seventeen, I knew Joy's story was one that needed to be told. But I didn't want to simply give a cliched account of domestic violence. I wanted to shed light on the inner workings of an abusive relationship.

All too often, we think of an abuser as a heartless monster. As outsiders, we look at the victim in an abusive relationship and can't imagine why they choose to stay. While Carl is, at times, monstrous, he is not a monster, leaving Joy torn between seeing Carl as both the boy she fell in love with and the abusive man he is.

I hope that *Wrong Girl Gone* not only intrigues readers, but speaks to them. That Joy's voice can be heard by anyone in a similar situation, and that her story may give people the strength and courage they need to see the truth.

Made in the USA
Las Vegas, NV
24 June 2022